FLIGHTS OF FEAR

Further Titles by Graham Masterton from Severn House

BLACK ANGEL
DEATH TRANCE
MANITOU
MIRROR
NIGHT PLAGUE
NIGHT WARRIORS
THE SWEETMAN CURVE

Also in this series

FORTNIGHT OF FEAR

FLIGHTS OF FEAR

Graham Masterton

This first world edition published in Great Britain 1995 by
SEVERN HOUSE PUBLISHERS LTD of
9–15 High Street, Sutton, Surrey SM1 1DF.
First published in the USA 1995 by
SEVERN HOUSE PUBLISHERS INC of
425 Park Avenue, New York, NY 10022.

British Library Cataloguing in Publication Data
Masterton, Graham
  Flights of Fear
  I. Title
  823.914

  ISBN 0-7278-4741-4

Typeset by Hewer Text Composition Services, Edinburgh.
Printed and bound in Great Britain by
Hartnolls Ltd, Bodmin, Cornwall.

CONTENTS

FOREWORD

You can fly to any corner of the globe, and visit any culture from Argentinian to Zulu – but everywhere you go, in every culture, you will always come across dark myths and terrifying legends.

Perhaps we created them to explain our fear of nature – of sickness, and drought, and other catastrophes beyond our control. Perhaps we created them so that we could better understand the nature of good and evil.

On the other hand, perhaps we didn't create them at all. Perhaps some of the blackest demons in the hierarchy of human terror were already here, waiting for us, before we evolved. Perhaps angels did fall from heaven, and nameless horrors ruled the Jurassic night.

So many cultures share similar demons that it isn't difficult to believe that there could be some truth in their existence. They may have different names, like Micantecutli from Mexico, the great Aztec lord of the dead, who crawled head downwards like a spider on its web, in order to harvest freshly dead souls; or Azazel, the Jewish scapegoat, who corrupted women by teaching them to use cosmetics, and taught their sons the crueller skills of war; or Ravana, the Indian equivalent of Satan; or Baba Yaga, the Slavic hag who ripped people open and lived in a house balanced on a single chicken leg.

But – different names or not – they all embody the

same fundamental fears that everybody feels. Fear of the dark. Fear of our families being killed or injured. Fear of poverty, and fear of pestilence.

Now you can visit some of the different cultures of the world, on a special flight into the most frightening regions of the human imagination. Your ticket is already booked, you have your passport in your hand.

If you have the nerve, I will take you to visit three continents – from the winter fogs of Bruges to the flower-painted hills of Fes; from autumnal New England to steamy Alabama. You will visit many different mythologies, too – from Roman Catholic to Australian Aboriginal.

Some of the places will be familiar to you. But these flights will show you what lies beneath the familiar . . . they will take you to places where travellers never normally dare to venture. And even when I bring you on your return flight home, you will still find that dread walks very close behind you, everywhere you go.

Find your seat, please. You don't have to fasten your safety belt, because the very last thing that you're going to be on these flights is safe. Sorry, it's much too late to get off.

Egg

Bayswater, London

On our way to the airport, let's pause for a moment in this crowded, cosmopolitan area of London just north of Hyde Park, a mixture of once elegant houses, apartment blocks, bedsitters, and some of the best ethnic restaurants in London. Bayswater is part of Paddington ("the settlement of Padda's people"), and up until 1860 it was little more than a village. But then the well-to-do began to build large houses here – followed, of course, by the less salubrious dwellings of those who made a living by servicing their needs. Paddington was chosen for the site of the terminus of the Great Western Railway in the 1860s, and the world's first underground railway was built beneath the streets of Bayswater. It was here, too, that Tom Ponting opened one of the first of the new "cash only" department stores.

Like many areas of London, Bayswater fell from gentility to semi-squalor in only a few decades. By the end of the century, the streets no longer echoed with the clatter of elegant horse-drawn carriages, but with the raucous cries of Irish dockers, selling oranges and nuts, hot potatoes and eggs.

This is the story of just one egg. But in this case, one egg was more than enough.

EGG

Michael knew there was something wrong with the egg as soon as he lifted it out of the pan. It was unnaturally heavy, and it seemed to be wrongly weighted, like one of those googly-men that you could never push over.

He cracked the shell with his signet ring, and broke off two or three pieces. Inside, the egg was a pale beige, and glistening with slime. Disgusted, he dropped it immediately into the pedal bin and refilled the saucepan with cold water. He lit the gas, but after a few seconds he switched it off again. He didn't feel like an egg now. He was squeamish at the best of times, and even the tiniest fleck of blood in an egg-yolk could put him off cooked breakfasts for weeks.

He reached for the muesli, and filled up his only cereal bowl with it.

He listened to Radio 2 as he sat at his formica-topped kitchen table, chewing muesli in solitude. It was only when he was eating that he was really conscious of being lonely, and muesli took so long to eat.

On the green-painted kitchen wall, the calendar boasted only two entries. This Thursday was his 32nd birthday; next Friday he was due at the dentist for Wsdm Tth!! The girl on the calendar had impossibly large breasts, and he had blacked out one of her teeth with Biro.

Outside the window, all he could see was the windowless

brick wall of the Bayswater Hotel next door, and a rhomboid of putty-coloured sky.

He opened the pedal bin to scrape away the last of his muesli. The egg was still lying amongst the used tea bags and the orange peel and the crumpled take-away container from last night's biryani. But much more of its shell had broken away, and now he could see that the pale beige flesh wasn't egg-white at all, but slimy skin; and that the egg contained a naked, half-hatched chick. What was more, the chick seemed to be stirring.

He tore off a piece of kitchen-roll and lifted the egg out of the pedal bin. He laid it carefully on the draining-board, and it was only then, with an extraordinary tightening feeling around his scalp, that he realized it wasn't a chick at all. Cupped in the last cracked portion of shell, face down, lay a child. A tiny, quivering child.

Michael tore off more kitchen-roll and folded it into a thick, layered pad. Swallowing with fear and revulsion, he lifted the slippery little creature out of its shell and laid it on the tissue. It was a boy. It lay gasping and waving its little arms, and twisting its head blindly from side to side, as if in search of a nipple.

He poured some milk into a saucer, dipped his finger into it, and touched it against the creature's lips. The creature immediately turned its head away, and started to sob – a weak, miniaturized cry that Michael found both frightening and touching.

"What's the matter, you don't like milk? What about something sweet?"

He tried the child with honey, with orange squash, with chocolate and with golden syrup. Each time it turned its head away, and its crying began to grow hysterical.

Michael went out into the hallway and picked up the phone. Liz, the redhead who lived in the flat immediately above his, came down the stairs in a short green skirt and a low-cut yellow T-shirt. He leaned over the banisters as she went downstairs, to watch her.

"Emergency, which service please?"

He took a deep breath, and then said nothing at all. Which service? Who do you call when you find a baby in a boiled egg?

"No . . . no thanks. Sorry. I made a mistake."

He went back into the kitchen. The baby was quiet now, lying on its back, its arms and its legs spread out. At first he thought it was dead but then he realized that it was breathing, sticky little baby-breaths.

Michael took the inner bag out of his muesli box, cut out the back with scissors, and laid the baby inside it. He stared at it for almost an hour, in bewilderment and wonder.

"What am I going to do with you?" he asked it.

He went to work. It was a slack day because it was mid-summer and nobody bought TVs and washing machines in mid-summer. He kept thinking about the tiny boy in his muesli box. Perhaps he had imagined it. Perhaps, by the time he got home, the boy would be dead.

At lunchtime, in the pizza restaurant, he asked Willowby, as off-handedly as he could, "Are babies ever born out of eggs, do you know? Ordinary eggs like chicken's eggs?"

Willowby had red spots and a silky adolescent moustache. "No wonder you've never got no girlfriends," he grinned.

When Michael returned home, he went straight into the kitchen. The muesli box was still there, the tiny baby boy was still there, and still asleep. Michael watched it, biting his thumbnail. It was impossible, but it was true; and for some reason he had been chosen to find it and to take care of it. He sat down, and bowed his head, and murmured, "Thank you, Blessed Virgin, for this miracle. I promise that I will feed him and care for him and bring him up in the way that You brought up Jesus. And I shall call him Ian. Amen."

Ian grew like all other babies grow, except that his diet was distinctly different from that of all other babies. Michael discovered on the second day that he had a taste for diluted wine vinegar, and gherkins, and anything else that was bitter or sour. However, he developed well and steadily, and by the end of his first year he was nearly as heavy as an ordinary child.

Michael gave up his job at Curry's and devoted all of his days to bringing up Ian. Everybody thought that they were father and son, even though Ian looked nothing like Michael at all. Michael was mousy: Ian was white-skinned and slender, with curly hair that was almost black, and eyes that were oddly colourless, as if they were windows, rather than eyes.

When he was four, they were sitting together in the kitchen eating fried eggs on toast when Ian asked, "Where did I come from?"

Michael stopped chewing. "I found you by accident."

"Aren't you my daddy, then?"

"Yes, because I love you. That's all anybody needs, to be a daddy."

"What if my real daddy comes looking for me?"

Michael stood up, and picked Ian up, and hugged him tight. "I'm your daddy now. I wouldn't let you go. Not ever."

Through all of Ian's childhood years, they played and

talked and told each other stories. Michael told Ian the story of Moomintroll, and the Hemulen. Ian told Michael the story of his real father, and how he would come to find him one day. Michael went to every school play, and during sports was always cheering Ian's team from the touchline. "Come on, Wood Park! Come on, Wood Park!" like all the other fathers, who were real fathers.

Michael took Ian on holidays to the Isle of Wight and Devon. They played cricket, and the sea retreated and turned the sand into prehistoric ribs that hurt their feet.

On Ian's seventeenth birthday, Michael took him for a curry in Queensway, and they walked back along the Bayswater Road together in the warm noisy night. Outside their flat, however, Ian said, "I have to go now."

"What?"

"I've come of age. My father's come to take me away. My real father."

"I don't know what you mean."

Unexpectedly, Ian took Michael in his arms and held him tight. "This wasn't meant to be," he whispered in Michael's ear. "I was supposed to be something quite different. But you loved me, and because you loved me, you changed me. You've changed more things than you know."

Without another word, he walked away. Michael lost sight of him almost immediately. There were too many people walking and talking and jostling. But then he glimpsed him just past the tube station, and a tall dark man was close beside him; a very tall man; and they were talking like people who had secrets to share.

Michael smelled flame on the wind; and incinerated promises; and vinegar.

*   *   *

"Father, I miss him."

"You weren't his real father, my son. His real father has more of a claim to him than you do."

"But I brought him up myself. He came out of an egg, and I brought him up myself."

"What do you mean he came out of an egg?"

"It's true. I cracked open an egg and there he was. All curled up."

"If you're telling me the truth, this was the Devil. This was Satan's son. Satan's children are hatched out of eggs, one out of every generation. You have sinned, my son, most grievously, by harbouring the child of the Prince of Darkness."

Michael was arrested early the next morning at Battle Perchery, in Sussex. He had smashed over seven hundred eggs. He told police, "I found one of them, and I saved him. There must be more."

They wiped the yolk from his arms and put him in a cell. He pressed his cheek against the green-painted wall and thought about Ian; and Ian's schooldays; and Ian's babyhood; and he was the first man in human history to cry for the Devil.

The Gray Madonna

Bruges, Belgium

Although it is such a crowded and popular tourist town, Bruges hasn't lost its feeling of medieval mysticism, especially on chill, autumnal days when the fog hangs over the canals, and the footsteps of unseen people clatter through its winding, cobbled streets. The capital of West Flanders, Bruges has kept its old city walls and its fortified gates, and the old city has some of the grandest Gothic buildings in Europe, especially the 14th-century cathedral of St Saveur and the church of Notre Dame. It was while I was walking through the statue collection in the church of Notre Dame that I was first inspired to write about the gray madonna. I had already seen the stone virgins that adorn the street corners of Bruges, but here was Michelangelo's Virgin & Child *– a statue that seems to have a life of its own. When you reach out to touch the Virgin's hand, you can hardly believe that it isn't going to be warm.*

Go to Bruges for its lace and its embroidery and its freshly made chocolates. Enjoy its cafés and its restaurants, and eat as many steamed mussels and waterzooi *chicken stew as you want. Take a boat trip around the canals, visit its art galleries and walk in its parks. But be careful of going down its side streets alone, and always look around you to see who might be following.*

THE GRAY MADONNA

He had always known that he would have to return to Bruges. This time, however, he chose winter, when the air was foggy and the canals had turned to the colour of breathed-on pewter, and the narrow medieval streets were far less crowded with shuffling tourists.

He had tried to avoid thinking about Bruges for three years now. Forgetting Bruges – really forgetting – was out of the question. But he had devised all kinds of ways of diverting his attention away from it, of mentally changing the subject, such as calling his friends or turning on the TV really loud or going out for a drive and listening to Nirvana with the volume set on Deaf.

Anything rather than stand on that wooden jetty again, opposite the overhanging eaves and boathouses of the 14th-century plague hospital, waiting for the Belgian police frogmen to find Karen's body. He had stood there so many times in so many dreams, a bewildered sun-reddened American tourist with his shoulder bag and his camcorder, while diseased-looking starlings perched on the steep, undulating tiles up above him, and the canal slopped and gurgled beneath his feet.

Anything rather than watch the medical examiner with her crisp, white uniform and her braided blonde hair as she unzipped the black vinyl body-bag and Karen's face appeared, not just white but almost green. "She would not have suffered much," in that guttural back-of-the-throat Flemish accent. "Her neck was broken almost at once."

"By what?"

"By a thin ligature, approximately eight millimetres in diameter. We have forensic samples, taken from her skin. It was either hemp or braided hair."

Then Inspector Ben De Buy from the Politie resting a nicotine stained hand on his arm and saying, "One of the drivers of the horse-drawn tourist carriages says that he saw your wife talking to a nun. This was approximately ten minutes before the boatman noticed her body floating in the canal."

"Where was this?"

"Hoogstraat, by the bridge. The nun turned the corner around Minderbroederstraat and that was the last the driver saw of her. He did not see your wife."

"Why should he have noticed my wife at all?"

"Because she was attractive, Mr Wallace. All of these drivers have such an eye for good-looking women."

"Is that all? She talked to a nun? Why should she talk to a nun? She's not a Catholic.

He had paused, and then corrected himself. "She *wasn't* a Catholic."

Inspector De Buy had lit up a pungent Ernte 23 cigarette, and breathed smoke out of his nostrils like a dragon. "Perhaps she was asking for directions. We don't know yet. It shouldn't be too difficult to find the nun. She was wearing a light gray habit, which is quite unusual."

Dean had stayed in Belgium for another week. The police came up with no more forensic evidence; no more witnesses. They published photographs of Karen in the newspapers, and contacted every religious order throughout Belgium, southern Holland and northern France. But

12

nobody came forward. Nobody had seen how Karen had died. And there were no nunneries where the sisters wore gray; especially the whitish-gray that the carriage driver claimed to have seen.

Inspector De Buy had said, "Why not take your wife back to America, Mr Wallace? There's nothing more you can do here in Bruges. If there's a break in the case, I can fax you, yes?"

Now Karen was lying in the Episcopalian cemetery in New Milford, Connecticut, under a blanket of crimson maple leaves, and Dean was back here, in Bruges, on a chilly Flanders morning, tired and jet-lagged, and lonelier than he had ever felt before.

He crossed the wide, empty square called 't Zand, where fountains played and clusters of sculptured cyclists stood in the fog. The real cyclists were far busier jangling their bells and pedalling furiously over the cobbles. He passed cafés with steamy, glassed-in verandahs, where doughy-faced Belgians sat drinking coffee and smoking and eating huge cream-filled pastries. A pretty girl with long black hair watched him pass, her face as white as an actress in a European art movie. In an odd way, she reminded him of the way that Karen had looked, the day that he had first met her.

With his coat collar turned up against the cold and his breath fuming, he walked past the shops selling lace and chocolates and postcards and perfume. In the old Flemish tradition, a flag hung over the entrance of every shop, bearing the coat of arms of whoever had lived there in centuries gone by. Three grotesque fishes, swimming through a silvery sea. A man who looked like Adam, picking an apple from a tree. A white-faced woman with a strange suggestive smile.

Dean reached the wide cobbled marketplace. On the far

13

side, like a flock of seagulls, twenty or thirty nuns hurried silently through the fog. Up above him, the tall spire of Bruges' Belfry loomed through the fog, six hundred tightly spiralling steps to the top. Dean knew that because he and Karen had climbed up it, panting and laughing all the way. Outside the Belfry the horse-drawn tourist carriages collected, as well as ice cream vans and hot dog stalls. In the summer, there were long lines of visitors waiting to be given guided tours around the town, but not today. Three carriages were drawn up side by side, while their drivers smoked and their blanketed horses dipped their heads in their nose-bags.

Dean approached the drivers and lifted one hand in greeting.

"Tour, sir?" asked a dark-eyed unshaven young man in a tilted straw hat.

"Not today, thanks. I'm looking for somebody . . . one of your fellow drivers." He took out the folded newspaper clipping. "His name is Jan De Keyser."

"Who wants him? He's not in trouble, is he?"

"No, no. Nothing like that. Can you tell me where he lives?"

The carriage drivers looked at each other. "Does anybody know where Jan De Keyser lives?"

Dean took out his wallet and handed them 100 francs each. The drivers looked at each other again, and so Dean gave them another 100.

"Oostmeers, about halfway down, left-hand side," said the unshaven young man. "I don't know the number but there's a small delicatessen and it's next to that, with a brown door and brown glass vases in the window."

He coughed, and then he said, "You want a tour, too?"

Dean shook his head. "No, thanks. I think I've seen everything in Bruges I ever want to see; and more."

14

He walked back along Oude Burg and under the naked lime trees of Simon Stevin Plein. The inventor of decimal currency stood mournfully on his plinth, staring at a chocolate shop across the street. The morning was so raw now that Dean wished he had brought a pair of gloves. He crossed and recrossed the canal several times. It was smelly and sullen and it reminded him of death.

They had first come to Bruges for two reasons. The first was to get over Charley. Charley hadn't even talked, or walked, or seen the light of day. But a sound-scan had shown that Charley would be chronically disabled, if he were ever born; a nodding, drooling boy in a wheelchair, for all of his life. Dean and Karen had sat up all evening and wept and drank wine, and finally decided that Charley would be happier if he remained a hope; and a memory; a brief spark that illuminated the darkness, and died. Charley had been terminated and now Dean had nobody to remember Karen by. Her china collection? Her clothes? One evening he had opened her underwear drawer and taken out a pair of her panties and desperately breathed them in, hoping to smell her, hoping to smell her. But the panties were clean and Karen was gone; as if she had never existed.

They had come to Bruges for the art, too: for the Groeninge Museum with its 14th-century religious paintings and its modern Belgian masters, for Rubens and Van Eycks and Magrittes. Dean was a veterinarian, but he had always been a keen amateur painter; and Karen had designed wallpaper. They had first met nearly seven years ago, when Karen had brought her golden retriever into Dean's surgery to have its ears checked out. She had liked Dean's looks right from the very beginning. She had always liked tall, gentle, dark-haired men ("I would have married Clark Kent if Lois Lane hadn't gotten in first").

15

But what had really persuaded her was the patience and affection with which he had handled her dog Buffy. After they were married, she used to sing *Love Me, Love My Dog* to him, and accompany herself on an old banjo.

Buffy was dead now, too. Buffy had pined so pitifully for Karen that Dean had eventually put him down.

Oostmeers was a narrow street of small, neat, row houses, each with its shining front window and its freshly painted front door and its immaculate lace curtains. Dean found the delicatessen easily because – apart from an antique dealers – it was the only shop. The house next door was much shabbier than most of its neighbours, and the brown glass vases in the window were covered in a film of dust. He rang the doorbell, and clapped his hands together to warm them up.

After a long pause, he heard somebody coming downstairs, and then coughing, and then the front door was opened about two inches. A thin, soapy-looking face peered out at him.

"I'm looking for Jan De Keyser."

"That's me. What do you want?"

Dean took out the newspaper cutting and held it up. "You were the last person to see my wife alive."

The young man frowned at the cutting for nearly half a minute, as if he needed glasses. Then he said, "That was a long time ago, mister. I've been sick since then."

"All the same, can I talk to you?"

"What for? It's all in the paper, everything I said."

"I'm just trying to understand what happened."

Jan De Keyser gave a high, rattling cough. "I saw your wife talking to this nun, that's all, and she was gone. I turned around in my seat, and saw the nun walk into Minderbroederstraat, into the sunshine, and then she was gone, too, and that was all."

16

"You ever see a nun dressed in gray like that before?"

Jan De Keyser shook his head.

"You don't know where she might have come from? What order? You know, Dominican or Franciscan or whatever?"

"I don't know about nuns. But maybe she wasn't a nun."

"What do you mean? You told the police that she was a nun."

"What do you think I was going to say? That she was a statue? I have two narcotics offences already. They would have locked me up, or sent me to that bloody stupid hospital in Kortrijk."

Dean said, "What are you talking about, statue?"

Jan De Keyser coughed again, and started to close the door. "This is Brugge, what do you expect?"

"I still don't understand."

The door hovered on the point of closing. Dean took out his wallet again, and ostentatiously took out three 100 BFr notes, and held them up. "I've come a long way for this, Jan. I need to know everything."

"Wait," said Jan De Keyser; and closed the door. Dean waited. He looked down the foggy length of Oostmeers, and he could see a young girl standing on the corner of Zonnekemeers, her hands in her pockets. He couldn't tell if she were watching him or not.

After two or three minutes, Jan De Keyser opened the door again and stepped out into the street, wearing a brown leather jacket and a chequered scarf. He smelled of cigarettes and linament. "I've been very sick, ever since that time. My chest. Maybe it was nothing to do with the nun; maybe it was. But you know what they say: once a plague, always a plague."

He led Dean back the way he had come, past the

canals, past the Gruuthuuse Museum, along Dijver to the Vismarkt. He walked very quickly, with his narrow shoulders hunched. Horses and carriages rattled through the streets like tumbrils; and bells chimed from the Belfry. They had that high, strange musical ring about them that you only hear from European bells. They reminded Dean of Christmases and wars; and maybe that was what Europe was really all about.

They reached the corner of Hoogstraat and Minderbroederstraat; by the bridge. Jan De Keyser jabbed his finger one way, and then the other. "I am carrying Germans; five or six-member German family. I am going slow because my horse is tired, yes? I see this woman in tight white shorts, and a blue T-shirt, and I look at her because she is pretty. That was your wife, yes? She has a good figure. Anyway, I turn and watch because she is not only pretty, she is talking to a nun. A nun in gray, quite sure of that. And they are talking as if they are arguing strongly. You know what I mean? Like, arguing, very fierce. Your wife is lifting her arms, like this, again and again, as if to say, 'What have I done? What have I done?' And the nun is shaking her head."

Dean looked around, frustrated and confused. "You said something about statues; and the plague."

"Look up," said Jan De Keyser. "You see on the corner of almost every building, a stone madonna. Here is one of the largest, life-size."

Dean raised his eyes, and for the first time he saw the arched niche that had been let into the corner of the building above him. In this niche stood a Virgin Mary, with the baby Jesus in her arms, looking sadly down at the street below.

"You see?" said Jan De Keyser. "There is so much to see in Brugge, if you lift your head. There is another world

18

on the second storey. Statues and gargoyles and flags. Look at that building there. It has the faces of thirteen devils on it. They were put there to keep Satan away; and to protect the people who lived in this building from the Black Death."

Dean leaned over the railings, and stared down into the water. It was so foggy and gelid that he couldn't even see his own face; only a blur, as if somebody had taken a black-and-white photograph of him, and jogged the camera.

Jan De Keyser said, "In the 14th Century, when the plague came, it was thought that the people of Brugge were full of sin, yes?, and that they were being given a punishment from God. So they made statues of the Holy Mary at every corner, to keep away the evil; and they promised the Holy Mary that they would always obey her, and worship her, if she protected them from plague. You understand this, yes? They made binding agreement."

"And what would happen if they didn't stick to this binding agreement?"

"The Holy Virgin would forgive; because the Holy Virgin always forgives. But the statue of the Holy Virgin would give punishment."

"The statue? How could the statue punish anybody?"

Jan De Keyser shrugged. "They made it, in the false belief. They made it with false hopes. Statues that are made with false hopes will always be dangerous; because they will turn on the people who made them; and they will expect the payment for their making."

Dean couldn't grasp this at all. He was beginning to suspect that Jan De Keyser was not only physically sick but mentally unbalanced, too; and he was beginning to wish that he hadn't brought him here.

But Jan De Keyser pointed up to the statue of the Virgin

Mary; and then at the bridge; and then at the river, and said, "They are not just stone; not just carving. They have all of people's hopes inside them, whether these hopes are good hopes; or whether these hopes are wicked. They are not just stone."

"What are you trying to tell me? That what you saw –?"

"The gray madonna," said Jan De Keyser. "If you offend her, you must surely pay the price."

Dean took out three more 100 BFr bills, folded them, and stuffed them into Jan De Keyser's jacket pocket. "Thanks, pal," he told him. "I love you, too. I flew all the way from New Milford, Connecticut, to hear that my wife was killed by a statue. Thank you. Drink hearty."

But Jan De Keyser clutched hold of his sleeve. "You don't understand, do you? Everybody else has told you lies. I am trying to tell you the truth."

"What does the truth matter to you?"

"You don't have to insult me, sir. The truth has always mattered to me; just like it matters to all Belgians. What would I gain from lying to you? A few hundred francs, so what?"

Dean looked up at the gray madonna in her niche in the wall. Then he looked back at Jan De Keyser. "I don't know," he said, flatly.

"Well, just give me the money, and maybe we can talk about morals and philosophy later."

Dean couldn't help smiling. He handed Jan De Keyser his money; and then stood and watched him as he hurried away, his hands in his pockets, his shoulders swinging from side to side. *Jesus*, he thought, *I'm getting old. Either that, or Jan De Keyser has deliberately been playing me along.*

All the same, he stood across the street, cater-corner from

20

the gray madonna, and watched her for a long, long time, until the chill began to get to his sinuses, and his nose started to drip. The gray madonna stared back at him with her blind stone eyes, calm and beautiful, with all the sadness of a mother who knows that her child must grow up, and that her child will be betrayed, and that for centuries to come men and women will take His name in vain.

Dean walked back along Hoogstraat to the marketplace, and he went into one of the cafés beside the entrance to the Belfry. He sat in the corner, underneath a carved wooden statue of a *louche*-looking medieval musician. He ordered a small espresso and an Asbach brandy to warm him up. A dark-looking girl on the other side of the café smiled at him briefly, and then looked away. The jukebox was playing *Guantanamera*.

He was almost ready to leave when he thought he saw a gray nun-like figure passing the steamed-up window.

He hesitated, then he got up from his table and went to the door, and opened it. He was sure that he had seen a nun. Even if it wasn't the same nun that Karen had been talking to, on the day when she was strangled and thrown into the canal, this nun had worn a light gray habit, too. Maybe she came from the same order, and could help him locate the original nun, and find out what Karen had said to her.

A party of schoolchildren were crossing the gray fan-patterned cobbles of the market, followed by six or seven teachers. Behind the teachers, Dean was sure that he could glimpse a gray robed figure, making its way swiftly toward the arched entrance to the Belfry. He started to walk quickly across the marketplace, just as the carillon of bells began to ring, and starlings rose from the rooftops all around the square. He saw the figure disappear into the foggy, shadowy archway, and he broke into a jog.

21

He had almost reached the archway when a hand snatched at his sleeve, and almost pulled him off balance. He swung around. It was the waiter from the café, pale-faced and panting.

"You have to pay, sir," he said.

Dean said, "Sure, sorry, I forgot," and hurriedly took out his wallet. "There – keep the change. I'm in a hurry, okay?"

He left the bewildered waiter standing in the middle of the square and ran into the archway. Inside, there was a large, deserted courtyard. On the right-hand side, a flight of stone steps led to the interior of the Belfry tower itself. There was nowhere else that the nun could have gone.

He vaulted up the steps, pushed open the huge oak door, and went inside. A young woman with upswept glasses and a tight braid on top of her head was sitting behind a ticket window, painting her nails.

"Did you see a nun come through here?"

"A nun? I don't know."

"Give me a ticket anyway."

He waited impatiently while she handed him a ticket and leaflet describing the history of the Belfry. Then he pulled open the narrow door which led to the spiral stairs, and began to climb up them in leaps and bounds.

The steps were extravagantly steep, and it wasn't long before he had to slow down. He trudged around and around until he reached a small gallery, about a third of the way up the tower, where he stopped and listened. If there *were* a nun climbing the steps up ahead of him, he would easily be able to hear her.

And – yes – he could distinctly make out the *chip – chip – chip* sound of somebody's feet on worn stone steps. The sound echoed down the staircase like fragments of granite dropping down a well. Dean seized the thick, slippery rope

22

that acted as a handrail, and renewed his climbing with even more determination, even though he was soaked in chilly sweat, and he was badly out of breath.

As it rose higher and higher within the Belfry tower, the spiral staircase grew progressively tighter and narrower, and the stone steps were replaced with wood. All that Dean could see up ahead of him was the triangular treads of the steps above; and all he could see when he looked down was the triangular treads of the steps below. For more than a dozen turns of the spiral, there were no windows, only dressed stone walls, and even though he was so high above the street, he began to feel trapped and claustrophobic. There were still hundreds of steps to climb to reach the top of the Belfry, and hundreds of steps to negotiate if he wanted to go back down again.

He paused for a rest. He was tempted to give it up. But then he made the effort to climb up six more steps and found that he had reached the high-ceilinged gallery which housed the clock's carillon and chiming mechanism – a gigantic medieval musical box. A huge drum was turned by clockwork, and a complicated pattern of metal spigots activated the bells.

The gallery was silent, except for the soft, weary ticking of a mechanism that had been counting out the hours without interruption for nearly five hundred years. Columbus's father could have climbed these same steps, and looked at this same machinery.

Dean was going to rest a moment or two longer, but he heard a quick, furtive rustling sound on the other side of the gallery, and caught sight of a light gray triangle of skirt just before it disappeared up the next flight of stairs.

"*Wait!*" he shouted. He hurried across the gallery and started to climb. This time he could not only hear the sound of footsteps, he could hear the swishing of well-starched cotton, and once or twice he actually saw it.

"Wait!" he called. "I don't mean to frighten you – I just want to talk to you!"

But the footsteps continued upward at the same brisk pace, and with each turn in the spiral the figure in the light gray habit stayed tantalizingly out of sight.

At last the air began to grow colder and fresher, and Dean realized that they were almost at the top. There was nowhere the nun could go, and she would *have* to talk to him now.

He came out onto the Belfry's viewing gallery, and looked around. Barely visible through the fog he could distinguish the orange rooftops of Bruges, and the dull gleam of its canals. On a clear day the view stretched for miles across the flat Flanders countryside, toward Ghent and Kortrijk and Ypres. But today Bruges was secretive and closed in; and looked more like a painting by Brueghel than a real town. The air smelled of fog and sewers.

To begin with, he couldn't see the nun. She must be here, though: unless she had jumped off the parapet. Then he stepped around a pillar, and there she was, standing with her back to him, staring out toward the Basilica of the Holy Blood.

Dean approached her. She didn't turn around, or give any indication that she knew that he was here. He stood a few paces behind her and waited, watching the faint breeze stirring the light gray cloth of her habit.

"Listen, I'm sorry if I alarmed you," he said. "I didn't mean to give you the impression that I was chasing you or anything like that. But three years ago my wife died here in Bruges, and just before she died she was seen talking to a nun. A nun in a light gray habit, like yours."

He stopped and waited. The nun remained where she was, not moving, not speaking.

"Do you speak English?" Dean asked her, cautiously. "If you don't speak English, I can find somebody to translate for us."

Still the nun remained where she was. Dean began to feel unnerved. He didn't like to touch her, or to make any physical attempt to turn her around. All the same, he wished she would speak, or look at him, so that he could see her face. Maybe she belonged to a silent order. Maybe she was deaf. Maybe she just didn't want to talk to him, and that was that.

He thought of the gray madonna, and of what Jan De Keyser had told him: "*They are not just stone; not just carving. They have all of people's hopes inside them; whether these hopes are good hopes, or whether these hopes are wicked.*"

For some reason that he couldn't quite understand, he shivered, and it wasn't only the cold that made him shiver. It was the feeling that he was standing in the presence of something really terrible.

"I, er – I wish you'd say something," he said, loudly, although his voice sounded off balance.

There was a very long silence. Then suddenly the carillon of bells started to ring, so loudly that Dean was deafened, and could literally feel his eyeballs vibrating in their sockets. The nun swivelled around – didn't turn, but smoothly swivelled, as if she were standing on a turntable. She stared at him, and Dean stared back, and the fear rose up inside him like ice-cold sick.

Her face was a face of stone. Her eyes were carved out of granite, and she couldn't speak because her lips were stone, too. She stared at him blind and sad and accusing, and he couldn't even find the breath to scream.

He took one step backward, then another. The gray madonna came gliding after him, blocking his way to the staircase. She reached beneath her habit and lifted out a thin braided ligature, made of human hair, the kind of ligature that depressed and hysterical nuns used to plait out of their own hair, and then use to hang themselves. Better to meet your Christ in Heaven than to live in fear and self-loathing.

Dean said, "Keep away from me. I don't know what you are, or *how* you are, but keep away from me."

He was sure that she smiled, very faintly. He was sure that she whispered something.

"What?" he asked. "*What?*"

She came closer and closer. She was stone, and yet she breathed, and she smiled, and she whispered, "*Charley, this is for Charley.*"

Again, he screamed at her, "*What?*"

But she caught hold of his left arm in a devastatingly strong grip, and she stepped up onto the platform that ran around the parapet, and with one irresistible turn of her back she rolled herself over the parapet and slid down the orange-tiled roof.

Dean shouted, "*No!*" and tried to tug himself free from her; but she wasn't an ordinary woman. She gripped him so tight and she weighed so much that he was dragged over the parapet after her. He found himself sliding and bumping over the fog-moist tiles, and at the end of the tiles was a lead gutter and then a sheer drop down to the cobbles of the Market, one hundred and seventy feet below.

With his right hand, he scrabbled to get a grip on the tiles. But the gray madonna was far too heavy for him. She was solid granite. Her hand was solid granite; no longer pliable, but still holding him fast.

26

She tumbled over the edge of the roof. Dean caught hold of the guttering, and for one moment of supreme effort he swung from it, with the gray madonna revolving around him, her face as calm as only the face of the Virgin Mary could be. But the guttering was medieval lead, soft and rotten, and slowly it bent forward under the weight, and then gave way.

Dean looked down and saw the market square. He saw horse-drawn carriages and cars and people walking in every direction. He heard the air whistling in his ears.

He clung to the gray madonna because that was the only solid thing he had to cling to. He embraced her as he fell. Hardly anybody saw him falling, but those who did lifted up their hands in horror in the same way that serious burns victims lift up their hands.

He dropped and dropped the whole height of Bruges' Belfry, two dark figures falling through the fog, holding each other tight, like lovers. Dean thought for one illogical instant that everything was going to be all right, that he was going to fall for ever and never hit the ground. But then suddenly he saw the rooftops much closer and the cobbles expanded faster and faster. He hit the courtyard with the gray madonna on top of him. She weighed over half a ton, and she exploded on impact, and so did he. Together, they were like a bomb bursting. Their heads flew apart. Stone arms and flesh arms jumped up into the air.

Then there was nothing but the muffled sound of traffic, and the echoing flap of starlings' wings as they resettled on the rooftops, and the jangling of bicycle bells.

Inspector Ben De Buy stood amongst the wreckage of

man and madonna and looked up at the Belfry, cigarette smoke and fog vapour fuming from his nose.

"He fell from the very top," he told his assistant, Sergeant Van Peper.

"Yes, sir. The girl who collects the tickets can identify him."

"And was he carrying the statue with him, when he bought his ticket?"

"No, sir, of course not. He couldn't even have lifted it. It was far too heavy."

"But it was up there with him, wasn't it? How did he manage to take a life-size granite statue of the Virgin Mary all the way up those stairs? It's impossible. And even if it *was* possible, why would he do it? You might need to weight yourself down to drown yourself, but to jump from the top of a belfry?"

"I don't know, sir."

"No, well, neither do I, and I don't think I really *want* to know."

He was still standing amongst the blood and the broken stone when one of his youngest detectives appeared, carrying something grayish-white in his arms. As he came closer, Inspector De Buy realized that it was a baby, made of stone.

"What's this?" he demanded.

"The infant Jesus," said the officer, blushing. "We found it on the corner of Hoogstraat, up in the niche where the stone madonna used to stand."

Inspector De Buy stared at the granite baby for a while, then held out his arms. "Here," he said, and the officer handed it over to him. He lifted it over his head, and then he smashed it onto the cobbles as hard as he could. It shattered into half a dozen lumps.

"Sir?" asked his sergeant, in puzzlement.

Inspector De Buy patted him on the shoulder. "Thou shalt worship no graven image, Sergeant Van Peper. And now you know why."

He walked out of the Belfry courtyard. Out in the market square, an ambulance was waiting, its sapphire lights flashing in the fog. He walked back to Simon Stevin Plein, where he had left his car. The bronze statue of Simon Stevin loomed over him, black and menacing in his doublet and hat. Inspector De Buy took out his car keys and hesitated for a moment. He was sure that he had seen Simon Stevin move slightly.

He stood quite still, right next to his Citroën, his key lifted, not breathing, listening, waiting. Anybody who saw him then would have believed that he was a statue.

J.R.E. Ponsford

Harrow, Middlesex

The story of J.R.E. Ponsford is set in a boys' public school somewhere in Southern England. My own sons boarded at Harrow, but at Harrow there was none of the bullying described in this story, and any resemblance is purely atmospheric. Much of the detail came from boys at other British public schools – Eton, Winchester, Westminster and Dulwich.

There is nothing quite like a British boys' public school, with its sexual segregation and its extraordinary rituals. The language is a tortured combination of the nursery and the voodoo lounge. They can't call a bell a bell, they have to call it "Ding-Dong".

Most of all, though, this flight will take you into a world to which only a wealthy and privileged few have access; a world where conformity is congratulated and "going into daddy's business" is the paramount ambition. It will also show you that conformity and privilege often breed a high sense of social duty.

Harrow School is perched on a hill with a matchless view of northwest London. Founded in 1571 by the wealthy yeoman John Lyon, it was originally intended for the education of poor boys, but is now one of the most expensive schools in the world. The fourth form room dates from 1611, and contains the names of famous pupils, cut into the panels – among them, Byron, Robert Peel, Sheridan, Palmerston and Winston Churchill (who couldn't stand the place).

Our hero finds his school intolerable, too. But in myth and legend, no matter how frightening, there is always an answer . . .

J.R.E. PONSFORD

The afternoon sun slanted through the pale amber glass of the cricket pavilion window, and illuminated it like a chapel. Faintly, through the open skylights, Kieran could hear the knocking of bat against ball, followed by shouts of encouragement and ripples of applause.

It was Thursday, First XI *v* Milton College, attendance obligatory. But Kieran hardly ever went to cricket matches. In fact, he kept away from every school event where Benson and his friends could find him. He had been here five weeks now, since the start of the Summer Half, and Benson and his friends still chased him and ragged him as badly as they had on his very first day.

It had all started while he was unpacking his trunk. Marker, the head boy of Mallards' House, tall and blonde-headed and spotty and noble, had strode breezily into his room while he was unpacking his pyjamas. "Any good at eccer, O'Sullivan?" he had asked.

Kieran had studied the Heaton School information booklet for new boys carefully, and he knew that "eccer" was school slang for any kind of games; just as "ducker" meant swimming; while "short ducker", perversely, meant a cross-country run.

"I'm good at cricket, sir," he had volunteered.

"You're Irish, aren't you, O'Sullivan? All right then: name three famous Irish cricketers. And you don't have

33

to call me 'sir'. You only call the beaks 'sir', and that's to their faces. Behind their backs you can call them anything you like."

Kieran had flushed. He was small for his age, curly headed, with a spattering of freckles across the bridge of his nose, and eyes as green as his mother's, green as those marbles they called "sea-green sailors". A scholarship boy.

"I don't think I know any Irish cricketers," he admitted.

"Well, exactly," Marker had told him. "But how about a house knock-about in the nets this afternoon?"

"All right," said Kieran. He had already been feeling homesick. His mother had seen him off at Shannon, and she had waved and waved until the airline bus had turned the corner around the terminal building, and she had probably kept on waving even when he couldn't see her. Ever since he had woken up in the morning, there had been a lump in Kieran's throat, and no matter how often he swallowed he hadn't been able to get rid of it.

On the plane he had closed his eyes and he had been able to smell his mother's perfume and feel her arms around him – his mother with her camel-coloured Marks & Spencer coat and her hair that was going grey on one side because of Stress.

"You've got some cricket kit, I suppose?" Marker had asked him.

"Yes, sir," Kieran had told him, and lifted out of the trunk the white V-necked cricket sweater with the yellow and brown house colours around the neck.

Marker had been looking casually out of the window, down at "yarder", three floors below, where some of the boys were already playing football. He had turned and smiled, his hair shining godlike in the sun, and then he had stared in disbelief.

"What on earth's *that*?"

That lump again; that unswallowable lump. "It's my cricket sweater, sir."

Marker had let out a huge great shout of laughter. "That's your cricket sweater? I've never seen anything like it! My God, what happened to it?"

His laughter had attracted two or three older boys who were walking down the corridor. They had stopped and looked, and then they had burst out laughing, too.

"That's not a cricket sweater! That's a caveman outfit!"

"You'll look like a Yeti in that!"

Kieran had clutched the sweater tight and tears had prickled his eyes.

"We haven't got very much money, sir. Granny O'Sullivan knitted it for me, from one of the school photographs."

Marker had laughed so much that his face had turned scarlet and tears had run down his cheeks. The other boys had screamed and yelled and kicked the panelled walls of the corridor. Kieran had sat on his bed and bitten his lip to stop himself from crying, his cricket sweater bundled in his lap.

Granny O'Sullivan had been so proud of it. She had kissed him and said, "Off to such a posh school, Kieran! Who'd have believed it? You'll be the smartest boy on the cricket pitch, believe me!"

Marker had soon forgotten about the cricket jumper. After all, he was lofty and mature, an upper VIth, and above all that kind of thing. But the other boys – the Removes – hadn't. The worst of them all had been Benson, a swarthy, thick-necked boy with black curly hair and boils and a black silky moustache. Benson was the youngest son of the Benson Camping Supplies family. His brother had been head of school and captain of squash, and his father drove a bronze Bentley Continental R and gave absurdly generous donations to the Heaton School fund. Benson's mother wasn't his mother at all, but his father's third wife – a young blonde woman with deeply-tanned skin and vivid green short-skirted suits. Benson called her The Stick Insect.

Kieran couldn't imagine how Benson hadn't been hurt by his father's divorces. Two divorces! Perhaps you got used to it. His own parents' divorce had cut him apart like broken glass. There had been so many rows, so much shouting, and then those long boring hours in the waiting rooms of solicitors' offices, with the rain pattering against the windows and the smell of old magazines. Then his father saying, with immense pride, those terrible words, worse than a death sentence, "You're a lucky boy, Kieran. You've won a scholarship to Heaton."

So here he sat in the upper gallery of the cricket pavilion on this hot July afternoon, listening to the distant sounds of First XI *v* Milton College, dreaming and thinking and waiting for the hours to go by. A wasp flew in through the skylight and bizzled around for a while, and then flew out again.

Kieran took his mother's last letter out of his pocket. Pale blue Basildon Bond, with rubbery glue on the top of each sheet. Not like the heavily embossed note-paper that everybody else received from their mothers, with house names like The Cedars and Crowhurst Lodge and Amherst. *My darling Kieran, I miss you so much. I go into your bedroom every day and turn down your bed, waiting for the day you come home. I'm sure you've made lots of friends, though. Rufus sends you a woof.*

He folded the letter up and tucked it back into his pocket. Gradually the sunlight in the cricket pavilion crept around, until it illuminated the tall glass case that stood in the very centre of the right-hand wall. Inside the case was propped a cricket bat, a pair of worn-out pads, and a pair of old-fashioned wicketkeeper's gloves, as well as a faded black-and-white striped blazer, a First XI tie and a black tasselled cap.

Kieran stood up and walked across to the case and looked inside. He had looked inside it almost every day, because he always came here after lessons, so that Benson and the others wouldn't find him. He sat here and did his prep and ate apples and Drifter bars and sometimes he even fell asleep. It was the one place in the whole school where he felt safe and secure.

In the back of the glass case stood the oak-framed photograph of J. R. E. Ponsford, School Cricket Captain 1931–36. Public schools' champion batsman, 1935. A handsome, smiling boy, with dark brushed-back hair and amused-looking eyes. Kieran had liked him from the moment he had first seen him. At least he smiled. At least he didn't call him "Granny O'Sullivan" like the other boys. At least he didn't steal his tuck and spill ink over his prep and drop his towel in the mud.

At least he didn't make him cry.

The afternoon wore on. Kieran sat down in the corner and took out the fountain pen and the writing pad that his mother had bought for him at the corner stores. He had written home almost every day. *Dear Mummy, I am very homesick but I am sure that I will get used to it. I have been playing a lot of cricket and the maths teacher Mr Barnett is nice. The food is not very nice we had grissle in the sheppers pie but I have plenty of tuck so not to worry.*

Lonely. He was so lonely.

But this time he looked at the sun-gilded case in the cricket pavilion, and then carefully wrote, in his best rounded handwriting: *Dear Mummy, I have made a good friend in the 6th Form his name is Ponsford. He has been very kind to me and takes me for net practice. He is the school's best batsman. He never rags me and won't allow any of the other boys to rag me either, even when they say things about me being Irish or having a cricket sweater that granny knitted.*

I am very happy here now so you mussnt worry. Ponsford is coaching me every evening so I expect that I will be chosen for the junior cricket team. I must go now as Ponsford is taking me for tea in the town.

He folded up the letter very small. It made him feel better, writing a letter like that, because he knew that it would make his mother feel better too. If he had actually known Ponsford, he was sure that Ponsford would have been just like that, too: generous and kind and protective. He imagined himself and Ponsford, walking down the hill with their hands in their pockets, chatting about cricket and what they were going to have for tea. There was a place called Café Café that all the Removes talked about. Their parents sometimes came at weekends and took them there for lunch and bought them beer too.

He lay on the floor and rested his head on his folded-up blazer and thought about playing cricket. He was bowling, Ponsford was batting. The sun was going down over the oak trees, and the late afternoon air was stitched with midges.

"Well done, O'Sullivan, that was a cracking ball!"

He slept. His closed eyelids trembled. His thumb crept

towards his mouth, but he didn't suck it. He hadn't sucked his thumb since he was three.

He woke up suddenly and the cricket pavilion was deep in gloom.

He stood up, and held up his wrist towards the window so that he could see what time it was. Oh, no! It was five minutes to ten. That meant that he had missed supper and callover and prep and everything! In a panic, he picked up his blazer and hurried along the gallery and down the stairs. He reached the front doors of the pavilion and tried to open them, but they were locked.

He rattled and rattled at the door handles but they wouldn't budge. He ran along to the far end of the pavilion, where they served the teas. All the windows were closed and locked; the door to the kitchen was locked, too.

He tried the ladies' toilets. Thank God, they were open! Even better, the window wasn't locked, either. He stood on the lavatory seat, climbed onto the windowsill, and opened it up. He was balanced awkwardly for a moment, and his heel caught a tin of Harpic. It dropped with a clatter and a splash into the lavatory, and he waited breathlessly for a moment, listening, in case anybody had heard him. There was silence, and then the clock over Big School ponderously chimed ten.

O clock (as the school song put it) *that measures out each day*

Of diligence and carefree play!

He dropped down from the window onto the verandah. He twisted his ankle, but it wasn't too bad. He started to run and hop across the cricket-pitch towards the dark, Gothic outline of Mallards.

He took a short cut back to the house by running

through the housemaster's garden. It was dark there, and heavily overgrown with sycamores, and with any luck nobody would see him. But as he ran round the back of the housemaster's garden shed, he collided at full tilt with four or five boys who were gathered in the shadows. Cigarettes were glowing in the darkness like fireflies.

"Hey, who's that?" yelped one of the boys.

A butane lighter flared. Kieran saw Muggeridge and Parker – and oh God – Benson too.

"God almighty, O'Sullivan. You smelly little bog dweller. You practically gave me a heart attack!"

"What are you doing out here? Shells are supposed to be tucked up in their beddy-weddies!"

"Yes, what are you doing out here, you little cretin? Spying, were you? Trying to get us into clag with Bonedome?" Bonedome was Mr Henderson, their housemaster, who had an angular, bony head with five long strands of hair combed meticulously across it.

Benson pushed his way forward and shoved Kieran in the chest. Kieran stumbled back across an old rusty lawn roller, and tore the seat of his trousers. He tried to get up but Benson pushed him again, and this time he fell right down between the roller and the side of the shed, scraping his ear against the splintery timber.

"You're a sneaky little cretin, O'Sullivan. What are you?"

"Leave me alone!" Kieran protested. He was already close to tears. He tried to get up yet again, but Benson this time punched him in the ribs.

"You're a sneaky little Irish cretin, that's what you are. You eat potatoes and you live in a bog and you say begorrah at the end of every sentence. And your old granny knitted your uniform."

40

Kieran managed to stand up. He said, "Leave me alone, Benson. I haven't done anything to you!"

"Oh yes, you have," said Benson, seizing the lapels of Kieran's blazer and screwing them around so that he almost choked him. "You've been breathing the same air as me, and living on the same planet. You're a horrible little apology for a person, O'Sullivan, and everything about you offends me. Everything!"

"Have you seen the bog dweller's cricket bag?" put in Muggeridge. "Is it real rhinoceros hide from Louis Vuitton, do you think?"

"Oh, I don't think so," said Benson, fiercely ruffling up Kieran's hair.

"Is it canvas and pigskin from Slazenger, do you think?"

"I doubt it," said Benson. His face was pressed so close to Kieran's that Kieran could smell the cigarettes on his breath. "I know, O'Sullivan. Why don't you tell us where your cricket bag comes from? I'm sure we all want one just like it!"

Kieran was weeping now. He couldn't help himself. His ankle throbbed and his ribs hurt and his face was bleeding, and even more humiliating his trousers were flapping open at the back and showing his underpants.

"Come on, O'Sullivan! Tell us where you got your cricket bag, and we'll let you go!"

"You know where I got it," he sobbed.

"Remind us," said Benson, ruffling his hair even more painfully. "I mean, it's got such a subtle label on it, hasn't it?"

"Dead subtle!" laughed Parker.

"It's just a plastic bag from the Co-Op," said Kieran.

"Did you hear that?" crowed Benson. "A plastic bag from the Co-Op! And we're supposed to live and breathe and rub shoulders and break our daily bread with a pathetic little Irish toe rag who carries his cricket kit – his *home-knitted* cricket kit, in a plastic bag from the Co-Op!"

"My father's getting me a proper one," said Kieran. "He's been away: he hasn't had time."

"Oh, your father's getting you a proper one? A plastic bag from Sainsbury's instead!"

"Your father's got all the time in the world!" Benson told him. "What your father hasn't got is any money!"

With that, Benson pushed him away. Kieran hurried off, smearing his tears with his hands. He had almost reached the back gate of the house when he heard footsteps rushing up behind him. The next thing he knew, Benson had kicked him in the back – so hard that he fell against the gatepost and almost knocked himself out.

"You're a bog dweller, O'Sullivan!" Benson raged at him. "You're a smelly Irish peasant!"

Kieran hobbled into yarder, and miserably pressed the combination lock that let him into the house. As he pushed open the door, he saw Bonedome standing by the house notice board, peering through his half-glasses at the cricket fixtures.

"My goodness, O'Sullivan!" Bonedome exclaimed. "Have you been run over?"

Matron dabbed his scrapes and his scratches with anti-septic, and gave him a paracetamol tablet and a glass of water. She was a bustling, friendly Australian woman whose husband worked for Qantas out at Heathrow Airport.

"Looks like you've been fighting, young man," she said, as she examined his cheek.

"Actually, I fell."

"Where from? The top of the clock tower?"

"I was late. I was trying to climb over the garden fence."

"You weren't down in the town, were you? Two Heaton boys were beaten up quite badly last term."

Kieran didn't answer. He had that lump in his throat again.

"You know what the Aborigines used to do, when they got the worst of a fight?"

Kieran shook his head.

"They used to make this special potion, and shake it over the spears and the loincloths of their dead warriors, and the dead warriors would come alive again and help them to fight their battles. Spooky, don't you think?"

"Yes," Kieran managed to say.

Matron gently ruffled his hair. "You go and get into bed. I'll bring you something warm to drink, and then you can get some sleep. Leave your trousers out and I'll sew them for you."

Kieran said, "All right," but he had to turn his face away so that Matron wouldn't see him crying.

Dear Mummy, things are going very well. I am very happy. I have been playing cricket for the Juniors and Ponsford says that he has rarely seen such a good all-rounder as me (which of course made me pleased). I have still been getting some ragging from a horrible boy called Benson but Ponsford warned him to stay away and now everything is okay. Ponsford's parents are extremely rich and they have a large house in the country, Kent, I think. He has invited me to stay for the half term with him.

My darling Kieran, I am so pleased that you are settling down so well at Heaton. We are all so proud that you are playing for the junior cricket team. Mr Murphy at the corner stores sends you his warmest congratulations! I am also very pleased that your friend Ponsford has invited you to spend half term with him. It would be an enormous help to me if you could, since I am rather short of £££ at the moment – usual problem!!! – and it would certainly save the air fare.

It was half term. Kieran stood in the upper gallery of the cricket pavilion with his face pressed against the glass display case, staring at the photograph of J.R.E. Ponsford. He tried to imagine what they might be doing together. Going to McDonald's for a Big Mac and a large milkshake? Practising cricket in Ponsford's huge, tree-shaded garden? Perhaps they would go swimming in the lake, and then have a big tea, with cakes and everything.

On the floor was a heap of cushions and blankets, and a bag filled with chocolate bars and crisps. He had been living off sweets and crisps for two days now, and he felt hungry and sick. He would have done anything for a hamburger or some fish and chips, but he didn't dare leave the pavilion in case one of the beaks caught sight of him. He knew that Mummy didn't have much money but he wished and wished that he hadn't made up that bit about Ponsford inviting him home for the holidays.

Next to his blankets was a small stack of books: *The Australian Outback, The Look-and-Learn Book of Aborigines, Nyungar Tradition* and *Thorn Bird Country.* He had taken them out of the school library before half term, and he had already found two mentions of the story that Matron had told him, about the potion that could bring dead warriors to life. It was part of the frightening *kadaitcha* magic practised in Queensland. The blood and the feathers of a bird were mixed with mud and crushed-up

44

bone, while the sorcerer chanted *epuldugger, epuldugger*, which meant "come to the place where the dead spirit rises up and takes revenge".

In Australia, the potion was made with emu feathers and emu blood, and the bones were either human or kangaroo. But Kieran didn't think that it would make any difference if he used any old bird, or any old bone. It was the magic that counted, the *kadaitcha*, the determination to do harm.

He unwrapped another Crunchie and ate it without enthusiasm. J. R. E. Ponsford smiled at him kindly from his glass case as if he were saying, "Chin up, old man! You can do it!" But Kieran stared back at him dejectedly and wondered whether he could.

On Sunday evening, the school grounds were noisy with Range Rovers and Jaguars and BMWs as the rest of the boys returned from their half-term holiday. Kieran hid in the house changing rooms until a quarter to nine, and then skirted around the outside of Mallards, and walked in through the front door as if he had just arrived.

"Good holiday, O'Sullivan?" Bonedome asked him. "And how was Ireland?"

"Full of bog peasants, as usual!" Benson remarked, pushing past them.

Bonedome gave an indulgent laugh. He didn't wait for Kieran to answer his question, but turned to a senior boy and said, "Congratulations on your father's CBE, Mason! You must be very proud of him!"

The bell rang for supper. Kieran was so hungry that he could hardly wait. He left the house and jogged across the fields and up the wide stone steps to the main school dining hall. A few other boys were running from other

45

houses, too – from Carlisle's and Headmaster's – so that they could be first in the queue.

The clock on top of Big School chimed nine, and a flock of starlings turned and wheeled around the clocktower. The school rooftops had been plagued with starlings this year; and it was a starling that Kieran had found this morning, limping along the verandah of the cricket pavilion with a broken wing. He had hesitated, and then killed it with a brick. He didn't like to think about it. He could still see its eye staring accusingly out of its squashed head.

He managed to be fifth in the queue in the dining hall. It was sausages tonight, as it always was on the nights they returned to school from half-term holidays. Kieran asked for three, with heaps of baked beans and mashed potatoes. He carried his plate carefully back along the line of jostling boys. The dining hall was filling up now, and the noise of laughing and hooting and shouting was almost deafening.

Kieran had almost reached the house table when somebody tripped him. He staggered, nearly caught his balance, but then his whole plateful of supper dropped onto his shirt and down his trousers. The plate dropped too, and broke in half.

"God!" said Benson. "These bog peasants are so stupid they can't even carry a plate!"

Kieran took a whole handful of beans and mashed potato from the front of his shirt and threw it in Benson's face. There was a huge roar of laughter, and a shout of "Fight! Fight! Fight!" Benson lunged at Kieran but Kieran dodged away, and then ran for the door.

"I'm going to kill you for this!" screamed Benson. He turned to Muggeridge and Parker, and said, "Come on, let's sort him out once and for all!"

Kieran flew down the steps outside the dining hall three at a time. But instead of running back towards the house, he vaulted the rosebeds that lined the pathway, and cut diagonally across the cricket pitch towards the pavilion. He ran as fast as he could, his shoes drumming on the hard grass. *Epuldugger, epuldugger!* Help me! *Epuldugger, epuldugger!* Help me!

He heard Benson and his friends running along the path. The far side of the pitch was so shadowy that they obviously couldn't see him at first. He had almost reached the safety of the pavilion when he heard Muggeridge whooping, "There he is! Bog peasant halloooo!"

Kieran ran around the pavilion to the toilet window. He dragged one of the heavy wrought-iron benches across, and climbed up on it, and scrambled onto the windowsill. He caught his pocket on the handle, but he managed to disentangle himself and drop down into the Ladies. He crossed the main pavilion floor and ran up the stairs.

Benson and his friends reached the pavilion only a few moments later, panting and swearing. Parker noisily shook the front door handles, but the door was locked. Then they ran round to the back and tried the back door, but that was locked, too.

"Where's he got to, the little cretin?" Benson demanded. "I'm going to wring his neck when I catch hold of him!"

It was then that Muggeridge caught sight of the open window. "There! He's climbed in there!"

"Then he's caught like a rat in a trap, isn't he?" said Benson.

The three of them climbed in through the window. They were much bigger and heavier than Kieran, and they were gasping by the time they had managed it.

"It isn't half dark. Where is this?"

"It's the Ladies' loo, for God's sake! Hey, careful! I nearly put my foot down it."

They crossed the pavilion floor. It was only ten past nine, but the evening was cloudy, and the interior of the pavilion was thick with clotted shadows.

"Any lights anywhere?" asked Muggeridge; but Benson said, "Better not. This is out of bounds except during cricket matches. Don't want the groundsmen coming around to find out who's in here."

Treading as quietly as they could, they reached the stairs.

"I'll bet you anything he's hiding up there."

They listened. The pavilion was silent, except for their own breathing and the occasional creak of an old timber.

Upstairs, at the very end of the gallery, Kieran was standing next to the glass display case. His chest was rising and falling because he had been running so hard, but he was completely calm, completely determined. He whispered, "*Epuldugger, epuldugger*, come to the place where the dead spirit rises up and takes revenge."

He unscrewed the jam jar which he had hidden behind the display case, and dipped his fingers into the potion. It was sticky and it smelled strongly of blood and rugby-field mud.

"*Epuldugger*," he chanted, louder this time. "*Crumbana coomera*. I give blood to the dead man. The dead spirit rises up and takes revenge."

With two fingers, he painted his potion all around the mahogany frame of the cabinet. "*Epuldugger*, help me!" he breathed. He closed his eyes as tight as he could, trying to believe, trying to believe. Tears ran freely down his cheeks. "*Epuldugger*, help me!"

He opened his eyes again, and unfastened the brass

catch on the display case door, and swung it open. The glass momentarily reflected the pale, moonlike clock face on the top of Big School. Inside the case it smelled of old, musty clothes and varnish.

Ponsford's cap, Ponsford's blazer, Ponsford's cricket flannels, all neatly folded. Ponsford's record-breaking cricket bat.

"*Epuldugger*," wept Kieran. "*Please!*"

Downstairs, Benson and his friends approached the foot of the staircase. "O'Sullivan!" Benson shouted. "We know you're up there, O'Sullivan! You'd better give yourself up before we come up and do something you seriously wouldn't like!"

They listened again, but all they could hear was the faintest scratching sound, and that could have been anything – a mouse or a bird.

"Come on," said Benson. Taking one slow step at a time, he began to climb the stairs, and his friends followed. They reached the upper gallery and stood peering into the amber-tinted gloom.

"O'Sullivan? Come on, O'Sullivan. We're missing our supper because of you, and that could mean death, or even worse."

"I say we lock the toilet window so that he has to stay here all night," Muggeridge suggested.

"I say we find the little bog dweller and beat him up," Benson insisted.

They took two or three steps forward. They stopped, straining their ears, straining their eyes.

"They've got a natural talent for cowardice, these Irish peasants," said Parker. "It's all they're any good at."

Benson said, "*Ssh!*"

They heard a slight scuffling sound. Then two sharp knocks. Then they heard somebody walking towards them; and what was strange was the rattling, rumbling noise that his shoes made on the parquet flooring. The sort of noise that cricket studs made.

Out of the shadows at the very far end of the gallery, a tall figure appeared. He was dressed all in white, and his face was white, too – as white as a photograph, as white as death. Most unnerving of all, his eyes were closed, and yet he walked towards them without any hesitation whatsoever.

He was wearing a black cricket cap, emblazoned with the HS insignia of Heaton School, and he was carrying a cricket bat. He wasn't carrying it casually, either. It was already raised to waist level in both hands, as if he were just about to hit a fast, hard ball from the other end of the pitch.

"Who the hell are *you*?" said Parker, but his voice was very much shriller than usual.

The young man in white didn't break his rattling, studded stride for even a second, even though his eyes remained closed. He came towards Parker at a fast walking pace and hit him on the side of the head with his cricket bat, with a terrible knocking sound that echoed all around the gallery.

Parker dropped to the floor without a sound. Muggeridge started to kneel down beside him, then thought better of it, but it was too late. The young man hit him across the shoulders, and then again, on the back of the head, and then again, and again, and Parker's right ear was reduced to a smashed piece of red gristle.

Benson, whining, tried to dodge back towards the stairs. But the young man in white came relentlessly after him, raising his bat high.

"Go away! Leave me alone!" Benson shouted at him, hoarsely. "You're mad, go away!"

The bat swung and hit him hard on the left shoulder.

"Leave me alone! Leave me alone!" he screamed.

The batsman hit Benson again, and this time his collarbone audibly snapped. He whimpered, and ducked, and turned, and tried to run towards the stairs, but Kieran was standing there, almost as pale as the cricketer, his eyes wide and staring, his hands raised, palms outwards, as if he were praying, or invoking a spirit.

"For God's sake, O'Sullivan!" Benson screamed at him.

But then the batsman hit him on the side of the head with a blow that would have sent a cricket ball way past the boundary, over the roof ridge of Big School, and out of sight. The end of the bat split. Benson's skull cracked, and he spun around and collapsed onto the floor.

Kieran stood over him, saying nothing, his hands still raised. He looked up at the silent white figure who was motionless now, white as a photograph, white as death. Tears sparkled in Kieran's eyes.

"Thank you," he whispered. "Thank you, thank you, thank you."

Kieran's mother sat in the housemaster's office holding her white vinyl handbag and looking pale. One of the senior boys, not realizing who she was, had remarked to his friends how pretty she was: a "Yummy Mummy" as they always called them. He hadn't had time to evaluate the Marks & Spencer summer dress or the cultured pearl necklace.

Bonedome sat behind his desk and steepled his hands and tried to look sad but sympathetic. This was almost impossible for a man who had never truly felt either emotion in the whole of his life, and resulted in an extraordinary grimace, as if he had just bitten into a lemon.

"You understand that Kieran will have to be suspended during the police investigation," he said. "We can't possibly risk any kind of repetition."

"But why Kieran?" asked his mother. "He told me on the phone that Ponsford did it."

Bonedome took off his glasses. "I'm sorry? Ponsford?"

"He said his friend Ponsford did it, to protect him. He said that Benson and the others had been bullying him, and so Ponsford had taught them a lesson. I mean – I know what he did was terrible, it went far beyond anything he should have done – but why suspend Kieran?"

"Ponsford," said Bonedome. Then, "*Ponsford?* We have nobody at Heaton named Ponsford."

"Well, that's ridiculous," said Kieran's mother, shaking her head and smiling. "Ponsford has been Kieran's closest friend ever since he's been here . . . he's been teaching him cricket . . . Kieran spent the half term holiday with him. J.R.E. Ponsford, Upper Sixth, captain of cricket."

Bonedome blinked. "J. R. E. Ponsford? J. R. E. Ponsford, captain of cricket?"

"Then you *do* know him?"

"My dear Mrs O'Sullivan, everybody at Heaton knows J. R. E. Ponsford. He was the greatest cricket champion the school ever produced."

Kieran's mother's smile faded away. "*Was?*" she said.

"I'm afraid so, Mrs O'Sullivan. J. R. E. Ponsford was educated at Heaton from 1931 to 1936. Subsequently, he joined the RAF as a bomber pilot, and went missing over the Dutch coast in the winter of 1942."

Kieran was still standing in front of the glass display case

52

in the cricket pavilion when his mother came to take him home. She put her arm around his shoulder, and held him close, and she still smelled like Mummy.

"I'm sorry," she said.

Kieran said nothing, but looked for the last time into the bright open eyes of J. R. E. Ponsford, and down at his famous cricket bat. A five centimetre crack bore witness to his last and greatest match.

Voodoo Child

Littlehampton, Sussex

The real heart of Voodoo Child *beats in Macon, Georgia, where the idea for this story first came to me, one sweltering night when my car radio played* Are You Experienced? *But Jimi Hendrix was so much a part of the psychedelic scene in London that I can never separate my memories of him from Notting Hill and Park Lane and all the places I used to spend my time when he was still alive. Littlehampton being one of them.*

I met Jimi only once, when we were taking photographs in Hyde Park. He said, "I was born on another planet, you know that?" I said, "I don't think you were, but you'll go back there."

Perhaps he did. But meanwhile, this story doesn't take place on another planet, but a plain and ordinary seaside resort on the Sussex coast, at the mouth of the River Arun. It's a dull little town, but its beaches are wonderful. The tide goes out for almost a mile, and you can walk ankle-deep until you think you can almost walk to France. You can stand all that distance away from land, with the sea breeze blowing in your face, and think of everybody you knew in days gone by; and what kind of devilry it was that took them away.

VOODOO CHILD

I saw Jimi ducking into S.H. Patel's newsagent on the corner of Clarendon Road and his face was ashy gray. I said to Dulcie, "Jesus, that's Jimi," and followed him inside, shop doorbell clanging. Mr Patel was marking up stacks of *Evening Standards* and said, "*New Musical Express* not in yet, Charlie," but all I could do was to shake my head.

I walked cautiously along the shelves of magazines and children's sweets and humorous birthday cards. I could hear Mrs Patel's television playing the theme tune from *Neighbours* somewhere in the back of the shop. There was a musty smell of Manila envelopes and candy shrimps and fenugreek.

I came around the corner of the shelves and Jimi was standing by the freezer cabinet looking at me wide-eyed; not sly and funny the way he always used to, but wounded almost, defensive. His hair was just the same, frizzy, and he was wearing the same sleeveless Afghan jacket and purple velvet flares; and even the same Navajo necklace. But his skin looked all white and dusty, and he really scared me.

"Jimi?" I whispered.

At first, he didn't say anything, but there was a chilliness around him and it wasn't just the freezer cabinet with its Birds Eye peas and Findus mixed carrots and Economy beefburgers.

"Jimi . . . I thought you were dead, man," I told him. I hadn't called anybody "man" for over fifteen years. "I was really totally convinced you were dead."

He sniffed, and cleared his throat, his eyes still wounded looking. "Hallo, Charlie," he said. He sounded hoarse and remote and blocked-up, the same way he sounded that last night I saw him, September 17, 1970.

I was so scared I could scarcely speak; but at the same time Jimi was so much the same that I felt weirdly reassured; like it was still 1970 and the past twenty years just hadn't happened. I could have believed that John Lennon was still alive and that Harold Wilson was still Prime Minister and that it was peace and love forever.

"I've been trying to get back to the flat, man," Jimi told me.

"What? What flat?"

"Monika's flat, man, in Lansdowne Crescent. I've been trying to get back."

"What the hell do you want to go back there for? Monika doesn't live there any more. Well, not so far as I know."

Jimi rubbed his face and ash seemed to fall between his fingers. He looked distracted, frightened, as if he couldn't think straight. But then I'd often seen him stoned out of his skull, talking weird talk, all about some planet or other where things were ideal, the godlike planet of Supreme Wisdom.

"Where the hell have you *been*?" I asked him. "Listen – Dulcie's outside. You remember Dulcie? Let's go and have a drink."

"I've got to get into that flat, man," Jimi insisted.

"What for?"

He stared at me as if I were crazy. "What for? Shit! What for, for fuck's sake."

I didn't know what to do. Here was Jimi, three feet in front of me, real, talking, even thought Jimi had been dead for twenty years. I never saw his actual dead body, and I never actually went to his funeral because I couldn't afford the fare, but why would the Press and his family have said that he was dead if he wasn't?

Monika had found him lying on the bed, cold, his lips purple from suffocation. The doctors at St Mary Abbot's Hospital had confirmed that he was dead on arrival. He had suffocated from breathing vomit. He had to be dead. Yet here he was, just like the old psychedelic days, Purple Haze and Voodoo Chile and Are You Experienc-c-ced?

The shop doorbell rang. It was Dulcie, looking for me. "Charlie?" she called. "Come on, Charlie, I'm dying for a drink."

"Why don't you come and have a drink with us?" I asked Jimi. "Maybe we can work out a way of getting you back in the flat. Maybe we can find out who the estate agent is, and talk to him. Courtney probably knows. Courtney knows everybody."

"I can't come with you, man, no way," Jimi said, evasively.

"Why not? We're meeting Derek and all the rest of them down at the Bull's Head. They'd really like to see you. Hey – did you read about Mitch selling your guitar?"

"Guitar?" he asked, as if he couldn't understand me.

"Your Strat, the one you used at Woodstock. He got something like a hundred and eighty grand for it."

Jimi gave a dry, hollow sniff. "Got to get into that flat, man, that's all."

"Well, come for a drink first."

"No way, man, can't be done. I'm not supposed to see nobody. Not even you."

"Then what are you going to do?" I asked him. "Where are you staying?"

"I ain't staying nowhere, man."

"You can stay with me. I've got a house in Clarendon Road now."

Jimi shook his head. He wasn't even listening. "I've got to get into the flat, that's all. No two ways about it."

"Charlie?" protested Dulcie. "What the hell are you doing?"

I felt a cold, dusty draft; and I turned around; and the Patels' multicoloured plastic curtain was swinging, but Jimi was gone. I dragged the curtain back and shouted, "Jimi!" But there was nobody in the Patels' armchair-crowded sitting room except a brown bare-bottomed baby with a runny nose and an elderly grand-mother in a lime-green sari, who stared at me with eyes as hostile as stones. Above the brown-tiled fire-place was a luridly coloured photograph of the Bhutto family.

I apologized, and retreated. Dulcie said, "What the hell's the matter with you? I've been waiting outside for ages."

"I saw Jimi," I told her.

"Jimmy who?" she demanded. She was young and blonde and pretty and tarty and always intolerant. Perhaps that was why I liked her so much.

"Hendrix, Jimi Hendrix. He was here, just now."

Dulcie stopped chewing gum and stared at me with her mouth open. "Jimi Hendrix? What do you mean, Jimi Hendrix?"

"I saw him, he was here."

"What are you talking about? You're out of your fucking tree, you are!"

"Dulcie, he was here, I swear to God. I've just been

60

talking to him. He said he had to get back into Monika's old flat. You know, the flat where he . . ."

"Pree-cisely," Dulcie mocked me. "The flat where he died."

"He was here, believe me. He was so damned close I could have touched him."

"You're mad," Dulcie declared. "Anyway, I'm not waiting any longer. I'm going down to the Bull's Head for a drink."

"Listen, wait," I told her. "Let's just go round to Monika's flat and see who lives there now. Maybe they know what's going on."

"I don't want to," Dulcie protested. "You're just being ridiculous. He's *dead*, Charlie. He's been dead for twenty years."

But in the end we went round to the flat and rang the doorbell. We saw the grubby net curtains twitching but it was a long time before we heard anybody coming to the door. A cold gray wind blew round the crescent. The railings were clogged with newspaper and empty crisp bags, and the trees were scrubby and bare.

"I don't suppose they even know that Jimi Hendrix used to live here," Dulcie sniffed.

Eventually the door was opened about an inch and a woman's pale face appeared.

"Yes?"

"Oh," I said. "I'm sorry to bother you, but I know somebody who used to live here, and they were wondering if you'd mind if they sort of came back and took a look around. You know, just for old times' sake."

The woman didn't answer. I don't think she really understood what I was on about.

"It wouldn't take long," I told her. "Just a couple of minutes. Just for old times' sake."

She closed the door without saying a word. Dulcie and I were left on the step, under a cold north London sky the colour of glue.

A black woman in a shiny Marks & Spencer's raincoat pushed a huge dilapidated pram across the street. The pram was crowded with children and shopping.

"Now what are you going to do?" asked Dulcie.

"Don't know," I told her. "Let's go and get that drink."

We drove down to the Bull's Head and sat by the window overlooking the Thames. The tide was out, and so the river was little more than a dull gray ribbon in a stretch of sloping black mud.

Courtney Tulloch was there and so were Bill Franklin and Dave Blackman and Margaret and Jane and I suddenly realized that I'd known all of them back in 1970 when Jimi was still alive. It was a strange feeling, like being in a dream.

What had John Lennon written? *"Yea though I wart through the valet of thy shadowy hut I will feed no norman."*

I asked Courtney whether he knew who was living in Monika's old flat but he shook his head. "All the old faces are gone now, man, long gone. It's all changed from what it used to be. I mean it was always run-down and seedy and all that, but everybody knew where they was, black and white, bus driver and whore. Nowadays these kids run riot. It's like the moon."

But Dave said, "I know who took that flat after Monika left. It was John Drummond."

"You mean *the* John Drummond?" I asked him. "John Drummond the guitarist?"

"That's right. But he was only there for a couple of months."

Dulcie said, "You're being really boring today, Charlie. Can I have another drink?"

I bought another round: snowball for Dulcie, Holsten Pils for me. Courtney was telling a joke about a new fast food chain for soul brothers called Blackdonald's. "You'd walk in, right, and there'd be these two big mommas in flowery print frocks talking away to each other, and after about ten minutes one of them would turn around and say, 'You *want* sometin'?'"

I hadn't realized that John Drummond had lived in the same flat as Jimi. For my money, John had been a better guitarist than Jimi; technically, anyway. He was always more single-minded, more creative. He'd been able to make his guitar talk in the same way that Jimi did, but the voice that had come out had been less confused than Jimi's, less angry, less frustrated; and he'd never played an uneven set like Jimi did at Woodstock; or a totally disastrous set like Jimi did at Seattle the last time he ever appeared at a concert in America. John Drummond had played first with Graham Bond and then with John Mayall and then his own "supergroup", the Crash.

John Drummond had reached number one both sides of the Atlantic with *Running A Fever*. But then, without warning, he'd suddenly retired, amid newspaper reports of cancer or multiple sclerosis or chronic heroin addiction, and that had been the last that anybody ever saw of him. That was – what? – 1973, 1974, something like that. I didn't even know if he was dead or alive.

That night in my one-bedroomed flat in Holland Park Avenue the telephone rang. It was Jimi. His voice sounded distant and powdery.

"*I can't talk for long, man. I'm in a call box in Queensway.*"

"I went to the flat, the woman wouldn't let me in."

"*I have to get in there, Charlie. No two ways about it.*"

"Jimi – I found something out. John Drummond had that flat after Monika. Maybe he could help."

"*John Drummond? You mean that young guy who kept hanging around wanting to play with the Experience?*"

"That's right, amazing guitarist."

"*He was shit. He couldn't play for shit.*"

"Oh come on, Jimi. He was great. *Running A Fever* was a classic."

There was a long silence on the other end of the phone. I could hear traffic, and Jimi breathing. Then Jimi said, "*When was that?*"

"When was what?"

"*That song you mentioned, 'Running A Fever', when was that?*"

"I don't know. Early seventy-four, I think."

"*And he was good?*"

"He was amazing."

"*Was he as good as me?*"

"If you want the God's honest truth, yes he was."

"*Did he sound like me?*"

"Yes, he did, except not many people would admit it, because he was white."

I looked down into the street. Traffic streamed endlessly past the front of my flat, on its way to Shepherds Bush. I thought of Jimi singing *Crosstown Traffic* all those years ago.

Jimi said, "*Where's this Drummond guy now? Is he still playing?*"

"Nobody knows where he is. He had a number one hit with *Fever* and then he quit. Warner Bros couldn't even find anybody to sue."

"*Charlie*," urged Jimi hoarsely, "*you've got to do me*

one favour. You've got to find this guy. Even if he's dead, and you can only find out where they buried him."

"Jimi, for Christ's sake. I wouldn't even know where to start."

"Please, Charlie. Find him for me."

He hung up. I stood by the window for a long time feeling frightened and depressed. If Jimi didn't know that John Drummond had played so well – if he wasn't aware that John had reached number one with *Running A Fever* – then where had he been for the past twenty years? Where had he been, if not dead?

I telephoned Nik Cohn and Nik met me in this stuffy afternoon drinking club in Mayfair. Nik had written the definitive work on pop in the 'sixties, *Awopbopaloopa Alopbamboom* and he had known just about everybody including the Beatles and Eric Burdon and Pink Floyd in their UFO days and Jimi of course, and John Drummond.

He hadn't seen John for yonks but about six years ago he had received a postcard from Littlehampton on the south coast, saying nothing much except that John was trying to get his mind and his body back together again.

"He didn't exactly explain what he meant," Nik told me. "But he was always like that. You got the feeling that he was always thinking about something else. Like trying to deal with something that was going on inside him."

Littlehampton in the middle of winter was windswept and bleak. The funfair was closed, the beach huts were closed, the Red Indian canoes were all tied together in the middle of the boating pond so that nobody could reach them. Fawn sand waved in flat horsetails across the promenade, and old lolly-wrappers danced across the tufted sea-grass.

I spent hours walking around the town centre looking for John Drummond; but that first afternoon I didn't see anybody between the ages of three and sixty-five. It started to rain – cold, persistent rain, and so I rang the doorbell at one of the redbrick Edwardian villas close to the seafront and booked myself a room for the night.

It wasn't much of a place to stay, but it was warm, and there were fish and chips for supper, in a small dining room which I shared with two travelling salesmen, an unmarried mother with a snotty wriggling boy in pee-stained dungarees, and a bristly-moustached retired colonel with leather armpatches on his jacket, and a habit of clearing his throat like a fusillade of gunshots.

Not a drum was heard, not a funeral note, as his corse to the ramparts we hurried.

Next morning it was still raining but I walked the silvery-gray streets all the same, looking for John Drummond. I found him totally by accident, in a pub on the corner of River Road, sitting in a corner with an untouched pint of McEwan's and a half-eaten packet of salt-and-vinegar crisps. He was smoking incessantly and staring at nothing.

He was thin, so much thinner than the last time I'd seen him, and his hair was graying and wild. He looked a bit like a geriatric Pete Townshend. He was dressed in tight black trousers and a huge black leather jacket with about fifty zippers and D-rings. He wore a lapel badge with a picture of three pairs of scampering legs on it and the motif *Running Men Tour 1986*.

I parked my lager next to his, and dragged up a chair. He didn't even look at me.

"John?" I said, without much confidence.

His eyes flicked across at me, and narrowed.

"John, it's Charlie. Charlie Goode. Don't you remember me?"

"Charlie Goode?" he asked, dully. Then, very slowly, as if recognition were penetrating his consciousness like a pebble falling into treacle, "Cha-a-arlie Goode! That's right! Charlie Goode! How are you keeping, man? I haven't seen you since . . . when was the last time I saw you?"

"Isle of Wight."

"So it was. Isle of Wight. Fuck me."

I lifted my beer and drank some, wiping my lips with the back of my hand. "I've been looking for you since yesterday," I told him.

He sucked at the butt of his cigarette, then crushed it out. He didn't make any comment, didn't even look as if he'd heard me.

"I'm not really sure why," I said, trying to sound light-hearted about it. "The thing is, Jimi asked me."

"Jimi asked you?"

"It sounds stupid, doesn't it?" I said, with a forced laugh. "But I met him in the street, in Notting Hill. He's still alive."

John took out another cigarette and lit it with a cheap plastic lighter. He didn't take his eyes off me once.

I said, more seriously, "He was trying to get back into Monika's old pad. He didn't say why. The thing is, he found out that you lived there for a bit, after he . . . well, after he stopped being around. He said I had to find you. He said it was crucial. Don't ask me why."

John blew out smoke. "You saw Jimi and Jimi told you to find me?"

"That's right. I know it sounds stupid."

"No, Charlie, it doesn't sound stupid."

I waited for him to say something else; to explain what was going on; but he wouldn't, or couldn't. He sat there and smoked and drank his beer and occasionally said, "Jimi asked you, fuck me." Or else he sang a snatch from one of Jimi's old songs. *"There's a Red House over yonder . . . that's where my baby stays . . ."*

In the end, though, he drained his glass and stood up and said, "Come on, Charlie. You'd better see what this is all about."

Hunched, spindly-legged, he led me through the rain. We crossed River Road and into Arun Terrace, a long road of small Victorian artisans' cottages with slate roofs and majolica-tiled porches. The hedges smelled of cat's pee and wet cigarette packets were snared in the shrubbery. John pushed open the gate of No 17 "Caledonian" and opened the front door with his own key. Inside it was gloomy and crowded with knickknacks. A miniature ship's wheel with a barometer in it, the plaster head of a grizzled Arab with a hawk on his shoulder, a huge ugly vase full of pink-dyed pampas grass.

"My room's upstairs," he said, and led the way up a flight of impossibly steep stairs, covered in red sculptured carpet. We reached the landing and he opened the door of a small bedsitting room; a plain cold British bedroom with a candlewick bedspread and a varnished wardrobe and a Baby Belling cooker. The only indication that this was the home of one of the best rock guitarists since Eric Clapton was a shiny black Fender Strat with fingermarks all over it.

John pulled over a ratty basketwork chair with a collapsed seat. "Make yourself at home," he told me. Then he sat down himself on the end of the bed, and took out his cigarettes again.

Cautiously, I sat down. I felt as if I were sitting down

at the bottom of a dry well. I watched John light up again and testily smoke. He was growing more agitated by the minute, and I couldn't work out why.

After a while, however, he started talking in a low, flat monotone. "Jimi was always talking about the time he used to tour with The Flames; years ago, before he got famous or anything, just after he left the Army Airborne. They played in some nameless town in Georgia, and Jimi got mixed up with this chick, I always remember what he said about her, 'foxy to the bone'. Anyway, he spent all night with her, even though he missed the tour bus, and even though this chick was married and she kept telling him that her husband would beat her when she got home.

"He told her he wanted to be famous, and she said, sure, you can be famous. At about four o'clock in the morning she took him to see this weird old woman, and this weird old woman gave him a voodoo. She said so long as he fed this voodoo, he'd be fine, and famous all over the world, and every wish he ever wished would come true. But the day he stopped feeding that voodoo, that voodoo would take back everything, and he'd be shit, that's all, just shit.

"But Jimi wanted fame more than anything else. He could play good guitar; but he wanted to play brilliant guitar. He wanted to be so fucking brilliant that nobody would even believe that he came from earth."

"So what happened?" I asked. The rain pattered against the window like a handful of currants.

John blew smoke out of his nose; shrugged. "She gave him the voodoo and the rest is history. He played with the Isley Brothers, Little Richard, Curtis Knight. Then he was famous; then he was gone. Why do you think he wrote that song *Voodoo Chile*? He was a voodoo child, that's all, and that was true."

"John, he's still alive," I insisted. "I saw him; I talked to him. I wouldn't be here, otherwise."

But John shook his head. "He's gone, Charlie. Twenty years gone. When he became famous he started to starve that voodoo but in retaliation the voodoo made him weak; made him crazy. He wanted to play for an audience; but the voodoo made him play music that was way beyond anything that an ordinary audience could understand. It was beyond anything that even great guitarists could understand. You remember Robin Trower, from Procul Harum? He went to see Jimi in Berlin and said that he was amazing, but the audience were out of it. Robin was one of the greatest guitarists ever but *he* was out of it. Jimi was playing guitar that nobody would understand for about a hundred fucking years.

"So Jimi tried to get rid of the voodoo but in the end the voodoo got rid of him. The voodoo cancelled him out, man. If you don't live with me, then you don't live at all. But you don't die, either. You're nothing; you're absolutely nothing. You're a slave, and a servant, and that's the way it's going to be for ever."

"Go on," I whispered.

"There was only one thing he could do; and that was to take the voodoo back to that little town in Georgia that he first got it from. That meant leaving his grave in Seattle and bumming his way back to England; finding the voodoo; and taking it back, in person, and making a gift of it; because if the person you're giving it back to doesn't accept it as a gift, it's still yours, man. Still yours, for ever."

I sat in that ridiculous chair with its collapsed bottom and I couldn't believe what I was hearing.

"What are you trying to tell me? That Jimi's turned into some kind of zombie? Like, the walking dead?"

John smoked, looked away, didn't even try to convince me.

"I saw him," I insisted. "I *saw* him; and he talked to me on the phone. Zombies don't talk to you on the phone."

"Let me tell you something, man," John told me. "Jimi was dead from the moment he accepted that voodoo. Same way I am."

"What do you mean?"

"You want me to show you?"

I swallowed. "I don't know. Maybe, yes. All right."

He stood up, awkwardly. He took off his scruffy black coat, and dropped it on to the bed. Then he crossed his arms and lifted up his T-shirt.

He was white-skinned and skeletal; so thin that I could see his ribs and his arteries, and his heart beating under his skin. But it was his stomach that shocked me the most. Tied tightly to his abdomen with thin ropes of braided hair was a flattish ebony figure, very African in appearance, like a small monkey. It was decorated with feathers and diseased-looking fragments of dried pelt.

Somehow, the monkey figure had become part of John. It was impossible to tell where the figure ended and John began. His skin seemed to have grown around the ebony head and enclosed, in thin translucent webbing, the crooked ebony claws.

John let me look at it for a while, then he dropped his T-shirt and covered it.

"I found it under the floorboards in Monika's hallway. It was all wrapped up in one of Jimi's old shirts. I'm pretty sure that Monika didn't know anything about it. I knew it was dangerous and weird but I wanted the fame, man. I wanted the money. I thought that I could handle it, just like Jimi thought that he could handle it.

"I wore it for a while, tied loose around my waist, under

my shirt, and I fed it bits and pieces just like you'd feed a pet animal. In return it kind of *sang* to me, it's hard to describe unless you've experienced it. It sang to me and all I had to do was play what it sang.

"But then it wanted more. It clung tighter and tighter and I needed it tighter, because when it was tighter it sang such amazing music, and I got better and better. One morning I woke up and it had dug a hole in my skin, and kind of forced its mouth inside me. It was sore, it really hurt, but the music was even better. I didn't even have to listen to it any more, it was right inside me. I didn't even have to feed it with scraps any more, because whatever I ate, it sucked right out for itself.

"It was only when it was taking stuff direct from my stomach that I realized what was really happening. And by that time I was playing music that nobody could relate to. By that time I was so far out that there was no coming back."

He paused, coughed. "Jimi took it off before it went into his gut. But he couldn't play shit without it. It's a need, man. It's worse than any drug you ever imagined in your whole life. He tried pills and booze and acid and everything, but until you've needed the voodoo you don't know the meaning of the word need."

"So what are you going to do?" I asked him.

"Nothing. Go on living."

"Couldn't you give it back to Jimi?"

"What, and commit suicide? This thing's part of me, man. You might just as well tear out my heart."

I sat with John talking about the 1960s until it began to grow dark. We talked about Bondy at the Brighton Aquarium; John Mayall and Chris Farlowe and Zoot Money at the All-Nighter in Wardour Street, where you could get bashed in the face just for looking at somebody else's bird. We talked about sitting on Tooting Graveney Common on cold sunny autumn afternoons listening to the Turtles on a Boots tranny. We talked about the Bo Street Runners and the Crazy World of Arthur Brown. The girls in the miniskirts and the white PVC boots. All gone, man. All vanished, like colourful transparent ghosts. It had never occurred to us at the time that it could ever end.

But one gray evening in 1970 I had walked down Chancery Lane and seen the *Evening Standard* poster "Jimi Hendrix Dead" and they might just as well have announced that our youth had shut up shop.

I left John just after eight o'clock. His room was so dark that I couldn't see his face. The conversation ended and I left, that's all. He didn't even say goodbye.

I walked back to the boarding house. As I stepped into the front door, the bristly-moustached colonel held up the heavy black telephone receiver and announced harshly, "It's for you."

I thanked him and he cleared his throat like a Bren gun.

"*Charlie? It's Jimi. Did you find him?*"

I hesitated. Then I said, "Yes. Yes, I did."

"*He's still alive?*"

"In a manner of speaking, yes."

"*Where is he, man? I have to know.*"

"I'm not sure that I ought to tell you."

"*Charlie – did we used to be friends?*"

"I suppose so."

"*Charlie, you have to tell me where he is. You have to.*"

His voice sounded so panicky that I knew I had to tell him. I heard myself saying the address like a ventriloquist. I didn't dare to think of what might happen if Jimi tried to get the voodoo back. Maybe I should have minded my own business, right from the very beginning. They always say that it's dangerous to mess around with the dead. The dead have different needs from the living; different desires. The dead are more bloody desperate than we can even guess.

I went round to John's place the next morning after breakfast. I rang the doorbell and a fussy old woman with a brindled cat on her shoulder let me in.

"Nothing but trouble, you young men," she complained, hobbling away down the hall. "Nothing but noise. Nothing but loud music. Hooligans, the lot of you."

"Sorry," I said, although I don't think she heard me.

I climbed the stairs to John's room. Outside on the landing, I hesitated. I could hear John's cassette player, and a tap running. I knocked, too softly for John to hear me. Then again, louder.

There was no answer. Only the trickling of the tap water and the cassette playing *Are you experienced . . . have you ever been experienced?*

"John?" I called. "John, it's Charlie!"

I opened the door. I knew what had happened even before I could fully understand what I was looking at. Jimi had got there before me.

John's torso lay on his dark, soaked bedspread, torn wide open, so that his lungs and his stomach and his liver were spread around in brightly-coloured profusion, interconnected with webs of fat and torn-apart skin. His head was floating in the brimful washbasin, bobbing up and down with the flow of the water. Every now and then his right eye peeped at me accusingly over the china rim. His severed legs had been pushed bloodily beneath the bed.

The voodoo was gone.

I spent a week in Littlehampton "helping the police with their inquiries". They knew I hadn't done it, but they strongly suspected that I knew who had. What could I tell them? "Of course, officer! It was Jimi Hendrix"? They'd have had me committed to one of those seaside mental homes in Eastbourne.

I never heard from Jimi again. I don't know how the dead travel the seas, but I know for a fact that they do. Those lonely figures standing by the rails of Icelandic-registered cargo ships, staring at the foamy wake. Those silent passengers on cross-country buses.

Maybe he persuaded the old woman to take the voodoo back. Maybe he didn't. But I've pinned the album cover of *Are You Experienced?* to my kitchen wall, and sometimes I look at it and like to think to myself that Jimi's at peace.

Sex Object

Boston, Massachusetts

There are few cities in the world with better restaurants, worse politicians, or more unpredictable sports teams. Jasper's, on Commercial Street, serves Wellfleet littleneck clams and roasted monkfish that you would cheerfully eat as your last meal. Politicians? Look no further than Ted Kennedy. Sports teams? Look no further than the Red Sox and the New England Patriots. When the Patriots were accused of sexual harassment by the Boston Herald's *Lisa Olson, the team's owner, Victor Kiam, said, "What do Lisa Olson and Saddam Hussein have in common? They've both seen Patriot missiles up close."*

Boston has everything that makes New England great: lobsters, boats, culture and money. It also has the same diseases as many other American cities. The slums of Blue Hill Avenue, the drug trafficking of Seaver Street. Mike Barnicle of the Boston Globe *describes the Athens of the North as "a poseur of a city; a quaint, dirty, provincial little-big-town without street signs".*

But of course Boston has more than its fair share of something else . . . doctors. From the New England Medical Center to the Brigham & Women's Hospital; from Massachusetts General to New England Deaconess,

Boston has some of the brightest, most innovative doctors anywhere. If you're sick, Boston is the place to go.

Or even if you feel like nothing much more than a change . . .

SEX OBJECT

She sat against the foggy afternoon light, perched straight-backed on the black Swedish chair, her ankles crossed. She wore a perfectly tailored Karl Lagerfeld suit and a black straw hat, and her legs were perfect too.

Dr Arcolio couldn't see her face clearly because of the light behind her. But her voice was enough to tell him that she was desperate, in the way that only the wives of very, very rich men are capable of being desperate.

The wives of ordinary men would never think about such things, let alone get desperate about them.

She said, "My hairdresser told me that you were the best."

Dr Arcolio steepled his hands. He was bald, dark and swarthy, and his hands were very hairy. "Your hairdresser?" he echoed.

"John Sant'Angelo . . . he has a friend who wanted to make the change."

"I see."

She was nervy, vibrant, like an expensive racehorse. "The thing was . . . he said that you could do it very differently from all the rest . . . that you could make it real. He said that you could make it *feel* real. Have real responses, everything."

Dr Arcolio thought about that, and then nodded. "This is absolutely true. But then I'm dealing with transplants, you understand, rather than modifications of existing tissue. It's just like heart or kidney surgery . . . we have to find a donor part and then insert that donor part and hope that there's no rejection."

"But if you found a donor . . . you could do it for me?"

Dr Arcolio stood up, and paced slowly around his office. He was a very short man, not more than five-feet-five, but he had a calmness and a presence which made him both fascinating to watch and impressive to listen to. He was dressed very formally, in a three-piece chalkstripe suit, with a white carnation in the buttonhole, and very highly polished Oxfords.

He crossed to the window and drew back the nets, and stood for a long while staring down at Brookline Place. It hadn't rained for nearly seven weeks now, and the sky over Boston was an odd bronze color.

"You realize that what you're asking me to do is very questionable, both medically and morally."

"Why?" she retorted. "It's something I want. It's something I *need*."

"But, Mrs Ellis, the operations I perform are normally to correct a physical situation that is chronically out of tune with my patients' emotional state. I deal with transsexuals, Mrs Ellis, men who have penises and testes but who are psychologically women. When I remove their male genitalia and give them female genitalia instead . . . I am simply changing their bodies in line with their minds. In *your* case, however –"

"In my case, doctor, I'm thirty-one years old, I have a husband who is wealthier than the entire state of Massachusetts, and if I don't have this operation then I will probably lose both him and everything I've ever dreamed of. Don't you think that falls into exactly the same category as your transsexuals? In fact, don't you think my need is greater than some of your men who want to turn into women simply because they like to wear high heels and garter belts and panties by Frederick's of Hollywood?"

Dr Arcolio smiled. "Mrs Ellis . . . I'm a surgeon. I perform operations to rescue people from deep psychological misery. I have to abide by certain strictly defined ethics."

"Dr Arcolio, *I* am suffering from deep psychological misery. My husband is showing every sign of being bored with me in bed and since I'm his fifth wife I think the odds on him divorcing me are growing steadily by the minute, don't you?"

"But what you're asking – it's so radical. It's *more* than radical. And permanent, too. And have you considered that it will disfigure you, as a woman?"

Mrs Ellis opened her black alligator pocketbook and took out a black cigarette, which she lit with a black enameled Dunhill lighter. She pecked, sucked, blew smoke. "Do you want me to be totally candid with you?" she asked.

"I think I insist on your being totally candid with me."

"In that case, you ought to know that Bradley has a real thing for group sex . . . for inviting his pals to make love to me, too. Last week, after that charity ballet at Great Woods, he invited seven of them back to the house. Seven well-oiled Back Bay plutocrats! He told me to go get undressed while they had martinis in the library. Then afterwards they came upstairs, all seven of them."

Dr Arcolio was examining his framed certificate from Brigham and Women's Hospital as if he had never seen it before. His heart was beating quickly: he didn't know why. Wolff-Parkinson-White syndrome? Or atrial fibrillation? Or maybe fear, with a subtle seasoning of sexual arousal? He said, as flatly as he could manage, "When I said candid . . . well, you don't have to tell me any of this. If I *do* decide to go ahead with such an operation, it will only be on the independent recommendations of your family doctor and your psychiatrist."

Mrs Ellis carried on her narrative regardless. "They climbed on top of me and all around me, all seven of them. I felt like I was suffocating in sweaty male flesh. Bradley penetrated me from behind; George Carlin penetrated me from the front. Two of them pushed their cocks into my mouth, until I felt that I was choking. Two forced their cocks into my ears. The other two rubbed themselves on my breasts.

"They got themselves a rhythm going like an Ivy League rowing team. They were roaring with every stroke. *Roaring*. I was like nothing at all, in the middle of all this roaring and rowing. Then the two of them climaxed into my mouth, and the other two into my ears, and the next two over my breasts. Bradley was the last. But when he was finished, and pulled himself out of me, I was dripping with sperm, all over me, dripping; and it was then that I knew that Bradley wanted an object, not a wife, not even a lover. An object."

Dr Arcolio said nothing. He glanced at Mrs Ellis but Mrs Ellis's face was concealed behind a sloping eddy of cigarette smoke.

"Bradley wants a sex object so I've decided that if he wants a sex object I'll *be* a sex object. What difference will it make? Except that Bradley will be happy with me and life will stay the same." She gave a laugh like a breaking champagne glass. "Rich, pampered, secure. And nobody will *know.*"

Dr Arcolio said, "I can't do it. It's out of the question."

"Yes," Mrs Ellis replied. "I knew you'd said that. I came prepared."

"Prepared?" Dr Arcolio frowned.

"Prepared with evidence of three genital transplants which you performed without the permission of the donors' executors. Jane Kestenbaum, August 12, 1987; Lydia Zerbey, February 9, 1988; Catherine Stimmell, June 7, 1988. All three had agreed to be liver, kidney, heart, eye and lung donors. Not one of them had agreed to have their genitalia removed.

She coughed. "I have all of the particulars, all of the records. You carried out the first two operations at the Brookline Clinic under the pretense of treating testicular cancer, and the third operation at Lowell Medical Center, on the pretext of correcting a double hernia."

"Well, well," said Dr Arcolio. "This must be the first time that a patient has *blackmailed* me into carrying out an operation."

Mrs Ellis stood up. The light suddenly suffused her face. She was spectacularly beautiful, with high Garboesque cheekbones, and a straight nose, and a mouth that looked as if it were just about to kiss somebody. Her eyes were blue as sapphires, crushed underfoot. To think that a woman who looked like this was begging him to operate on her, *bullying* him into operating on her, was almost unthinkable.

"I can't do it," he repeated.

"Oh, no, Dr Arcolio. You *will* do it. Because if you don't, all of the details of your nefarious operations will go directly to the District Attorney's office, and then

83

you will go directly to jail. And with you locked up, think of all those transsexual men who are going to languish in deep psychological misery, burdened with a body that is so chronically out of tune with their minds."

"Mrs Ellis –"

She stepped forward. She was threateningly graceful, and nearly five inches taller than he was, in her gray high heels. She smelled of cigarettes and Chanel No 5. She was long-legged, and surprisingly large-breasted, although her suit was cut so well that her bosom didn't seem out of proportion. Her earrings were platinum, by Guerdier.

"Doctor," she said, and for the first time he detected the slight Nebraska drawl in her undertones, "I need this life. In order to keep this life, I need this operation. If you don't do it for me, then so help me, I'll ruin you, I promise."

Dr Arcolio looked down at his desk diary. It told him, in his own neat writing, that Mrs Helen Ellis had an appointment at 3:45. God, how he wished that he hadn't accepted it.

He said, quietly, "You'll have to make three guarantees. One is that you're available to come to my clinic on Kirkland Street in Cambridge at an hour's notice. The second is that you tell absolutely nobody apart from your husband who undertook the surgery for you."

"And the third?"

"The third is that you pay me a half-million dollars in negotiable bonds as soon as possible, and a further half-million when the operation is successfully completed."

Mrs Ellis nodded the slightest of nods.

Dr Arcolio said, "That's agreed then. Christ. I don't know who's the crazier, you or me."

In the dead of February, Helen Ellis was lunching at Jasper's on Commercial Street with her friend Nancy Pettigrew when the maître d' came over and murmured in her ear that there was a telephone call for her.

She had just been served with a plateful of nine Wellfleet littlenecks with radish-chili salsa, and a glass of chilled champagne.

"Oh . . . whoever it is, tell them I'll call back after lunch, would you?"

"Your caller said it was very urgent, Mrs Ellis."

Nancy laughed. "It isn't your secret lover, is it, Helen?"

The maître d' said, soberly, "The gentleman said that time was of the essence."

Helen slowly lowered her fork. Nancy frowned at her and said, "Helen? Are you all *right*? You've gone white as a sheet."

The maître d' pulled out Helen's chair for her and escorted her across the restaurant to the phone booth. Helen picked up the receiver and said, "Helen Ellis here," in a voice as transparent as mineral water.

"*I have a donor,*" said Dr Arcolio. "*Do you still want to go through with it?*"

Helen swallowed. "Yes. I still want to go through with it."

"*In that case, come immediately to Cambridge. Have you eaten anything or drunk anything?*"

"I was just about to have lunch. I ate a little bread."

"*Don't eat or drink any more. Come at once. The sooner you get here, the greater the chance of success.*"

"All right," Helen agreed. Then, "Who was she?"

"*Who was who?*"

"The donor. Who was she? How did she die?"

"It's not important for you to know that. In fact it's better psychologically if you don't."

"Very well," said Helen. "I can be there in twenty minutes."

She returned to her table. "Nancy, I'm so sorry . . . I have to leave right now."

"When we're just about to start lunch? What's happened?"

"I can't tell you, I'm sorry."

"I knew it," said Nancy, tossing down her napkin. "It *is* a lover."

"Let me explain what I have been able to do," said Dr Arcolio.

It was nearly two months later, the first week in April. Helen was sitting in the white-tiled conservatory of their Dedham-style mansion on the Charles River, on a white wickerwork daybed heaped with embroidered cushions. The conservatory was crowded with daffodils. Outside, however, it was still very cold. The sky above the glass cupola was the colour of rainwashed writing ink, and there was a parallelogram of white frost on the lawns where the sun had not yet come around the side of the house.

"In your usual run-of-the-mill transsexual operation, the testes are removed, and also the erectile tissue of the penis. The external skin of the penis is then folded back into the body cavity in a kind of rolled-up tube, creating an artifical vagina. But of course it *is* artificial, and very unsatisfactory in many ways, particularly in its lack of full erotic response.

"What *I* can do is give my patients a *real* vagina. I can remove from a donor body the entire vulva including the muscles and erectile tissue that surround it, as well as the

86

vaginal barrel. I can then transplant them onto and *into* the recipient patient.

"Then – by using microsurgery techniques which I helped to develop at MIT, all of the major nerve fibers can be 'wired into' the recipient patient's central nervous system . . . so that the vagina and clitoris are just as capable of erotic arousal as they were within the body of the donor."

"I've been too sore to feel any arousal," said Helen, with a tight, slanted smile.

"I know. But it won't be long. You're making excellent progress."

"Do you think I'm really crazy?" asked Helen.

"I don't know. It depends what your goals are."

"My goals are to keep this lifestyle which you see all around you."

"Well . . ." said Dr Arcolio, "I think you'll probably succeed. Your husband can't wait for you to be fit for lovemaking again."

Helen said, "I'm sorry I made you betray your ethics."

Dr Arcolio shrugged. "It's a little late for that. And I have to admit that I'm really quite proud of what I've been able to achieve."

Helen rang the small silver bell on the table beside her. "You'll have some champagne, then, Baron Frankenstein?"

On the second Friday in May she came into the gloomy, high-ceilinged library where Bradley was working and posed in the center of the room. It was the first time that she had ever walked into the library without knocking first. She wore a long, scarlet, silk robe, trimmed with lace, and scarlet stiletto shoes. Her hair was softly curled and tied up with a scarlet ribbon.

She stood there with her blue eyes just a little misted

and the faintest of smiles on her lips, her left hand on her hip in a subtle parody of a hooker waiting for a curb crawler.

"Well?" she asked. "It's four o'clock. Way past your bedtime."

Of course Bradley had known all along that she was standing there, and even though he was frowning intently at the land possession documents in his hands, he wasn't able to decipher a single word. At last he looked up, tried to speak, coughed, cleared his throat.

"Is it ready?" he managed to ask, at last.

"*It?*" she queried. She had new-found confidence. For the first time in a long time, she had something that Bradley seriously desired.

"I mean, are *you* ready?" he corrected himself. He stood up. He was a very heavily built, broad-shouldered man of fifty-five. He was silver haired, with a leonine head that would have looked handsome as a piece of garden statuary. He was one of the original Boston Ellises – shipping magnates, landowners, newspaper publishers – and now the largest single broker of laser technology in the Western world.

He slowly approached her. He wore a blue-and-white striped cotton shirt, pleated blue slacks and fancy maroon suspenders. It was a look that the Ellises cherished: the look of a hands-on newspaper publisher, or a wheeler-and-dealer in smoke-filled rooms. It was dated but it had its own special Bostonian charisma.

"Show me," he said. He spoke in a low, soft rumble. Helen *felt* what he said, rather than heard it. It was like distant thunder approaching.

"In the bedroom," she said. "Not here."

He looked around the library with its shelves of antique leather-bound books and its gloomy paintings of Ellis

88

ancestors. In one corner of the library, close to the window, stood the same flatbed printing press that Bradley's great-great-grandfather had used to print the first editions of the *Beacon Hill Messenger*.

"What better place than here?" he wanted to know. She may have something that he seriously desired, but his wish was still her command.

She let the scarlet silk robe slip from her shoulders, and whisper to the floor, where it lay like a shining pool of sudden blood. Underneath, she wore a scarlet quarter-cup bra which lifted and divided her large white breasts, but didn't cover them. Her nipples wrinkled as dark pink as raspberries.

But it was the scarlet silk triangle between her legs that kept Bradley's attention riveted. He tugged his necktie loose and opened his collar, and his breathing came harsh and shallow.

"Show me," he repeated.

"You're not frightened?" she asked him. Somehow she sensed that he might be.

He fixed her with a quick, black-eyed stare. "Frightened? What the hell are you talking about? You may have been the one who suggested it but I'm the one who paid for it. Show me."

She tugged loose the scarlet string of her panties, and they fell to the floor around her left ankle, a token shackle of discarded silk.

"Jesus," whispered Bradley. "It's fantastic."

Helen had bared her pale, plump-lipped, immaculately-waxed sex. But immediately above her own sex was another, just as plump, just as inviting, just as moist. Only an oval scar showed where Dr Arcolio had sewn it into her lower abdomen, a scar no more disfiguring than a mild first-degree burn.

Eyes wide, speechless, Bradley knelt on the carpet in front of her, and placed the palms of his hands against her thighs. He stared at her twin vulvas in almost ferocious erotic delight.

"It's fantastic. It's fantastic. It's the most incredible thing I've ever seen."

He looked up at her. "Can I touch it? Does it feel just like the other one?"

"Of course you can touch it," said Helen. "You paid for it. It's yours."

Trembling, Bradley stroked the smooth lips of her new sex. "You can feel that? You can really feel it?"

"Of course. It feels good."

He touched her second clitoris, until it began to stiffen. Then he slipped his middle-finger into the warm, moist depths of her second vagina.

"It's fantastic. It feels just the same. It's incredible. Jesus! It's incredible!"

He strode to the library door, kicked it shut, and then turned the key. He strode back to the middle of the room, snapping off his suspenders, tearing off his shirt, stumbling out of his pants. By the time he had reached Helen he was naked except for his large stripey shorts. He pulled those off, revealing a massive crimson erection.

He pushed her onto the carpet and he thrust himself furiously into her, no preliminaries, no foreplay, just raging explosive lust. First he pushed himself into her new vagina, then into her own vagina, then into her bottom. He went from one to the other like a starving man who can't choose between meat, bread and candy.

Frightened at first, taken aback by the fury of his sexual attack, Helen didn't feel anything but friction and spasm. But as he thrust and thrust and grunted with exertion, she began to experience a sensation between her legs that was quite unlike anything that she had ever felt before: a sensation that was doubled in intensity, trebled. A sensation so overwhelming that she gripped the rug with both hands, unsure if the pleasure wasn't going to be too great for her mind to be able to accept. As Bradley plunged into her second vagina again and again, she felt as if she were going to go mad, or die.

Then – like a woman caught swimming in a warm black tropical swell – she was carried away.

She opened her eyes to hear Bradley on the telephone. He was still naked, his heavy body white and hairy, his penis hanging down like a plum in a sock.

"George? Listen George, you have to get up here. You have to get up here *now*! It's the most fantastic thing you ever experienced in your life. George, don't argue, just drop everything and get your ass up here as fast as you can. And don't forget your toothbrush: you won't be going home tonight, I promise you!"

Just before dawn, she opened her eyes. She was lying naked in the middle of the emperor-sized bed. On her right side, Bradley was pressed up close to her, snoring heavily, his hand possessively cupping her second sex. On her left side, George Carlin was snoring in a different key, as if he were dreaming, and *his* hand was cupping her original sex. Her bottom felt sore and stretched, and her mouth was dry with that unmistakeable arid taste of swallowed semen.

She felt strange; almost as if she were more than one woman. Her second vagina had brought her a curious duality of personality, as well as a duality of body. But she felt more secure. Bradley had told her over and over that she was wonderful, that she was spectacular, that he would never think of leaving her, ever.

Dr Arcolio, she thought, you would be proud of me.

Winter again. She met Dr Arcolio at Hamersley's. Dr Arcolio had put on a little weight. Helen was thinner, almost gaunt, and she had lost weight off her breasts.

She toyed with a plate of sautéed skate. There were shadows under her eyes the same colour as the brown butter.

"What's wrong?" he asked her. He had ordered smoked and grilled game hen with peach chutney, and was eating at a furious speed. "You've had no problems, everything's great."

She put down her fork. "I'm having problems with rejection," she said, and he heard the same dull note of despair that he had heard when she first consulted him.

"Rejection? What are you talking about? The last time we checked, we couldn't tell where your tissues ended and the donor tissues began. That vagina has become part of *you*, Helen."

"I don't mean that kind of rejection, Eugene. I mean that it rejects Bradley."

"It rejects Bradley? I'm sorry, I don't follow. In what way does it reject Bradley?"

"It was all right to begin with, but these days it clenches up whenever he tries to put himself inside it. It stays dry whenever he tries to stimulate it."

"How about your original vagina?"

"No problem at all."

Dr Arcolio frowned at his lunch. "Maybe there's been some kind of glitch in the nerve connections."

"I don't think it's anything to do with the nervous system. It's just not enough."

"You have two vaginas and it's not enough?" he hissed

at her. A bearded man at the next table turned and stared at him in surprise.

Helen said, "It was wonderful to start with. We made love five or six times a day. He adored it. He made me walk around naked for days on end, so that he could stare at me and put his fingers up me whenever he felt like it. I gave him shows, like erotic performances, with candles and vibrators and once I did it with his two Great Danes."

Dr Arcolio swallowed his mouthful with difficulty. "Wow," was all he could say.

There were tears hovering on the edge of Helen's eyes. "I did all of that but it wasn't enough. It just wasn't enough. Now he scarcely bothers any more. He says we've done everything that we could possibly do. We had an argument last week and he called me a freak."

Dr Arcolio laid his hand on top of hers, trying to be comforting. "I had a feeling this might happen. I talked to a sex therapist friend of mine a little while ago. She said that once you start going down this road with human sexuality – once you get into sado-masochism or you start nipple-piercing or labia-piercing or tattooing or any other kind of heavyweight perversion – it becomes an obsession, and you never get satisfied. You start chasing a mirage of ultimate excitement that doesn't exist. Good sex is being exciting with what you've got."

He sat back, and fastidiously wiped his mouth with his napkin. "I can have you in for corrective surgery early next week. Fifty thousand in advance, fifty thousand on completion, scarcely any scar."

Helen frowned. "You can get donors that quick?"

"I'm sorry?" said Dr Arcolio. "You won't need any more donors. We'll simply take out the second vagina and close up."

93

"Doctor, I believe we're talking at cross-purposes here," Helen told him. "I don't want this second vagina removed. I want two more."

There was a very long silence. Dr Arcolio licked his lips, and then drank a glass of water, and then licked his lips again. "You want *what*, did you say?"

"Two more. You can do it, can't you? One in the lower half of each breast. Bradley will adore it. Then I can have one man in each breast, and three inside, and two in my mouth, and Bradley will adore it."

"You want me to transplant vaginas into your *breasts*? Helen, for God's sake, what I've done already is advanced enough. Not to mention ethically appalling and totally illegal. This time, Helen, no. No way. You can send all of your incriminating particulars about my transsexual surgery to the DA, or wherever you damn well like. But no. I'm not doing it. Absolutely not."

Bradley's Christmas present that year was to invite six of his friends for a stag supper. They ate flame-grilled steak, and drank four jugs of dry martinis between them, and then they roared and laughed and tilted into the bedroom, where Helen was waiting for them, naked, not moving.

They took one look at her and they stopped roaring. They approached her in disbelief, and stared at her, and she remained quite still, with everything exposed.

In drunken wide-eyed wonder, two of them clambered astride her. One of them was the president of a Boston savings bank. Helen didn't know the other one, but he had a ginger moustache, and ginger hair on his thighs. They took hold of her nipples between finger and thumb and lifted up her heavy breasts, as if they were lifting up dishcovers at an expensive restaurant.

94

"My God," said the president of the savings bank. "It's true. It's fucking true."

With gradually mounting grunts of excitement, the two men pushed their reddened erections deep into the slippery apertures that had opened up beneath Helen's nipples.

They forced themselves deep into her breasts, deep into soft warm tissue, and twisted her nipples until she winced with pain.

Two more crammed themselves into her mouth, so that she could scarcely breathe. But what did it matter, Bradley was whooping with delight, Bradley loved her, Bradley wanted her. Bradley would never grow tired of her now, not after this. And even if he did, she could always find new ways to please him.

He didn't grow tired of her. But then, he didn't have very much longer to live. On September 12, two years later, she woke up to find that Bradley was lying dead, his dead hand cupping her original vulva. Bradley was buried in the grounds of the Dedham-style house overlooking the Charles River; in that strange pretense that the dead can still see, or even care where they are.

Dr Arcolio came to the house and drank champagne and ate little bits of fish and artichoke and messy little barbecued ribs. Everybody spoke in very hushed voices. Helen Ellis had kept herself to herself throughout the funeral, and had been heavily veiled in black. Now she had retreated to her private apartments and left Bradley's family and business friends and political henchmen to enjoy his wake without her participation.

After a while, however, Dr Arcolio climbed the echoing marble stairs and tiptoed along to her room. He tapped three times on the door before he heard her say, indistinctly, "Who is it? Go away."

"It's Eugene Arcolio. Can I talk to you?"

There was no reply, but after a very long time, the doors were opened, and left open, and Dr Arcolio assumed that this must be an invitation for him to go inside.

Cautiously, he entered. Helen was sitting by the window on a stiff upright chair. She was still veiled.

"What do *you* want?" she asked him. Her voice was muffled, distorted.

He shrugged. "I just came by to say congratulations."

"Congratulations?"

"Sure . . . you got what you wanted, didn't you? The house, the money. Everything."

Helen turned her head towards him, and then lifted her veil. He wasn't shocked. He knew what to expect. After all, he had undertaken all of the surgery himself.

In each of her cheeks, a vulva gaped. Each vulva was pouting and moist, a surrealistic parody of a *Rustler* centre spread. A barely-comprehensible collage of livid flesh and composed beauty and absolute horror.

It had been Helen's last act of complete subservience, to sacrifice her looks, so that Bradley and his friends had been able to penetrate not only her body but her face.

Dr Arcolio had pleaded with her not to do it, but she had threatened suicide, and then murder, and then she had threatened to tell the media what he had done to her already.

"It's reversible," he had reassured himself, as he had meticulously sewn vaginal muscles into the linings of her cheeks. "It's totally reversible."

Helen looked up at him. "You think I got what I wanted?" Every time she spoke, the vaginal lips parted slightly.

He had to turn away. The sight of what he had done to her was more than he could bear.

"I didn't get what I wanted," she said, and tears began to slide down her cheeks, and drip from the curved pink labia minora. "I wanted vaginas everywhere, all over me, so that Bradley could have twenty friends for the night, a hundred of them all at once, in my face, in my thighs, in my stomach, under my arms. He wanted a sex object, Eugene, and I would have been happy, you know, being his sex object."

Dr Arcolio said, "I'm sorry. I think this was my fault, as much as yours. In fact, I think it was *all* my fault."

That afternoon he went back to his office overlooking Brookline Square where Helen Ellis had first consulted him. He stood by the window for a long time.

Was it right, to give people what they wanted, if what they wanted was perverse and self-sacrificial, and flew in the face of God's creation?

Was it right to mutilate a beautiful woman, even if she craved mutilation?

How far did his responsibilities go? Was he a butcher, or was he a saint? Was he close to Heaven; or dancing on the manhole cover of Hell? Or was he nothing more than a surgical parody of Ann Landers, solving marital problems with a scalpel, instead of sensible suggestion?

He lit the first cigarette he had smoked in almost a month, and sat at his desk in the gathering gloom. Then – when it was almost dark – his secretary Esther knocked on the door, and opened it, and said, "Doctor?"

"What is it, Esther? I'm busy."

"Mr Pierce and Mr De Scenza. They came for their six o'clock appointment."

Dr Arcolio crushed out his cigarette, and waved the smoke away. "Oh, shit. All right. Show them in."

John Pierce and Philip De Scenza came into his office and stood in front of his desk like two schoolboys summoned to report to the principal. John Pierce was young and blonde and wore an unstructured Italian suit with rolled-up sleeves. Philip De Scenza was older and heavier and darker, in a hand-knitted plum coloured sweater, and baggy brown slacks.

Dr Arcolio reached across his desk and shook their hands. "How are you? Sorry . . . I've been a little preoccupied this afternoon."

"Oh . . . we understand," said Philip De Scenza. "We've been pretty busy ourselves."

"How are things coming along?" asked Dr Arcolio. "Have you experienced any problems? Any pain?"

John Pierce shyly shook his head. Philip De Scenza made a circle with his finger and his thumb and said, "Perfect, doctor. Two thousand percent perfect. Fucking-A, if you don't mind my saying so!" Dr Arcolio stood up and cleared his throat. "You'd better let me take a look, then. Do you want a screen?"

"A *screen*?" John Pierce giggled.

Philip De Scenza dismissively flapped his hand. "We don't need a screen."

While Dr Arcolio waited, John Pierce unbuckled his belt, tugged down his zipper, and wriggled out of his toothpaste-striped boxer shorts.

"Would you bend over, please?" asked Dr Arcolio; and John Pierce gave a little cough, and did as he was told.

Dr Arcolio spread his muscular bottom to reveal two perfect crimson anuses, both tightly wincing, one above the other. Around the upper anus there was a star-shaped pattern of more than ninety stitches, but they had all

98

healed perfectly, and there were only the faintest diagonal scars across his buttocks.

"Good," said Dr Arcolio, "that's fine. You can pull up your pants again now."

He turned to Philip De Scenza, and all he had to do was raise an eyebrow. Philip De Scenza lifted his sweater, dropped his pants, and stood proudly brandishing his improved equipment. One dark penis, like a heavy fruit, surmounted by yet another dark penis; and four hairy testicles hanging at the sides.

"Any difficulties?" asked Dr Arcolio, lifting both penises with professional detachment and examining them carefully. Both began to stiffen a little.

"Timing, that's all," shrugged Philip De Scenza, with a sideways smile at his friend. "I still haven't managed a simultaneous climax. By the time I've finished, poor John's usually getting quite sore."

"General comfort?" asked Dr Arcolio tightly.

"Over so soon?" Philip De Scenza flirted. "That's not very good value, doctor. A hundred dollars for two seconds' fondle. You should be ashamed of yourself."

That evening, John Pierce and Philip De Scenza went to Le Bellecour on Muzzey Street for dinner. They held hands all the way through the meal.

Dr Arcolio picked up a few groceries and then drove home in his metallic blue Rolls-Royce, listening to *La Boheme* on the stereo. He glanced in the rearview mirror from time to time, and thought he was looking tired. Traffic was heavy and slow on the Turnpike, and he felt thirsty, so he took an apple out of the bag beside him and took a bite.

He thought about Helen; and he thought about John Pierce and Philip De Scenza; and he thought about all of the other men and women whose bodies he had skillfully changed into living incarnations of their own sexual fantasies.

Something that Philip De Scenza had said kept nagging him. *You should be ashamed of yourself.* Although Philip De Scenza had been joking, Dr Arcolio suddenly understood that, yes, he should be ashamed of what he had done. In fact, he *was* ashamed of what he had done. Ashamed that he had used his surgical genius to create such erotic aberrations. Ashamed that he had mutilated so many beautiful bodies.

But as well as being painful, this surge of shame was liberating, too. Because men and women were more than God had made them. Men and women were able to reinvent themselves, and to derive strange new pleasures from pain and humiliation and self-distortion. Who was to say that it was right or that it was wrong? Who could define the perfect human being? If it was wrong to give a woman a second vagina, was it also wrong to repair a baby's harelip?

He felt chastened; but also uplifted. He finished his apple and tossed the core out onto the highway. Ahead of him he could see nothing but a Walpurgis procession of red brake lights.

In her house, alone, Helen wept salt tears of grief and sweet tears of sex; which mingled and dropped on her hands, so that they sparkled like diamond engagement rings.

The Taking of Mr Bill

Kensington Gardens, London

Walking across Kensington Gardens today, it's hard to imagine that in the 16th century, these were the market gardens and orchards which supplied much of London's population with fresh fruit and vegetables. William III came to live here in 1689, purchasing Nottingham House from the 1st Earl of Nottingham and having it extensively remodelled by Christopher Wren. The royal presence guaranteed Kensington's fashionable status, although it remained little more than a village until the mid 19th century, and it wasn't reached by the railway until the 1860s.

Kensington Gardens still has a special place in the psyche of the wealthy children whose nannies walked them here in their perambulators, and who sailed their boats on the Round Pond, and they are still haunted by the legend of one strange and exceptional boy.

THE TAKING OF MR BILL

It was only a few minutes past four in the afternoon, but the day suddenly grew dark, thunderously dark, and freezing cold rain began to lash down. For a few minutes, the pathways of Kensington Gardens were criss-crossed with bobbing umbrellas and au pairs running helter-skelter with baby buggies and screaming children.

Then, the gardens were abruptly deserted, left to the rain and the Canada geese and the gusts of wind that ruffled back the leaves. Marjorie found herself alone, hurriedly pushing William in his small navy blue Mothercare pram. She was wearing only her red tweed jacket and her long black pleated skirt, and she was already soaked. The afternoon had been brilliantly sunny when she left the house, with a sky as blue as dinner plates. She hadn't brought an umbrella. She hadn't even brought a plastic rain-hat.

She hadn't expected to stay with her Uncle Michael until so late, but Uncle Michael was so old now that he could barely keep himself clean. She had made him tea and tidied his bed, and done some hoovering while William lay kicking and gurgling on the sofa, and Uncle Michael watched him, rheumy-eyed, his hands resting on his lap like crumpled yellow tissue paper, his mind fading and brightening, fading and brightening, in the same way that the afternoon sunlight faded and brightened.

She had kissed Uncle Michael before she left, and he had clasped her hand between both of his. "Take good care of that boy, won't you?" he had whispered. "You never know who's watching. You never know who might want him."

"Oh, Uncle, you know that I never let him out of my sight. Besides, if anybody wants him, they're welcome to him. Perhaps I'll get some sleep at night."

"Don't say that, Marjorie. Never say that. Think of all the mothers who have said that, only as a joke, and then have wished that they had cut out their tongues."

"Uncle . . . don't be so morbid. I'll give you a ring when I get home, just to make sure you're all right. But I must go. I'm cooking chicken chasseur tonight."

Uncle Michael nodded. "Chicken chasseur . . ." he said, vaguely. Then, "Don't forget the pan."

"Of course not, Uncle. I'm not going to burn it. Now, make sure you put the chain on the door."

Now she was walking past the Round Pond. She slowed down, wheeling the pram through the muddy grass. She was so wet that it scarcely made any difference. She thought of the old Chinese saying, "Why walk fast in the rain? It's raining just as hard up ahead."

Before the arrival of the Canada geese, the Round Pond had been neat and tidy and peaceful, with fluttering ducks and children sailing little yachts. Now, it was fouled and murky, and peculiarly threatening, like anything precious that has been taken away from you and vandalized by strangers. Marjorie's Peugeot had been stolen last spring, and crashed, and urinated in, and she had never been able to think of driving it again, or even another car like it.

She emerged from the trees and a sudden explosion of cold rain caught her on the side of the cheek. William was awake, and waving his arms, but she knew that he would be hungry by now, and that she would have to feed him as soon as she got home.

She took a short cut, walking diagonally through another group of trees. She could hear the muffled roar of London's traffic on both sides of the garden, and the rumbling, scratching noise of an airliner passing overhead, but the gardens themselves remained oddly empty, and silent, as if a spell had been cast over them. Underneath the trees, the light was the colour of moss-weathered slate.

She leaned forward over the pram handle and cooed, "Soon be home, Mr Bill! Soon be home!"

But when she looked up she saw a man standing silhouetted beside the oak tree just in front of her, not more than thirty feet away. A thin, tall man wearing a black cap, and a black coat with the collar turned up. His eyes were shaded, but she could see that his face was deathly white. And he was obviously waiting for her.

She hesitated, stopped, and looked around. Her heart began to thump furiously. There was nobody else in sight, nobody to whom she could shout for help. The rain rattled on the trees above her head, and William let out one fitful yelp. She swallowed, and found herself swallowing a thick mixture of fruit cake and bile. She simply didn't know what to do.

She thought: There's no use running. I'll just have to walk past him. I'll just have to show him that I'm not afraid. After all, I'm pushing a pram. I've got a baby. Surely he won't be so cruel that he'll –

You never know who's watching. You never know who might want him.

Sick with fear, she continued to walk forward. The man remained where he was, not moving, not speaking. She would have to pass within two feet of him, but so far he had shown no sign that he had noticed her, although he must have done; and no sign at all that he wanted her to stop.

She walked closer and closer, stiff legged, and mewling softly to herself in terror. She passed by him, so close that she could see the glittering raindrops on his coat, so close that she could *smell* him, strong tobacco and some dry, unfamiliar smell, like hay.

She thought: Thank God. He's let me pass.

But then his right arm whipped out and snatched her elbow, and twisted her around, and flung her with such force against the trunk of the oak that she heard her shoulder blade crack and one of her shoes flew off.

She screamed, and screamed again. But he slapped her face with the back of his hand, and then slapped her again.

"What do you want?" she shrieked. "What do you want?"

He seized the lapels of her jacket and dragged her upright against the harsh-ribbed bark of the tree. His eyes were so deep-set that all she could see was their glitter. His lips were almost blue, and they were stretched back across his teeth in a terrifying parody of a grin.

"What do you want?" she begged him. Her shoulder felt as if it were on fire, and her left knee was throbbing. "I have to look after my baby. Please don't hurt me. I have to look after my baby."

She felt her skirt being torn away from her thighs. Oh God, she thought, not that. Please not that. She started to collapse out of fear and out of terrible resignation, but the man dragged her upright again, and knocked her head so hard against the tree that she almost blacked out.

She didn't remember very much after that. She felt her underwear wrenched off. She felt him forcing his way into her. It was dry and agonizing and he felt so *cold*. Even

106

when he had pushed his way deep inside her, he still felt cold. She felt the rain on her face. She heard his breathing, a steady, harsh *Hah! Hah! Hah!* Then she heard him swear, an extraordinary curse like no curse that she had ever heard before.

She was just about to say "My baby", when he hit her again. She was found twenty minutes later standing at a bus stop in the Bayswater Road, by an American couple who wanted to know where to find Trader Vic's.

The pram was found where she had been forced to leave it, and it was empty.

John said, "We should go away for a while."

Marjorie was sitting in the window seat, nursing a cup of lemon tea. She was staring across the Bayswater Road as she always stared, day and night. She had cut her hair into a severe bob, and her face was as pale as wax. She wore black, as she always wore black.

The clock chimed three on the mantelpiece. John said, "Nesta will keep in touch – you know, if there's any development."

Marjorie turned and smiled at him weakly. The dullness of her eyes still shocked him, even now. "Development?" she said, gently mocking his euphemism. It was six weeks since William had disappeared. Whoever had taken him had either killed him or intended to keep him for ever.

John shrugged. He was a thickset, pleasant looking, but unimaginative man. He had never thought that he would marry; but when he had met Marjorie at his younger brother's 21st, he had been captivated by her mixture of shyness and wilfulness, and her eccentric imagination. She had said things to him that no girl had ever said to him before – opened his eyes to the simple magic of everyday life.

But now that Marjorie had closed in on herself, and communicated nothing but grief, he found that he was increasingly handicapped; as if the gifts of light and colour and perception were being taken away from him. A spring day was incomprehensible unless he had Marjorie beside him, to tell him why it was all so inspiring.

She was like a woman who was dying; and he was like a man who was gradually going blind.

The phone rang in the library. Marjorie turned back to the window. Through the pale afternoon fog the buses and the taxis poured ceaselessly to and fro. But beyond the railings, in Kensington Gardens, the trees were motionless and dark, and they held a secret for which Marjorie would have given anything. Her sight, her soul, her very life.

Somewhere in Kensington Gardens, William was still alive. She was convinced of it, in the way that only a mother could be convinced. She spent hours straining her ears, trying to hear him crying over the bellowing of the traffic. She felt like standing in the middle of Bayswater Road and holding up her hands and screaming "Stop! Stop, for just one minute! Please, stop! I think I can hear my baby crying!"

John came back from the library, digging his fingers into his thick chestnut hair. "That was Chief Inspector Crosland. They've had the forensic report on the weapon that was used to cut your clothes. Some kind of gardening implement, apparently – a pair of clippers or a pruning hook. They're going to start asking questions at nurseries and garden centres. You never know."

He paused, and then he said, "There's something else. They had a DNA report."

Marjorie gave a quiet, cold shudder. She didn't want to start thinking about the rape. Not yet, anyway. She could deal with that later, when William was found.

When William was found, she could go away on holiday and try to recuperate. When William was found, her heart could start beating again. She longed so much to hold him in her arms that she felt she was becoming completely demented. Just to feel his tiny fingers closing around hers.

John cleared his throat. "Crosland said that there was something pretty strange about the DNA report. That's why it's taken them so long."

Marjorie didn't answer. She thought she had seen a movement in the gardens. She thought she had seen something small and white in the long grass underneath the trees, and a small arm waving. But – as she drew the net curtain back further – the small, white object trotted out from beneath the trees and it was a Sealyham, and the small waving arm was its tail.

"According to the DNA report, the man wasn't actually alive."

Marjorie slowly turned around. "What?" she said. "What do you mean, he wasn't actually alive?"

John looked embarrassed. "I don't know. It doesn't seem to make any sense, does it? But that's what Crosland said. In fact, what he actually said was, the man was dead."

"*Dead?* How could he have been dead?"

"Well, there was obviously some kind of aberration in the test results. I mean, the man couldn't have been *really* dead. Not clinically. It was just that –"

"Dead," Marjorie repeated, in a whisper, as if everything had suddenly become clear. "The man was *dead*."

John was woken by the telephone at five to six that Friday morning. He could hear the rain sprinkling against the bedroom window, and the grinding bellow of a garbage truck in the mews at the back of the house.

"It's Chief Inspector Crosland, sir. I'm afraid I have some rather bad news. We've found William in the fountains."

John swallowed. "I see," he said. Irrationally, he wanted to ask if William were still alive, but of course he couldn't have been, and in any case he found that he simply couldn't speak.

"I'm sending two officers over," said the chief inspector. "One of them's a woman. If you could be ready in – say – five or ten minutes?"

John quietly cradled the phone. He sat up in bed for a while, hugging his knees, his eyes brimming. Then he swallowed, and smeared his tears with his hands, and gently shook Marjorie awake.

She opened her eyes and stared up at him as if she had just arrived from another country. "What is it?" she asked, throatily.

He tried to speak, but he couldn't.

"It's William, isn't it?" she said. "They've found William."

They stood huddled together under John's umbrella, next to the gray, rain-circled fountains. An ambulance was parked close by, its rear doors open, its blue light flashing. Chief Inspector Crosland came across – a solid, beef-complexioned man with a dripping moustache. He raised his hat, and said, "We're all very sorry about this. We always hold out hope, you know, even when it's pretty obvious that it's hopeless."

"Where was he found?" asked John.

"Caught in the sluice that leads to the Long Water. There were a lot of leaves down there, too, so he was difficult to see. One of the maintenance men found him when he was clearing the grating."

"Can I see him?" asked Marjorie.

John looked at Crosland with an unspoken question: How badly is he decomposed? But Crosland nodded, and took hold of Marjorie's elbow, and said, "Come with me."

Marjorie followed him obediently. She felt so small and cold. He guided her to the back of the ambulance, and helped her to climb inside. There, wrapped in a bright red blanket, was her baby, her baby William, his eyes closed, his hair stuck in a curl to his forehead. He was white as marble, white as a statue.

"May I kiss him?" she asked. Crosland nodded.

She kissed her baby and his cheek was soft and utterly chilled.

Outside the ambulance, John said, "I would have thought – well, how long has he been down there?"

"No more than a day, sir, in my opinion. He was still wearing the same Babygro that he was wearing when he was taken, but he was clean and he looked reasonably well nourished. There were no signs of abuse or injury."

John looked away. "I can't understand it," he said.

Chief Inspector Crosland laid a hand on his shoulder. "If it's any comfort to you, sir, neither can I."

All the next day, through showers and sunshine, Marjorie walked alone around Kensington Gardens. She walked down Lancaster Walk, and then Budge's Walk, and stood by the Round Pond. Then she walked back beside the Long Water, to the statue of Peter Pan.

It had started drizzling again, and rainwater dripped from the end of Peter's pipes, and trickled down his cheeks like tears.

The boy who never grew up, she thought. Just like William.

111

She was about to turn away when the tiniest fragment of memory scintillated in her mind. What was it that Uncle Michael had said, as she left his flat on the day that William had been taken?

She had said, "I'm cooking chicken chasseur tonight."

And *he* had said, "Chicken chasseur . . ." and then paused for a very long time, and added, "Don't forget the pan."

She had assumed he meant saucepan. But why would he have said "Don't forget the pan"? After all, he hadn't really been talking about cooking. He had been warning her that somebody in Kensington Gardens might be watching her. He had been warning her that somebody in Kensington Gardens might want to take William.

Don't forget the Pan.

He was sitting on the sofa, bundled up in maroon woollen blankets, when she let herself in. The flat smelled of gas and stale milk. A thin shaft of sunlight the colour of cold tea was straining through the net curtains; and it made his face look more sallow and withered than ever.

"I was wondering when you'd come," he said, in a whisper.

"You expected me?"

He gave her a sloping smile. "You're a mother. Mothers understand everything."

She sat on the chair close beside him. "That day when William was taken . . . you said 'Don't forget the Pan.' Did you mean what I think you meant?"

He took hold of her hand and held it in a gesture of infinite sympathy and infinite pain. "The Pan is every mother's nightmare. Always has been, always will be."

"Are you trying to tell me that it's not a story?"

"Oh . . . the way that Sir James Barrie told it – all

112

fairies and pirates and Indians – *that* was a story. But it was founded on fact."

"How do you know that?" asked Marjorie. "I've never heard anyone mention that before."

Uncle Michael turned his withered neck toward the window. "I know it because it happened to my brother and my sister and it nearly happened to me. My mother met Sir James at a dinner in Belgravia, about a year afterwards, and tried to explain what had happened. This was in 1901 or 1902, thereabouts. She thought that he might write an article about it, to warn other parents, and that because of his authority, people might listen to him, and believe him. But the old fool was such a sentimentalist, such a fantasist . . . he didn't believe her, either, and he turned my mother's agony into a children's play.

"Of course, it was such a successful children's play that nobody ever took my mother's warnings seriously, ever again. She died in Earlswood Mental Hospital in Surrey in 1914. The death certificate said 'dementia', whatever that means."

"Tell me what happened," said Marjorie. "Uncle Michael, I've just lost my baby . . . you have to tell me what happened."

Uncle Michael gave her a bony shrug. "It's difficult to separate fact from fiction. But in the late 1880s, there was a rash of kidnaps in Kensington Gardens . . . all boy babies, some of them taken from prams, some of them snatched directly from their nanny's arms. All of the babies were later found dead . . . most in Kensington Gardens, some in Hyde Park and Paddington . . . but none of them very far away. Sometimes the nannies were assaulted, too, and three of them were raped.

"In 1892, a man was eventually caught in the act of trying to steal a baby. He was identified by several nannies as the man who had raped them and abducted their charges. He was tried at the Old Bailey on three specimen charges of murder, and sentenced to death on June 13, 1893. He was hanged on the last day of October.

"He was apparently a Polish merchant seaman, who had jumped ship at London Docks after a trip to the Caribbean. His shipmates had known him only as Piotr. He had been cheerful and happy, as far as they knew – at least until they docked at Port-au-Prince, in Haiti. Piotr had spent three nights away from the ship, and after his return, the first mate remarked on his 'moody and unpleasant mien'. He flew into frequent rages, so they weren't at all surprised when he left the ship at London and never came back.

"The ship's doctor thought that Piotr might have contracted malaria, because his face was ashy white, and his eyes looked bloodshot. He shivered, too, and started to mutter to himself."

"But if he was hanged –" put in Marjorie.

"Oh, he was hanged, all right," said Michael. "Hanged by the neck until he was dead, and buried in the precincts of Wormwood Scrubs prison. But only a year later, more boy babies began to disappear from Kensington Gardens, and more nannies were assaulted, and each of them bore the same kind of scratches and cuts that Piotr had inflicted on his victims.

"He used to tear their dresses, you see, with a baling hook."

"A baling hook?" said Marjorie, faintly.

Uncle Michael held up his hand, with one finger curled. "Where do you think that Sir James got the notion for Captain Hook?"

"But I was scratched like that, too."

"Yes," nodded Uncle Michael. "And that's what I've

been trying to tell you. The man who attacked you – the man who took William – it was Piotr."

"What? That was over a hundred years ago! How *could* it have been?"

"In the same way that Piotr tried to snatch me, too, in 1901, when I was still in my pram. My nanny tried to fight him off, but he hooked her throat and severed her jugular vein. My brother and my sister tried to fight him off, too, but he dragged them both away with him. They were only little, they didn't stand a chance. A few weeks later, a swimmer found their bodies in the Serpentine."

Uncle Michael pressed his hand against his mouth, and was silent for almost a whole minute. "My mother was almost mad with grief. But somehow, she *knew* who had killed her children. She spent every afternoon in Kensington Gardens, following almost every man she saw. And – at last – she came across him. He was standing amongst the trees, watching two nannies sitting on a bench. She approached him, and she challenged him. She told him to his face that she knew who he was; and that she knew he had murdered her children.

"Do you know what he said? I shall never forget my mother telling me this, and it still sends shivers down my spine. He said, 'I never had a mother, I never had a father. I was never allowed to be a boy. But the old woman on Haiti said that I could stay young for ever and ever, so long as I always sent back to her the souls of young children, flying on the wind. So that is what I did. I kissed them, and sucked out their souls, and sent them flying on the wind.'"

"But do you know what he said to my mother? He said 'Your children's souls may have flown to a distant island, but they can still live, if you wish them to. You can go to their graves, and you can call them, and they'll

115

come to you. It takes nothing more than a mother's word.'

"My mother said, 'Who are you? *What* are you? And he said 'Pan', which is nothing more nor less than Polish for 'Man'. That's why my mother called him 'Piotr Pan'. And that's where Sir James Barrie got the name from.

"And here, of course, is the terrible irony: Captain Hook and Peter Pan weren't enemies at all, not in real life. They were one and the same person."

Marjorie stared at her Uncle Michael in horror. "What did my great-auntie do? She didn't call them, did she?"

Uncle Michael shook his head. "She insisted that their graves should be covered in heavy slabs of granite. Then – as you know – she did whatever she could to warn other mothers of the danger of Piotr Pan."

"So she really believed that she could call her children back to life?"

"I think so. But, as she always said to me, what can life amount to, without a soul?"

Marjorie sat with her Uncle Michael until it grew dark, and his head dropped to one side, and he began to snore.

She stood in the chapel of rest, her face bleached white by the single ray of sunlight that fell from the clerestory window. Her dress was black, her hat was black. She held a black handbag in front of her.

William's white coffin was open, and William himself lay on a white silk pillow, his eyes closed, his tiny eyelashes curled over his deathly-white cheek, his lips slightly parted, as if he were still breathing.

On either side of the coffin, candles burned; and there were two tall vases of white gladioli. Apart from the murmuring of traffic, and the occasional rumbling of a Central Line tube train deep beneath the building's foundations, the chapel was silent.

Marjorie could feel her heart beating, steady and slow.

My baby, she thought. My poor sweet baby.

She stepped closer to the coffin. Hesitantly, she reached out and brushed his fine baby curls. So soft, it crucified her to touch them.

"William," she breathed.

He remained cold and still. Not moving, not breathing.

"William," she repeated. "William, my darling, come back to me. Come back to me, Mr Bill."

Still he didn't stir. Still he didn't breathe.

She waited a moment longer. She was almost ashamed of herself for having believed Uncle Michael's stories. Piotr Pan indeed! The old man was senile.

Softly, she tiptoed to the door. She took one last look at William, and then she closed the door behind her.

She had barely let go of the handle, however, when the silence was broken by the most terrible high-pitched scream that she had ever heard in her life.

In Kensington Gardens, beneath the trees, a thin dark man raised his head and listened, and listened, as if he could hear a child crying in the wind. He listened, and he smiled, although he never took his eyes away from the young woman who was walking towards him, pushing a baby buggy.

He thought, *God bless mothers everywhere.*

Rug

Münster, Germany

I first made my acquaintance with Münster when my father was serving with the British Forces in Germany. It lies on the Dortmund-Ems canal, about 100 kilometres north of Dusseldorf, and was once a bishopric, with prince-bishops who ruled everything around them.

Like many towns in Westphalia, it suffered severe bomb damage during the war, and even though many of its 12th- and 13th-century buildings have been painstakingly restored, you always have the feeling when you walk through Münster that you are looking at a copy of its prewar glory, and that the soul has somehow gone out of it.

There are still some impressive relics left – Münster cathedral, which has some fine Romanesque and Gothic sculpture; the 14th-century Church of Our Lady with its inspired Gothic tower. The famous Gothic facade of the Rathaus, dating from 1335, was destroyed by bombing, but has been faithfully copied.

What Münster retains is its medieval atmosphere; a gray town on a wide gray plain. It also retains its legends and its superstitions, its local folk tales. Rug *is an adaptation of a story that was told to me by a Münster baker, as he cut me a large slice of apfelküchen and squirted heaps of cream on it.*

What he told me may be nothing more than imagination, a spooky yarn to be told around a winter stove. But on the other hand, it may come closer to explaining the real truth of many terrible incidents that have plagued Westphalia since the turn of the century – the curse of the Wolfshaut.

You don't understand what Wolfshaut *means? You very soon will.*

RUG

Two days later, and nearly 75 kilometres away, a tall woman entered an antique shop close to the 13th-century Buddensturm, in the cathedral town of Münster. The doorbell jangled on a spring; the morning sunlight illuminated antlers and stags' heads and display cases of stuffed foxes.

The shop owner appeared from behind a curtain, smoking a cigarette. The woman was standing against the light, so that it was difficult for him to see her face.

"*Ich möchte eine Relsedecke,*" she said.

"*Eine Relsedecke, gnadige Frau?*"

"*Ja. Ich möchte ein Wolfshaut.*"

"*Ein Wolfshaut? Das ist rar.* Very difficult to find, you understand?"

"Yes, I understand. But you can find me one, yes?"

"*Ich weiss nicht.* I can try."

The woman took out a small black purse, unfastened the clasp, and gave the shop owner 1,000DM, neatly folded. "Deposit," she said. "*Depositum.* If you can find me a wolfskin rug, I will pay you more. Much more."

She wrote a telephone number on the back of one of his cards, blew it dry and gave it to him.

"Don't fail me," she said.

But when she had left the shop (the doorbell still ringing) the shop owner stood still for a very long time. Then he opened one of the drawers underneath his counter and took out a dark, tarnished nail. A steel nail, heavily plated with silver.

They didn't come looking for wolfskins very often, but when they did they were usually desperate, which made them even more vulnerable than ever. Still, he needed the practice. He needed to tease her along. He needed to build up her hopes. He needed to make her believe that here, at last, was a man that she could trust.

Then it would be tree time. The hammer and the heart.

The woman didn't look back at the shop as she left it. Even if she *had* done, she may not have understood the significance of its name. After all, one beast simply passed on its ferocity to the next; not caring about names or heritage or marital vows. The only thing that was important was the skin, the *Wolfshaut*, the hairy covering that gave everything meaning.

But the name of the shop was "Bremke: Jagerkunst", and its business was not only the art and artefacts of hunting, but the relentless pursuit of the hunters themselves.

John found the wolf on the third day, when everybody else had gone to Paderborn for the horse trials. He had pleaded an earache (earaches were always best because nobody could prove whether you really had one or not, and you were still allowed to read and listen to the radio). The truth was, though, that he was already homesick, and he didn't feel like doing anything but sitting by himself and thinking miserably about Mummy.

The Smythe-Barnetts were very kind to him. Mrs Smythe-Barnett always kissed him goodnight, and their two daughters Penny and Veronica tried their best to involve him in everything they did. But the truth was that he was too sad to be much fun, and he shunned affection because it made a terrible prickly lump rise up in his throat, like a sea urchin, and his eyes fill with tears.

He stood in the bay window in the front of the house watching the Smythe-Barnetts drive away with their smartly varnished horsebox in tow. The exhaust from Col. Smythe-Barnett's Land Rover drifted away between the scabby plane trees, the street fell silent again. It was one of those colourless autumn mornings when he could easily believe that he would never see blue sky again, ever. From Aachen to the Teutoburger Wald, the north German plains were suffocating under a comforter of grayish-white cloud.

In the kitchen, John could hear the German maid singing as she mopped the beige-tiled floor – *Wooden Heart* in German. Everybody was singing it because Elvis had just released *GI Blues*.

He knew that everything would be better next week. His father had ten days' leave, and they were going to take a Rhine steamer to Koblenz, and then they were going to spend a week at the Forces recreation center at Winterberg, among the pine forests of the Sauerland. But that still couldn't ease the homesickness of staying with a strange family in a strange country, with his parents so recently divorced. His grandmother had said something about "all those long separations . . . a man's only human, you know." John wasn't at all sure what she meant by "only human". It sounded to him like only *just* human – as if beneath those pond green cardigans and those tattersall-check shirts there throbbed the heart of a creature far more primitive.

He had even heard Mummy saying about his father: "He can be a beast at times", and he thought of his father arching back his head and baring his teeth, his

123

eyes filled up with scarlet and his hands crooked like claws.

He went into the kitchen, but the floor was still wet and the maid shooed him away. She was a big-faced woman in black, and she smelled of cabbagey sweat. It seemed to John that all Germans smelled of cabbagey sweat. Penny had taken him on the bus to Bielefeld yesterday afternoon, and the smell of cabbagey sweat had been overwhelming.

He went out into the garden. The lawns were studded with fallen apples. He kicked one of them so that it hit the side of the stable. John had already been told off for trying to feed the Smythe-Barnetts' horse with apples. "They give him gripes, you stupid boy," Veronica had snapped at him. How was *he* supposed to know? The only horse he had ever seen at close quarters was the milkman's horse from United Dairies, and that wore a permanent nosebag.

He sat on the swing and creaked backward and forward for a while. The garden was almost unbearably silent. Still, this was better than being introduced to all of the Smythe-Barnetts' haw-hawing friends in Paderborn. He had seen them packing their picnic lunch and it was salami and fatty beef sandwiches.

He looked up at the huge suburban house. It was typical of large family residences built in Germany between the wars, with an orange-tiled roof and fawn concrete-rendered walls. There must have been another similiar house next door, but Bielefeld had been badly bombed, and now there was nothing left but a wild orchard and brick foundations.

John heard a harsh croaking noise. He looked up and saw a stork perched on the chimney – a real live stork. It was the first one he had ever seen, and he could hardly believe it was real. It was like an omen, a warning of things to come. It stayed on the chimney for only a few moments, turning its beak imperiously from right to left, its feathers ruffled. Then it flew away, with an audible *flap*, *flap*, *flap* of its wings.

While he was looking up, John noticed for the first time that there was a dormer window in the roof: only a small one. There must be an attic or another bedroom right at the top of the house. If there was an attic, there might be something interesting in it, like relics from the war, or an unexploded bomb, or books about sex. He had found a book about sex in the attic at home: *Everything Newlyweds Should Know*. He had traced Fig 6 – The Female Vulva – and coloured it pink.

He went back inside the house. The maid was in the living room now, polishing the furniture and filling the air with the aroma of lavender and cabbagey sweat. John climbed the stairs to the first landing, where the walls were hung with photographs of Penny and Veronica on Jupiter, each photograph decorated with a red rosette. He was glad he hadn't gone with them to Paderborn. Why should he care if their stupid horse managed to jump over a whole lot of poles?

He climbed the second flight of stairs. He hadn't been up here before. This was where Col. and Mrs Smythe-Barnett had their "sweet". John didn't know why they felt it necessary to eat their pudding in their bedroom. He supposed it was just another of those things that snobby people like the Smythe-Barnetts always did, like having silver napkin rings and serving tomato ketchup in a dish.

The floorboards creaked. Through the half-open doors, John could see the corner of the Smythe-Barnetts' bed, and Mrs Smythe-Barnett's dressing table, with its array of silverbacked brushes. He listened for a moment. Downstairs, the maid had started to vacuum-clean the living room carpet. Her cleaner made a roaring drone like a German bomber. She wouldn't be able to hear him at all.

Cautiously, he crept into the Smythe-Barnetts' bedroom, and across to the dressing table. In the mirror, he could see a solemn, white-faced boy of eleven with a short prickly haircut and sticky-out ears. This of course was not him but simply his external disguise, the physical manifestation he adopted in order to put up his hand during school register and say, "Present, miss!"

On the dressing table lay a half-finished letter on blue deckle-edged notepaper, with a fountain pen lying across it. It read "Very disturbed and withdrawn, but I suppose that's only natural under the circumstances. He cries himself to sleep every night, and suffers nightmares. He also seems to find it very difficult to get along with other children. It will obviously take a great deal of time and –"

He stared at his pasty face in the mirror. He looked like a photograph of his father when his father was very young. *Very disturbed and withdrawn*. How could Mrs Smythe-Barnett have written that about him? He wasn't disturbed and withdrawn. It was just that what was inside him, he wanted to keep inside. Why should he let Mrs Smythe-Barnett know how unhappy he was? What did it have to do with *her*?

He tiptoed out of the Smythe-Barnetts' bedroom and quietly closed the door. The German maid was still leading a full-scale raid over London Docks. He walked along to the end of the corridor, and it was there that he discovered a small cream-painted door which obviously led up to the attic. He opened it. Inside, there was a steep flight of hessian-carpeted stairs. It was very gloomy up there, although a little of the gray, muted daylight managed to penetrate. John could smell mustiness, and dust, and an odd smell like onion flowers.

He climbed the stairs. As he did so, he came face to face with the wolf.

It was lying flat on the floor, facing him. Its eyes were yellow and its teeth were bared, and its dry, purplish tongue was hanging out. Its hairy ears were slightly moth-eaten, and there was a baldish patch on the side of its snout, but that did nothing to detract from its ferocity. Even if its body was utterly empty, and it was now being used as a rug, it was still a wolf, and a huge wolf at that – the biggest wolf that John had ever seen.

He looked around the attic. Apart from a partitioned-off area at the far end, to house the water tanks, it had been converted into a spare bedroom which ran the whole length and breadth of the house. Behind the wolf there was a solid brass bed, with a sagging mattress on it. Three ill-assorted armchairs were arranged by the window, and an old varnished chest of drawers stood beneath the lowest part of the eaves.

There was a framed photograph hanging by the side of the dormer window. The top of the frame was decorated with dried flowers, long ago leached of any colour. The photograph showed a fair-haired girl standing by the side of a suburban road somewhere, one eye closed against the sunlight. She was wearing an embroidered halter-top dress and a white blouse.

John knelt down beside the wolf-rug and examined it closely. He reached out and touched the tips of its curving teeth. It was incredible to think this had once been a real animal, running through the woods, chasing after hares and deer, maybe even people.

He stroked its fur. It was still wiry and thick, mostly

black, with some gray streaks around the throat. He wondered who had shot it, and why. If he had a wolf, he wouldn't shoot it. He would train it to hunt people down, and tear their throats out. Particularly his maths teacher, Mrs Bennett. She would look good with her throat torn out. Blood creeping across the pages of *School Mathematics Part One* by H.E. Parr.

He buried his nose in the wolf-rug's flanks and breathed in, to find out if it still smelled at all like animal. All he could detect, however, was dust, and a very faintly leathery odour. Whatever wolf-scent this beast had ever possessed, it had been dried up with age.

For an hour or two, until it was lunchtime, he played hunters. Then he played Tarzan, and wrestled with the wolf-rug all over the bedroom. He clamped its jaws around his wrist, and grunted and heaved in an effort to prevent it from biting off his hand. Finally he managed to get it onto its back, and he stabbed it again and again with his huge imaginary jungle knife, ripping out its guts, and twisting the blade deep into its heart.

A few minutes after twelve, he heard the maid calling him. He straightened the rug, and hurried quickly and quietly downstairs. The maid was ready to leave, in hat and coat and gloves, all black. On the kitchen table there was a plateful of cold salami and gherkins and buttered bread, and a large glass of warm milk, on the surface of which the yellow cream had already begun to form into blobby clusters.

That night, after the Smythe-Barnetts returned, all tired and noisy and smelling of horses and sherry, John lay in his small bed staring at the ceiling and thinking of the wolf. It was so proud, so fierce, and yet so dead, lying gutted on the attic floor with its eyes staring at nothing at all. It had been a beast at times, just like his father; and perhaps one day it could be a beast again. There was no telling with creatures like that, as his grandmother had once said, with her hand cupped over the telephone receiver, as if he wouldn't be able to hear.

The wind was getting up and clearing away the cloud; but at the same time it was making the plane tree branches dip and thrash, so that strange spiky shadows shuddered and danced across the ceiling of John's bedroom, shadows like praying mantises, and spider legs, and wolf claws.

In the eye of the coming gale he closed his eyes and tried to sleep. But the spider legs danced even more frantically on the ceiling, and the praying mantises dipped and shivered, and every quarter-hour the Smythe-Barnetts' hall clock struck the Westminster chimes, as if to remind themselves all through the night how correct they were, both in timing and in taste.

And then at a quarter past two in the morning he heard a scratching sound coming down the attic stairs. He was sure of it. The wolf! The wolf was climbing down the attic stairs with arched back and bristled tail, its eyes gleaming amber as garnets in the darkness, its breath panting *Hah-hah-HAH-hah*! *Hah-hah-HAH-hah*!, ripe with wolfishness and bloodlust.

He heard it running along the corridor, past the Smythe-Barnetts' sweet, hungry, hungry, hungry. He heard it sniffing at door locks, growling in its throat. He heard it pause at the head of the second floor staircase, and then plunge downwards, coming his way.

It began to run really fast now, its tail beating against the walls of the corridor. Its eyes opened wide and yellow, and its ears stiffened up. It was coming after him, coming to take its revenge. He shouldn't have fought it, shouldn't have wrestled it, and for all that his jungle knife was imaginary, he had still intended to cut its heart out, he had still *wanted* to do it, even if he hadn't.

He heard the wolf thudding toward his bedroom door, louder and louder, and then the door burst open and John shot up in bed and screamed and screamed, his eyes tight shut, his fists clenched, wetting his pyjamas in sheer terror.

Mrs Smythe-Barnett came into the room and took him in her arms. She switched on his bedside lamp and cuddled him and shushed him. He put up with her cuddling for two or three minutes and then he had to pull away. His wet pyjama trousers were rapidly chilling, and he felt so embarrassed that he could have happily died at that moment. Yet he had no alternative but to stand shivering in a dressing gown while she patiently changed the bed for him, and brought him clean pyjamas, and tucked him up. A tall big-nosed woman in a long nightdress, wearing a scarf to cover the rollers in her hair. Saintly, in a way, but a Bernini saint; marble-perfect, always able to cope. He so much missed his mummy, who couldn't cope with anything, or not very well.

"You had a nightmare," said Mrs Smythe-Barnett, stroking his forehead.

"It's all right. I'm all right now," John told her, almost crossly.

"How's your earache?" she asked him.

"Better, thanks. I saw a stork."

"That's nice. Actually, storks are quite common around here; but the local people think they're bad luck. They say that if a stork perches on your roof, somebody in the house will get the very worst thing they ever feared. I think that's why they say that storks bring babies! But I don't believe in superstitions like that, do you?"

John shook his head. He couldn't understand where the

wolf had gone. The wolf had come running down the stairs and along the corridor and down the second flight of stairs and along the corridor and –

And here was Mrs Smythe-Barnett, stroking his forehead.

He took the bus into Bielefeld the next day, on his own this time. He suffered the cabbagey sweat and the Ernte 23 cigarettes, squashed between a huge woman dressed in black and a thin youth with a long hair growing out of the mole on his chin.

He went to the cake shop and bought an apfelstrudel with piles of squirty cream on it, which he ate as he walked along the street. When he saw his reflection in shop windows he couldn't believe how young he was. He went into a bookshop and looked through some illustrated art books. Some of them had pictures of nudes. He found an etching by Hans Bellmer of a pregnant women being penetrated by two men at once, her baby crowded to one side of her womb by two thrusting penises. Her head was thrown back to swallow the penis of a third man, faceless, anonymous.

He was about to leave the bookshop when he saw an etching of a wolf on the wall. On closer inspection, however, it wasn't a wolf at all, but a man with the face of a wolf. The caption, in black Gothic lettering, read Wolfmensch. John went up and peered at it more closely. The man-wolf was standing in front of an old German town, with crowded rooftops. On one of those rooftops perched a stork.

He was still staring at the picture when the bookshop proprietor approached him – a small, balding, thin-cheeked man with yellowish skin and a worn-out gray suit, and breath that was thick with tobacco.

"You're English?" he asked.

John nodded.

"You're interested in wolf-men?"

"I don't know. Not specially."

"Well, anyway, this picture in which you show so much interest, his is our famous local wolf-man, from Bielefeld. His real name was Schmidt, Gunther Schmidt. He lived – you see the dates here – from 1887 to 1923. He was the son of a schoolmaster."

"Did he ever kill anybody?" asked John.

"Yes, they say so," nodded the bookshop proprietor. "They say he killed many young women, when they were out walking in the woods."

John said nothing, but stared at the wolf-man in awe. The wolf-man looked so much like the rug in the Smythe-Barnetts' attic – eyes and fangs and hairy ears – but then he supposed that all wolves looked much the same. Met one wolf-man, met them all.

The bookshop proprietor hooked the picture down from the wall. "Nobody knows how Gunther Schmidt became a wolf-man. Some people say that his ancestor was bitten by a wolf-man mercenary during the Thirty Years' War. There's a legend, you see, that when the Diet of Ratisbon called back General Wallenstein, he brought in some very strange mercenaries to help him. He was beaten by Gustavus at the battle of Lutzen, but many of Gustavus's men had terrible wounds, throats torn open, and suchlike. Well, perhaps it isn't true. But it's true that the battle of Lutzen was fought under a full moon, and you know what they say about wolf-people. Women, as well as men."

"Werewolves," said John, feeling awed.

"That's right, werewolves! Here, let me show you this book. It has pictures of all of the incidents of werewolves, during the past fifty years. It's a very interesting book, if you like to be scared!"

From the shelf just above his desk, he took down a large album, covered with brown paper. He opened it out, and beckoned John to take a look.

"Here! This is one for the werewolf enthusiast! Lili Bauer, killed on the night of April 20, 1921, in Tecklenburg, her throat was torn open. And here is Mara Thiele, found dead in the Lippe, July 19, 1921, also throat torn open . . . *und so weiter, und so weiter.*"

"Who's this?" asked John. He had found a photograph of a girl in a halter-top dress, with a white blouse, and blonde hair, standing by a suburban road, one eye squinched against the sunlight.

"This one . . . Lotte Bremke, found dead in the woods close to Heepen, August 15, 1923. Again, throat ripped out. The last victim, this is what it says. After that, nobody heard from Gunther Schmidt anything more . . . although here, look. A human heart was found nailed to a tree in Waldstrasse, with the message, here is the heart of the wolf."

John stared at the photograph of Lotte Bremke for a long time. He was sure that it was the same girl whose photograph was nailed up in the attic at the Smythe-Barnetts' house. But could that mean that Lotte Bremke had lived there once? And if she had – where had the wolf-skin come from? Had Lotte Bremke's father killed the wolf-man, perhaps, and nailed his heart to a tree, and kept his skin as a gruesome souvenir?

He closed the book and handed it back. The bookshop proprietor was watching him with pale, disinterested eyes, their pupils the colour of cold tea.

"Well?" said the bookshop proprietor. "*Was glaubst du?*"

"I'm not really interested in werewolves," John told him. There were far worse things than werewolves, like wetting the bed in front of Mrs Smythe-Barnett.

"But you stared at this picture," the bookshop proprietor smiled.

"I was just interested."

"Well . . . of course. But don't forget that the beast is not inside us. This is important to remember when dealing with wolf-men. The beast is not inside us. *We are inside the beast, versteh?*"

John stared at him. He didn't know what to say. He felt as if this man could read everything that he was thinking, like an open book lying on a shallow riverbed. All that was required to turn the pages was to get one's fingers wet.

John took the bus back to Heepen. It was nearly half-past five and the sky was indigo. The moon hung over the Teutoburger Wald like the bright face of God. When he arrived back at the Smythe-Barnetts' house, all the lights were lit, Penny and Veronica were giggling in the kitchen, and Col. Smythe-Barnett was entertaining six or seven fellow officers in the living room (roars of laughter, clouds of cigarette smoke).

Mrs Smythe-Barnett came into the kitchen and for the first time John was pleased to see her. She was wearing a glittery cocktail dress but her face was dark with rage. "Where have you been?" she shouted, and she was so angry that it took him a moment or two to understand that she was shouting at him.

"I went to Bielefeld," he said, weakly.

"You went to Bielefeld without telling us! We've been frantic! Gerald had to call the local polizei, for God's sake, and you don't have any idea how much he hates asking for help from the locals!"

134

"I'm sorry," he said. "I thought it was all right. We went on Tuesday. I thought it was all right to go today."

"For God's sake, isn't it enough that we're wet-nursing you? You've only been here four days and you've been nothing but trouble! No wonder your parents broke up!"

John sat with his head bowed and said nothing. He didn't understand adult drunkenness. He didn't understand that people could exaggerate things that irritated them, and not really mean it, and say sorry the next morning, and it was all forgotten. He was eleven.

Veronica set his supper in front of him. It was a cold chicken leg, with gherkins. He had asked especially not to be given warm milk, because he didn't like it. Instead, he had a glass of flat Coca-Cola.

In bed that night, he crunched himself up and cried as if his heart would split into pieces.

But at two o'clock in the morning, he opened his eyes and he was perfectly calm. The moon was shining so brightly through his bedroom curtains that it could have been daylight. Dead daylight, the world of the dead, but daylight all the same.

He climbed out of bed and looked at himself in his little mirror. A boy with a face made of silver. He said, "Lotte Bremke." That was all he had to say. He knew that she had lived here, when the house was first built. He knew what had happened to her. Some things are so obvious to children that they blink in disbelief when adults fail to understand. Lotte Bremke's father had done what any father would do, and hunted down the wolf-man, and killed him, somehow, and nailed his heart (*Smash!* Quiver! *Smash!* Quiver) to the nearest plane tree.

John glided to the bedroom door, and opened it. He

walked along the corridor with feet like glass. He walked up the stairs, and along the second corridor, with feet like glass. He reached the cream-painted door that led to the attic, and opened it.

He climbed the stairs.

Sure enough, the wolf-rug was waiting for him, with gleaming yellow eyes and bristly fur. John crawled across the rough hessian carpet on hands and knees and stroked it, and whispered, "Wolf-man, that's what you were. Don't deny it. You were on the outside, weren't you? You were the skin. That was the difference; that was what nobody understood. Werewolves are wolves turned into men, not men turned into wolves! And you ran round their houses, didn't you, and ran through their woods, and caught them, and bit them, and tore their throats out, and killed them!

"But they caught you, didn't they, wolf, and they took out the man who was hiding inside you. They took out all of your insides, and left you with nothing but your skin.

"Still, you shouldn't worry. I can be your man now. I can put you on. You can be a rug one minute, and a real wolf the next."

He stood up, and lifted the rug up from the floor. It had felt heavy when he had been wrestling with it this afternoon, but now it felt even heavier, almost as heavy as a live wolf. It took him all of his strength to lift it around his shoulders, and to drape the empty legs around him. He perched the head on top of his own head.

He trailed around the attic, around and around. "I am the wolf, and the wolf is me," he breathed to himself. "I am the wolf, and the wolf is me."

He closed his eyes. He flared his nostrils. I'm a wolf now, he thought to himself. Fierce and fast and dangerous. He could imagine himself running through the woods of

136

Heepen, in between the trees, his paws padding soft and deadly over the thick carpet of pine needles.

He opened his eyes. Now was the time to get his revenge. The wolf's revenge! He climbed down the stairs with his tail beating thump, thump, thump on the treads behind him. He pushed open the attic door and began to lope along the corridor, toward the slightly open door of the Smythe-Barnetts' bedroom.

He growled deep down in his throat, and saliva began to drip from the sides of his mouth. He made hardly any sound at all as he approached the Smythe-Barnetts' door.

I am the wolf, and the wolf is me.

He was only three or four feet away from the door when it suddenly and silently opened, and the corridor was filled with moonlight.

John hesitated for a moment, and growled again.

Then something stepped out of the Smythe-Barnetts' bedroom that made the real hair rise on the back of his neck, and turned his soul to water.

It was Mrs Smythe-Barnett, and yet it wasn't. She was naked, tall and naked – but she was more than naked, she was *raw*. Her body glistened with white bone and tightly stretched membranes, and John could even see her arteries pulsing, and the fan-like tracery of her veins.

Inside her long, narrow ribcage, her lungs rose and fell in a quick, obscene panting.

Her face was horrifying. It seemed to have stretched out into a long bony snout, and her lips were drawn tightly back over her teeth. Her eyes glittered yellow. Wolf-yellow.

"*Where's my skin?*" she demanded, in a voice that was halfway between a hiss and a growl. "*What are you doing with my skin?*"

John let the wolf-rug drop from his shoulders and slide down onto the floor. He couldn't speak. He couldn't even breathe. He watched in helpless dread as Mrs Smythe-Barnett dropped down onto her hands and knees, and seemed to slither into the wolf-rug like a naked hand slithering into a furry glove.

"I didn't *mean* to –" he managed to choke out, but then the claws burst into his windpipe, knocking him backward against the wall. He swallowed, so that he could scream, but all that he swallowed was a half-pint of warm blood.

The wolf-rug came after him and there was nothing he could do to stop it.

John's father arrived at the house shortly after eight-thirty the following morning, as he did every morning, so that he could see John for five or ten minutes before he went to work. His German driver kept the engine of the khaki Volkswagen running, because it was so cold this morning, well below five degrees.

He went up the steps, his swagger stick tucked under his arm. To his surprise, the front door was wide open. He pressed the doorbell, and then stepped inside the house.

"David? Helen? Anyone at home?"

He heard a strange mewing noise coming from the kitchen.

"Helen? Is everything all right?"

He walked through to the back of the house. In the kitchen he found the German maid sitting at the table, still dressed in her hat and coat, her handbag in front of her, shaking and shivering with shock.

"What's wrong?" John's father demanded. "Where is everybody?"

"*Etwas shrecklich,*" the maid quivered. "All family dead."

138

"What? What do you mean, 'All family dead'?"

"Upstairs," said the maid. "All family dead."

"Call my driver. Tell him to come inside. Then telephone the police. *Polizei*, got it?"

Filled with terrible apprehension, John's father climbed the stairs. On the first-floor landing, he found the bedroom doors ajar, and spattered with blood. The smiling photographs of Penny and Veronica lay smashed on the carpet, the red gymkhana rosettes trampled and torn.

He went close to the girls' bedroom doors and looked inside. Penny lay sprawled on her back, her neck so furiously ripped open that her head was almost separated from her body. Veronica lay face down, her white nightgown stained dark red.

Grim faced, John's father went to the bedroom where John was sleeping. He opened the door, but inside the bed was empty, and there was no sign of John. He swallowed dryly, and said a prayer to himself. Please God, let him still be alive.

He climbed further. The second-storey corridor was sprayed with squiggles and question marks of blood. In the Smythe-Barnetts' bedroom, Col. Smythe-Barnett lay on his back staring at the ceiling, his larynx torn out. He looked as if he were wearing a bib of blood. No sign of Helen Smythe-Barnett anywhere.

The door that led to the staircase was decorated all over with bloody handmarks. John's father opened it, took a deep breath, and slowly climbed up to the attic.

The room was filled with sunlight. As he climbed up, he found himself confronted by a rug made of wolfskin, with the wolf's head still attached. The wolf's jaws were dark with congealing blood, and its fur was matted.

There was something concealed by the rug that raised it in a slight hump. John's father hesitated for a very

139

long time, and then took hold of the edge of the rug and lifted it up.

Underneath it were the half-digested remains of a young boy.

Mother of Invention

Cliveden, Berkshire

Cliveden is a huge Victorian house which stands high on a hill overlooking the River Thames near Maidenhead. Once the home of the Astor family, it became notorious in the 1960s when it was the setting for liaisons between the British War Minister John Profumo and the good-time girl Christine Keeler. Along with its extensive woods and gardens, the house was given to the National Trust in 1942 by the 2nd Viscount Astor – his son, the 3rd Viscount, added Taplow Court Woods to the estate in 1954.

Cliveden is now open as a country house hotel, and you can spend the weekend roaming its panelled halls and admiring its antiques – or you can simply lunch there, and take a walk down the hill to the Thames to digest your meal (although – a warning – it's a stiff climb back up to the house again).

For a few hours, however, you can pretend that you're a viscount, and that you have everything that life has to offer. As this story shows, though, some people want more *than life has to offer.*

MOTHER OF INVENTION

He left her sitting on the sun-blurred verandah under the cherry blossoms which showered down softly all around her like the confetti on her wedding day, all those years ago.

She was seventy-five now: her hair shone white, her neck was withered, her eyes were the colour of rainwashed irises. But she still dressed elegantly, the way that David always remembered her, with pearl necklaces and silk dresses, and although she was old she was still very beautiful.

David could remember his father dancing around the dining room with her, and saying that she was the Queen of Warsaw, the most stunning woman that Poland had ever produced, from a nation which was renowned for its stunning women.

"There is no woman to equal your mother: there never will be," his father had said, on his eighty-first birthday, as they walked slowly together beside the Thames, at the foot of the steep hill which led up to Cliveden. Dragonflies had darted over the dazzling water; oarsmen had shouted and a girl had screamed with glee. Three days later, his father was dead, quite peacefully, in his sleep.

David's tan suede shoes crunched across the gravel. Bonny was already waiting for him in his decrepit blue open-topped MG, applying a violently-pink shade of lipstick in the rearview mirror. Bonny was his second wife, and eleven years younger than he was – blonde, still child-faced, funny – and totally different from Anne, his first wife, who had been brunette and very serious and *lank*, somehow. His mother still didn't approve of Bonny. She rarely said anything, but he could tell that she thought her thoroughly ill-behaved for taking a loving husband away from his family. As far as his mother was concerned, marriages were made in heaven, even if they often descended into hell.

"Your father would have had some very strong words to say to you, David," she had told him, staring at him resentfully, unblinking, her head tilted to one side, her fingers fiddling with her diamond engagement ring and her wedding band. "Your father said that a man should always stay faithful to one woman, and one woman only."

"Father loved you, mother. That was easy for him to say. I didn't love Anne at all."

"Then why did you marry her and give her children and make the poor girl's life an absolute misery?"

David still didn't really know the answer to that. He and Anne had met at college and somehow they had just got married. The same thing had happened to dozens of his friends. Twenty years later they were sitting in mortgaged houses in the suburbs staring out of the window and wondering what happened to all those laughing, golden-legged girls they *should* have married.

What he did know, however, was that he loved Bonny in a way that he had never loved Anne. With Bonny, he could understand for the very first time what it was that his father had seen in his mother. A captivating look about her that was almost angelic; an overwhelming femininity; a softness of skin; a shining of hair. He could sit and watch her for hours sometimes, as she sat at her drawing board,

144

painting wallpaper designs. He could have watched her for a living, if only it had paid a salary.

"How was she?" asked Bonny, as David eased himself into the car. He was a tall man, very English looking in his rust-coloured sweater and his fawn twill trousers. He had inherited his mother's deep-set Polish eyes and her dead-straight hair, but his Englishness was established beyond doubt by the same long, handsome face as his father, and his insistence on driving the tiniest of sports cars, even though he was six foot two inches tall.

"She was fine," he said, as he started up the engine. "She wanted to know where you were."

"Hoping I'd left you for ever, I suppose?"

He swung the car in a wide semicircle, and headed off down the long avenue of pollarded lime trees which gave The Limes Retirement Home its name.

"She doesn't want to break us up, not any more," said David. "She can see how happy I am."

"Perhaps that's the problem. Perhaps she thinks that the longer you and I stay together, the less chance there's going to be of you going back to Anne."

"I wouldn't go back to Anne for all the Linda McCartney meat-free foods in her freezer." He checked his watch, the Jaeger-le-Coultre that had once belonged to his father. "Talking of food, we'd better get back. Remember we promised to drop in to see Aunt Rosemary on the way back."

"How could I ever forget?"

"Oh, come on, Bonny, I know she's odd, but she's been part of the family for years."

"So long as she doesn't start dribbling, I don't mind."

"Don't be unkind."

They reached the gates of the nursing home, and turned east, toward the motorway, and London. The late-afternoon sun flickered through the trees, so that they looked as if they were driving through a Charlie Chaplin movie.

"Does your Aunt Rosemary ever visit your mother?" asked Bonny.

David shook his head. "Aunt Rosemary isn't my real aunt. She was more like my father's secretary, although I never saw her doing any secretarial work. I don't know who she is, exactly. She came to stay with us when I was about twelve or thirteen and after that she never left . . . not until father died, anyway. Then she and mother had some kind of falling-out."

"Your mother isn't exactly the forgiving kind, is she?"

They drove for a while in silence, then David said, "Do you know what she showed me today?"

"You mean apart from her continuing disapproval?"

David ignored that remark. He said, "She showed me an old photograph of her whole family – her grandfather, her grandmother, her mother and her father and her three brothers and her, all standing outside the Wilanow Palace in Warsaw. They were all very good-looking, as far as I can see."

"When was this photograph taken?"

"I think it was about 1924 . . . mother would have been five or six, that's all. But it gave me an idea for her birthday present. I thought I might see if I could trace her life back to when she was born . . . I know Father had hundreds of photographs and letters and stuff. I could make her a kind of 'This Is Your Life' book."

"Won't it take an awful lot of work? You've still got that thesis to finish for the Wellcome Foundation."

He shook his head. "The whole attic is crammed to the rafters with photograph albums and diaries. Father kept them all in immaculate order. He was that kind of man.

146

Very neat, very precise. A perfectionist. Well . . . he'd have to be."

"Where did he meet your mother?"

"In Warsaw, in 1937. Didn't I tell you? He went to Poland to assist the great Magnus Stothard when Sir Magnus was called to operate on Count Szponder, to remove a tumour on his spine. Unsuccessfully, I'm afraid. My mother came with her family to one of the dinners the Szponder family gave in Sir Magnus's honor . . . this was *before* the operation, I might add. My mother wasn't an aristocrat, but her father was very respectable . . . something in shipping, I think. In those days, my mother's name was Katya Ardonna Galowski. She always used to tell me that she wore a gray silk dress with lace on the collar, and sang a song called *The Little Song Thrush*. Apparently my father sat staring at her with his mouth open. He invited her to spend a holiday in Cheltenham, which she did, in the following spring. Of course things started looking rather threatening in Poland, so she stayed in England, and she and my father were married, and that was that."

"Did your mother never see her family again?"

David said, "No. Her brothers joined the Polish Resistance and nobody ever found out what happened to them. Her father and mother were denounced as Jews by one of her father's business partners, and were sent to Birkenau."

They were joining the M4 now, and he had to adjust his rearview mirror because Bonny had altered it when she was putting on her lipstick. A huge truck blared its horn at them, and David had to swerve back into the feeder lane as it came bellowing past.

"You're taking your life into your hands," said Bonny. Then, as they rejoined the motorway, and picked up speed, "Do you remember that programme, 'Your Life In Their Hands'? That surgery thing, where they showed you people having operations?"

"Of course I do. Father was on one of them, doing a liver transplant."

"Really? I didn't know that."

David nodded proudly. "They called him the Tailor of Gloucester, because his suturing was always so incredibly neat. He said the trouble with today's surgeons is that their mummies never taught them to sew. He always used to sew on his own buttons and take up his own trouser cuffs. I think he would have embroidered his patients if he ever had half a chance."

David's hand was resting on the gear-shift, and Bonny laid her hand on top of it. "It's strange to think that if some old Polish count hadn't had a tumour on his spine, and if Hitler hadn't invaded Poland, we wouldn't be together now."

Aunt Rosemary lived in a small bungalow in New Malden, in an uninspiring street that was straddled by pylons. Her front garden was covered in concrete, which had been scored with a crazy paving pattern, and a concrete birdbath stood in the centre of it, with a headless concrete robin perched on the rim. The hedge was tangled with last autumn's leaves and crisp bags.

David rang and Aunt Rosemary slowly heaved her way to the door. When she opened it up, they could smell lavender furniture polish and liniment, and the sourness of unchanged flower-vase water.

Aunt Rosemary was in her mid-seventies. She was almost handsome, but she walked with a terrible crab-like limp, and all of her movements were haphazard and unco-ordinated. She had told David that she suffered from

148

chronic arthritis, made worse by the treatment that doctors had given her in Paris in the 1920s. In those days, the latest thing was to inject the joints of arthritis sufferers with gold, a technique that was not only ruinously expensive but permanently crippling.

"David, you came," she said, her lower lip sloping in a parody of a smile. "Will you have time for some tea?"

"We'd love to," said David. "Wouldn't we, Bonny?"

"Oh yes," Bonny agreed. "We'd love to."

They sat in the small gloomy sitting room drinking weak PG Tips and eating rock cakes with cherries in them. Aunt Rosemary had to keep a handkerchief gripped in her hand in case cake crumbs poured out of the side of her mouth.

Bonny tried to look at something else. The clock on the mantelpiece, the china figurines of racehorses, the goldfish flapping in its murky bowl.

Before they left, David went to the toilet. Bonny and Aunt Rosemary sat in silence for a while. Then Bonny said, "I was asking David earlier why you never go to visit his mother."

"Oh," said Aunt Rosemary, dabbing her mouth. "Well, she and I were very close at one time. But she was the kind who always took and never gave. A very selfish woman, in ways that you wouldn't understand."

"I see," said Bonny, uncomfortably.

Aunt Rosemary laid a distorted hand on hers. "No, dear. I don't really think that you do."

David spent almost the entire weekend up in the attic. Fortunately, Bonny didn't mind too much, because she had a wallpaper design to finish for Sanderson's, a new range based on the 19th-century fabric designs of Arthur Mackmurdo, all curling leaves and flowers in the arts-and-crafts style. The attic was airless and rather too warm, but it was well-lit, with a dormer window looking out over the lawns, and a cushioned window seat where David could sit and sort through some of his father's old documents and photograph albums.

The albums smelled like musty old clothes and unopened closets: the very essence of yesterday. They contained scores of pictures of smiling young medical students in the 1920s, and people in boaters and striped summer blazers having picnics. His father had been photographed with lots of pretty girls, but after March, 1938, he was only ever photographed with one girl – Katya Ardonna Galowska – and even though she was his own mother, David could clearly see why his father had adored her so much.

Their wedding day – April 12, 1941. His mother had worn a smart tilted Robin Hood hat and a short dress with a bolero top. His father had worn a tight double-breasted suit, and spats. Yes, *spats*! They looked as glamorous as film stars, the pair of them, like Laurence Olivier and Vivien Leigh, and their eyes had that odd, unfocused brightness of the truly happy. The truly happy look only inward, dazzled by their own delight.

David in his mother's arms, the day after he was born. There was a larger print of this photograph in the drawing room downstairs, in a silver frame. David when he was eleven months old, sleeping in his mother's arm. Her face was limned by the sunlight that shone through the leaded-glass window, her wispy curls shone like traveller's joy. Her eyes were slightly hooded, as if she were dreaming, or thinking of another land. She was so magnetically beautiful that David found it almost impossible to turn the page – and when he did, he had to turn back again, just for another look.

The date on the photograph was August 12, 1948.

He kept on leafing through the album. There he was,

150

at the age of two, his first visit to the circus. His first Kiddi-Kar. Oddly, though, no sign of his mother – not until January, 1951, when she was pictured next to a frozen pond somewhere, wrapped up in furs, her face barely visible.

She appeared fairly consistently until September, 1951. She was standing at the end of Sea View pier on the Isle of Wight (a pier that was later blown down in a storm). She was wearing a wide-brimmed hat and a calf-length floral dress, and white strappy shoes. Her face was hardly visible in the shadow of her hat, but she seemed to be laughing.

Then again, his mother seemed to disappear. There were no photographs of her until November, 1952, when she had attended Lolly Bassett's wedding at Caxton Hall, in London. She wore a gray suit with a pleated skirt. She looked extremely thin, almost emaciated. Her face was still beautiful but slightly *lumpy* in a way, as if she were recovering from a beating, or hadn't slept well.

Throughout the first five photograph albums that he looked at, David discovered seven material gaps in his mother's appearance . . . almost as if she had taken seven extended vacations throughout his early childhood. When he came to think about it, she *had* been away now and again, but he had always been so well looked after by Auntie Iris (his father's maiden sister) that it had never really occurred to him until now how extended those absences must have been. He remembered that his mother had been ill a great deal, in those days, and that she had been obliged to stay in her bedroom for weeks on end, with the curtains tightly drawn. He remembered tiptoeing into her bedroom to kiss her goodnight, and scarcely being able to find her in the darkness. He remembered touching her soft, soft face, and feeling her soft, soft hair; and smelling her perfume and something else, some strong, penetrating smell, like antiseptic.

But then, in 1957, she had reappeared, as strong and as beautiful as ever before, and the sun had shone in every room, and his father had laughed, and he had thought sometimes that he must have the best parents that any boy could wish for.

There was a sixth album, bound in black leather, but it was fastened with a lock, and he couldn't find the key. He made a mental note to himself to look through his father's desk.

He turned back to the photograph of his mother in 1948, and laid the flat of his hand on it, as if he could somehow absorb some understanding of what had happened through the nitrates on the paper.

All through his early life, it seemed as if his mother had come and gone, come and gone, like the sunlight on a cloudy afternoon.

He parked outside Northwood Nursing Home and spent some time wrestling the MG's waterproof cover into place, because it looked like rain.

Inside, he found the registrar's office down at the end of a long linoleum-floored corridor, which echoed and smelled of wax polish. The registrar was a tired looking woman in a lilac cardigan who noisily clicked extra strong mints around her teeth, making little sucking noises. She made it more than obvious that David's request was extremely tiresome, and that she could have been doing something much more important instead (such as making Nescafé).

David waited while she leafed through the record book, making a performance of turning each page.

"Yes . . . here we are. July 3, 1947. Mrs Katerina

Geoffries. Blood group O. Medical history, measles, chicken pox, mild scarlatina. Live male birth – I presume that's you? – weighing 7lbs 4ozs."

David peered over the desk. "There's another note there, in red ink."

"That's because somebody has checked her medical record at a later date."

"I see. Why would anybody want to do that?"

"Well, in this case, because of her accident."

"Accident? What accident?"

The registrar stared at him very oddly, her eyes magnified by her spectacles. "You are who you say you are?" she asked him.

"Of course. Why shouldn't I be?"

The registrar closed the book with an emphatic slap. "It just strikes me as rather peculiar that you don't know about your mother's accident."

David pulled out his wallet, and showed the registrar his driving licence and a letter from the Borough Council. "I'm David Geoffries. Mrs Katya Geoffries is my mother. Look . . . here's a photograph of us together. I don't know why she never told me about her accident. Perhaps she didn't think that it was very important."

"I would say that it was extremely important – at least as far as your mother was concerned."

"But why?"

The registrar opened the book again, and turned it around so that David could read what was written in red ink. "Senior med. reg. from Middlesex Hosp. inquired blood grp. & med. history urgent 2 a.m. 14/09/48 (unable contact GP). Mrs G. seriously crushed car accident."

Underneath, in black ink, in another hand: "Mrs Geoffries deceased 15/09/48."

David looked up. He felt as if he had been breathing

in nitrous oxide at the dentist – light-headed and echoey and detached from everything around him. "This must be a mistake," he heard himself saying. "She's still alive, and perfectly well, and living at The Limes. I saw her only yesterday."

"Well, if that's the case, I'm very pleased," said the registrar, making a loud rattle with her mint. "Now, if you can excuse me –"

David nodded, and stood up. He left the Nursing Home and stood on the steps outside, while the rain began to spot the red-asphalt driveway, and the wind began to rise.

He found a copy of the death certificate at Somerset House. Mrs Katerina Ardonna Geoffries had died on September 15, 1948, in the Middlesex Hospital, cause of death multiple internal injuries. His mother had been killed and here was the proof.

He visited the offices of the *Uxbridge Gazette* and leafed through amber-coloured back issues in the morgue. There it was: in the issue dated September 18, complete with a photograph. A few minutes after midnight, a Triumph Roadster had run through a red traffic light at Greenford, and collided with a lorry carrying railway-lines. David recognized the car at once. He had seen it in several photographs at home. It hadn't occurred to him that it had failed to reappear after September, 1948.

His mother was dead. His mother had died when he was only a year old. He had never known her, never talked to her, never played with her.

So who was the woman in The Limes? And why had she pretended for all of these years that *she* was his mother?

He went back home. Bonny had made him a devastatingly hot chilli con carne, one of his favourites, but he found that he could only pick at it.

"What's the matter?" she asked him. "You're so pale! You look as if you need a blood transfusion."

"My mother's dead," he said; and then he told her the whole story.

They left their supper and sat on the sofa with glasses of wine and talked about it. Bonny said, "What I can't understand is why your father never told you. I mean, it wouldn't have upset you, would it? You wouldn't have remembered her."

"It wasn't just me he didn't tell. He didn't tell anybody. He called her Katya and he told everybody how they had met in Poland before the war . . . he used to call her the Queen of Warsaw. Why would he have done that, if it wasn't her at all?"

They pored over the photograph albums again. "These later pictures," said Bonny, "they certainly *look* like your mother. She's got the same hair, the same eyes, the same profile."

"No . . . here's a difference," said David. "Look . . . in this picture of her holding me when I was eleven months old, look at her ear lobes. They're very small. But look at *this* picture taken in 1951. There's no doubt about, she's got different ears."

Bonny went to her easel and came back with her magnifying glass. They scrutinized the woman's hands, her feet, her shoulders. "There . . . she has three moles on her shoulder in this picture, but not in this one."

At last, with the bottle of wine almost empty, they sat back and looked at each other in bewilderment.

"It's the same woman, yet it isn't the same woman. She keeps changing, very subtly, from year to year."

"My father was a brilliant surgeon. Maybe he was giving her cosmetic surgery."

"To make her ear lobes bigger? To give her moles where she didn't have moles before?"

David shook his head. "I don't know . . . I can't understand it at all."

"Then perhaps we'd better ask the only person who really knows . . . your mother, or whoever she is."

She sat with her face half in shadow. "I am Katya Ardonna," she said. "I always have been Katya Ardonna, and I will remain Katya Ardonna until the day I die."

"But what about the accident?" David insisted. "I've seen my mother's death certificate."

"I am your mother."

He went through the photograph albums again and again, searching for clues. He had almost given up when he found a photograph of his mother at Kempton Park racecourse in 1953, arm in arm with a smiling brunette. The caption read, "Katya & Georgina, lucky day at the races!!"

Clearly visible on her friend Georgina's shoulder were three moles.

Georgina's father sat by the window, staring sightlessly out at the traffic on the Kingston Bypass through his grimy net curtains. He wore a frayed gray cardigan and a resentful tortoiseshell cat sat in his lap and gave David an unblinking death stare.

"Georgina went out on New Year's Eve, 1953, and that was the last anybody ever saw of her. The police were very good about it, they did their best, but there was no clue to go on, not one. I can see her face like it was yesterday. She turned round and said, 'Happy New Year, Dad!' I can

156

hear it now. But after that night, I never had one happy new year, not one."

David said to his mother, "Tell me about Georgina."

"Georgina?"

"Georgina Philips, she was a friend of yours. One of your best friends."

"Why on earth do you want to know about her? She went missing, disappeared."

David said, "I think I've found out where she is. Or at least, I think I know where part of her is."

His mother stared at him. "My God," she said. "After all these years . . . I never thought that anybody would ever find out."

She stood in the centre of her room, wearing nothing but her pale peach dressing gown. Bonny stood in the corner, right in the corner, fearful but fascinated. David stood close to his mother.

"He worshipped me, that was the trouble. He thought I was a goddess, that I wasn't real. And he was so possessive. He wouldn't let me talk to other men. He was always telephoning me to make sure where I was. In the end, I began to feel that I was trapped, that I was suffocating. I had too much whisky to drink and I went for a drive.

"I don't remember the accident. All I remember is waking up in your father's clinic. I was terribly crushed, the lorry had driven right over my pelvis. You were right, of course, I *was* dead. But your father took possession of my body, and took me to Pinner.

"You probably didn't know very much about your father's work with electrical galvanization. He had found a way of stimulating life into dead tissue by injecting it with

157

negatively-charged minerals and then inducing a massive positive shock. He had perfected it in wartime for the War Office . . . and of course they had been only too happy to supply him with dead soldiers to experiment on. The first man he brought back to life was a Naval petty officer who had drowned in the Atlantic. The man's memory was badly impaired, but your father found a way of preventing that from happening by using amino acids."

She paused, and then she said, "I was killed in that accident, all those years ago, and I should have stayed dead. But your father revived me. Not only that, he rebuilt me, so that I was almost as perfect as I had been when he first met me.

"My legs were crushed beyond repair . . . he gave me new legs. My body was pulped . . . he gave me a new body. New heart, lungs, liver, pelvis, pancreas . . . new arms, new ribs, new breasts."

She dropped the shoulder of her dressing gown. "There," she said, "look at my back."

David could barely see the scar that his father's surgery had left on his mother's back. The faintest of silvery lines, where Georgina's arm had been sewn onto somebody else's shoulder.

"How much of you is really you?" he asked her, hoarsely. "How much of you is Katya Ardonna?"

His mother said, "Over the years, your father used six different women, restoring me piece by piece to what I once was."

"And you let him do it? You let him murder six women so that he could use their body parts, just for you?"

"Your father was beyond my control. Your father was beyond anybody's control. He was a great surgeon, but he was obsessed."

"I still can't believe you allowed him to do it."

His mother lifted her dressing gown again. "I suffered years of agony, David . . . years when I was scarcely conscious from one month to the next. It was like living in a dream, or a nightmare. Sometimes I used to wonder if I was actually dead."

"But how did he get away with it, killing all of those women? How did he get rid of the bodies?"

From around her neck, Katya Ardonna took a small silver key. "You've seen that black leather album in the attic? The one that's locked? Well, this key will open it. This key will let you know everything that you ever want to know, and more."

They looked through the album in silence. It was a complete photographic record of his father's surgical reconstruction of his mother's shattered body. Page by page, year after year, they could follow his progress as he painstakingly put her back together again. The surgical techniques were extraordinary – even involving a kind of micro-surgery, to reconnect nerve fibres and tiny blood capillaries.

First of all, they saw how David's father had sewn new limbs onto his mother's shattered body – then replaced her ribcage and her lungs and all of her internal organs.

After years of meticulous surgery, she had emerged as perfect as she was today. The same beautiful woman that his father had met in Poland in 1937 – almost flawless, finely proportioned, and scarcely scarred at all.

She smiled from the album like the Queen of Warsaw.

But the photographs told a darker story, too. Stage by horrifying stage, they showed what David's father had done with the limbs and the organs that had been surplus to his needs. He hadn't wrapped them up in newspaper, or burned them, or buried them, or dissolved them in acid.

159

He had painstakingly sutured them together, muscle to muscle, nerve to nerve. Every photograph was a grisly landscape of veins and membranes and bloody flesh. Glutinous chasms opened up; glutinous chasms were closed. Blood welled scarlet over thin connective tissues; blood was drained away.

Neither of them had ever seen the human body opened up like this. It was a monstrous garden of grisly vegetables: livers shining like aubergines, intestines heaped like cauliflower curds, lungs as big as crumpled pumpkins.

Out of this riot of skin and bone and offal, out of all of these rejects, David's scrupulous father had been able to create another woman. Of course, she wasn't as beautiful as Katya Ardonna . . . he had pillaged the best from six women's bodies to restore Katya Ardonna's beauty, the way he had remembered it to be.

But she had been presentable enough, under the circumstances. And she had given him the opportunity to practise his suturing skills, and some of his new ideas on connecting nerve fibres.

And she had *lived*, just as Katya Ardonna had lived – six murder victims tangled into one living woman.

The last few photographs in the album showed the woman's toes being sewn on, and the skin being closed over her open leg-incisions.

The very last picture showed the day that the bandages had come off this new woman's face. She was bruised and stunned, and her eyes were out of focus. But with a sickening, surging sensation of disgust, they saw the desperate, lopsided face of David's Aunt Rosemary.

Bridal Suite

Sherman, Connecticut

The Litchfield Hills are the ideal setting for a Gothic, romantic horror story. Drive up in fall, when the trees are turning, and the countryside smells and tastes like Hallowe'en. This is real pumpkin country, where witches ride on broomsticks and the leaves whirl even when there's nobody there.

Sherman, Connecticut, has kept its feeling of witchery far longer than towns in Europe, because economic necessity has reduced its population to commuters and retired folk, and modern development has passed it by. You can still find dark, dilapidated coaching-inns; and huge abandoned houses with lichen-blurred windows and sagging tennis nets.

It may be less than two hours' drive from the centre of Manhattan, but that, in a way, completes its strangeness. You can travel so quickly from modern metropolitan bustle to 17th-century silence that you can scarcely believe it.

And when things go strangely awry, you can scarcely believe that, either . . . ,

BRIDAL SUITE

They arrived in Sherman, Connecticut, on a cold fall day when the leaves were crisp and whispery, and the whole world seemed to have crumbled into rust. They parked their rented Cordoba outside the front steps of the house, and climbed out. Peter opened the trunk and hefted out their cases, still new, with price tags from Macy's in White Plains, while Jenny stood in her sheepskin coat and smiled and shivered. It was a Saturday, mid-afternoon, and they had just been married.

The house stood amongst the shedding trees, white weather-boarded and silent. It was a huge old colonial, 1820 or thereabouts, with black-paint railings, an old coach lamp over the door, and a flagged stone porch. All around it stretched silent leafless woods and rocky outcroppings. There was an abandoned tennis court, with a sagging net and rusted posts. A decaying roller, overgrown with grass, stood where some gardener had left it, at some unremembered moment, years and years ago.

There was utter silence. Until you stand still in Sherman, Connecticut, on a crisp fall day, you don't know what silence is. Then suddenly a light wind, and a scurry of dead leaves.

They walked up to the front door, Peter carrying the suitcases. He looked around for a bell, but there was none.

Jenny said: "Knock?"

Peter grinned. "With that thing?"

On the black-painted door was a grotesque corroded brass knocker, made in the shape of some kind of howling creature, with horns and teeth and a feral snarl. Peter took hold of it tentatively and gave three hollow raps. They echoed inside the house, across unseen hallways and silent landings. Peter and Jenny waited, smiling at each other reassuringly. They had booked, after all. There was no question but they had booked.

There was no reply.

Jenny said: "Maybe you ought to knock louder. Let me try."

Peter banged louder. The echoes were flat, unanswered. They waited two, three minutes more. Peter, looking at Jenny, said: "I love you. Do you know that?"

Jenny stood on tippy-toes and kissed him. "I love you, too. I love you more than a barrelful of monkeys."

The leaves rustled around their feet and still nobody came to the door. Jenny walked across the front garden to the living room window and peered in, shading her eyes with her hand. She was a small girl, only five-two, with long fair hair and a thin oval face. Peter thought she looked like one of Botticelli's muses, one of those divine creatures who floated two inches off the ground, wrapped in diaphanous drapery, plucking at a harp. She was, in fact, a *sweet* girl. Sweet-looking, sweet-natured, but with a slight sharpness about her that made all that sweetness palatable. He had met her on an Eastern Airlines flight from Miami to La Guardia. He had been vacationing, she had been visiting her retired father. They had fallen in love, in three months of beautiful days that had been just like one of those movies, all out-of-focus swimming scenes and picnics in the grass and running in slow motion across

164

General Motors Plaza while pigeons flurried around them and passing pedestrians turned and stared.

He was an editor for Manhattan Cable TV. Tall, spare, given to wearing hand-knitted tops with floppy sleeves. He smoked Parliament, liked Santana and lived in the village amidst a thousand LPs, with a grey cat that liked to rip up his rugs, plants and wind chimes. He loved Doonesbury and never knew how close it got to what he was himself.

Some friends had given them a polythene bag of grass and a pecan pie from the Yum-Yum Bakery for a wedding present. Her father, dear and white haired, had given them three thousand dollars and a water bed.

"This is crazy," said Peter. "Did we book a week at this place or did we book a week at this place?"

"It looks deserted," called Jenny, from the tennis court.

"It looks more than deserted," complained Peter. "It looks run down into the ground. *Cordon bleu* dining, they said in *Connecticut*. Comfortable beds and all facilities. It looks more like Frankenstein's castle."

Jenny, out of sight, suddenly called: "There's someone here. On the back terrace."

Peter left the cases and followed her around the side of the house. In the flaking trees, black-and-white wood warblers flurried and sang. He walked around by the tattered tennis court nets, and there was Jenny, standing by a deck chair. In the chair, asleep, was a gray-haired woman, covered by a blanket of dark green plaid. On the grass beside her was a copy of the New Milford newspaper, stirred by the breeze.

Peter bent over the woman. She had a bony, well-defined face, and in her youth she must have been pretty. Her mouth was slightly parted as she slept, and Peter could see her eyeballs moving under her eyelids. She must have been dreaming of something.

165

He shook her slightly, and said: "Mrs Gaylord?"

Jenny said: "Do you think she's all right?"

"Oh, she's fine," he told her. "She must have been reading and just dozed off. Mrs Gaylord?"

The woman opened her eyes. She stared at Peter for a moment with an expression that he couldn't understand, an expression that looked curiously like suspicion, but then, abruptly, she sat up and washed her face with her hands, and said: "Oh, dear! My goodness! I think I must have dropped off for a while."

"It looks that way," said Peter.

She folded back her blanket, and stood up. She was taller than Jenny, but not very tall, and under a gray plain dress she was as thin as a clothes horse. Standing near her, Peter detected the scent of violets, but it was a strangely closeted smell, as if the violets had long since died.

"You must be Mr and Mrs Delgordo," she said.

"That's right. We just arrived. We knocked, but there was no reply. I hope you don't mind us waking you up like this."

"Not at all," said Mrs Gaylord. "You must think that I'm awful . . . not being here to greet you. And you just married, too. Congratulations. You look very happy with each other."

"We are," smiled Jenny.

"Well, you'd better come along inside. Do you have many bags? My handyman is over at New Milford this afternoon, buying some glass fuses. I'm afraid we're a little chaotic at this time of year. We don't have many guests after Rosh Hashanah."

She led the way towards the house. Peter glanced at Jenny and shrugged, but Jenny could only pull a face. They followed Mrs Gaylord's bony back across the untidy lawn and in through the door of a sun room, where a faded billiard table mouldered, and yellowed, framed photographs of smiling young men hung next to yachting trophies and varsity pennants. They passed through a set of smeary French doors to the living room, dark and musty and vast, with two old screened fireplaces, and a galleried staircase. Everywhere around there was wood panelling, inlaid flooring and dusty drapes. It looked more like a neglected private house than a "*cordon bleu* weekend retreat for sophisticated couples".

"Is there . . . anybody else here?" asked Peter. "I mean, any other guests?"

"Oh, no," smiled Mrs Gaylord. "You're quite alone. We are very lonely at this time of year."

"Could you show us our room? I can always carry the bags up myself. We've had a plenty hard day, what with one thing and another."

"Of course," Mrs Gaylord told him. "I remember my own wedding day. I couldn't wait to come out here and have Frederick all to myself."

"You spent your wedding night here too?" asked Jenny.

"Oh, yes. In the same room where you will be spending yours. I call it the bridal suite."

Jenny said: "Is Frederick – I mean, is Mr Gaylord –?"

"Passed over," said Mrs Gaylord. Her eyes were bright with memory.

"I'm sorry to hear that," said Jenny. "But I guess you have your family now. Your sons."

"Yes," smiled Mrs Gaylord. "They're all fine boys."

Peter took his luggage from the front doorstep and Mrs Gaylord led them up the staircase to the second-floor landing. They passed gloomy bathrooms with iron claw-footed tubs and amber windows. They passed bedrooms with unslept-in beds and drawn blinds. They passed a

167

sewing room, with a silent pedal sewing machine of black enamel and inlaid mother-of-pearl. The house was faintly chilly, and the floorboards creaked under their feet as they walked towards the bridal suite.

The room where they were going to stay was high-ceilinged and vast. It had a view of the front of the house, with its driveway and drifts of leaves, and also to the back, across the woods. There was a heavy carved-oak closet, and the bed itself was a high four-poster with twisting spiral posts and heavy brocade drapes. Jenny sat on it, and patted it, and said: "It's kind of hard, isn't it?"

Mrs Gaylord looked away. She seemed to be thinking about something else. She said: "You'll find it's most comfortable when you're used to it."

Peter set down the cases. "What time do you serve dinner this evening?" he asked her.

Mrs Gaylord didn't answer him directly, but spoke instead to Jenny. "What time would you like it?" she asked.

Jenny glanced at Peter. "Around eight would be fine," she said.

"Very well. I'll make it at eight," said Mrs Gaylord. "Make yourself at home in the meanwhile. And if there's anything you want, don't hesitate to call me. I'm always around someplace, even if I am asleep at times."

She gave Jenny a wistful smile and then, without another word, she left the room, closing the door quietly behind her. Peter and Jenny waited for a moment in silence until they heard her footsteps retreating down the hall. Then Jenny flowed into Peter's arms, and they kissed. It was a kiss that meant a lot of things: like, I love you, and thank you, and no matter what everyone said, we did it, we got married at last, and I'm glad.

He unbuttoned her plain wool going-away dress. He

slipped it from her shoulder and kissed her neck. She ruffled his hair with her fingers and whispered: "I always imagined it would be like this."

He said: "Mmh."

Her dress fell around her ankles. Underneath, she wore a pink gauzy bra through which the darkness of her nipples showed and small gauzy panties. He slipped his hand under the bra and rolled her nipples between his fingers until they knurled and stiffened. She opened his shirt, and reached around to caress his bare back.

The fall afternoon seemed to blur. They pulled back the covers of the old four-poster bed and then, naked, scrambled between the sheets. He kissed her forehead, her closed eyelids, her mouth, her breasts. She kissed his narrow muscular chest, his flat stomach.

From behind the darkness of her closed eyes, she heard his breathing, soft and urgent and wanting. She lay on her side, with her back to him, and she felt her thighs parted from behind. He was panting harder and harder, as if he was running a race, or fighting against something, and she murmured: "You're worked up. My God, but I love it."

She felt him thrust inside her. She wasn't ready, and by his unusual dryness, nor was he. But he was so big and demanding that the pain was a pleasure, too, and even as she winced she was shaking with pleasure. He thrust and thrust and thrust, and she cried out, and all the fantasies she'd ever dreamed of burst in front of her closed eyes – fantasies of rape by brutal Vikings with steel armour and naked thighs, fantasies of being forced to show herself to prurient emperors in bizarre harems, fantasies of being assaulted by a glossy black stallion.

He was so fierce and virile that he overwhelmed her, and she seemed to lose herself in a collision of love and ecstasy. It took her whole minutes to recover, minutes that were measured out by a painted pine wall clock that ticked and ticked, slow as dust falling in an airless room.

She whispered: "You were fantastic. I've never known you like that before. Marriage must definitely agree with you."

There was no answer. She said: "Peter?"

She turned, and he wasn't there. The bed was empty, apart from her. The sheet was rumpled, as if Peter had been lying there, but there was no sign of him.

She said, in a nervous voice: "Peter? Where are you?"

There was silence, punctuated only by the clock.

She sat up. Her eyes were wide. She said, so softly that nobody could have heard: "Peter? Are you there?"

She looked across the room, to the half-open door that led to the bathroom suite. Late sunlight fell across the floor. Outside, in the grounds, she could hear leaves shifting and the faint distant barking of a dog.

"Peter – if this is supposed to be some kind of a game –"

She got out of bed. She held her hand between her legs and her thighs were sticky with their lovemaking. She had never known him to fill her with such a copious flow of semen. It was so much that it slid down the inside of her leg on to the rug. She lifted her hand, palm upwards, and frowned at it in bewilderment.

Peter wasn't in the bathroom. He wasn't under the bed, or hiding under the covers. He wasn't behind the drapes. She searched for him with a pained, baffled doggedness, even though she knew that he wasn't there. After ten minutes of searching, however, she had to stop. He had gone. Somehow, mysteriously, gone. She sat on the end of the bed and didn't know whether to giggle with frustration or scream with anger. He must have gone someplace. She hadn't heard the door open and

170

close, and she hadn't heard his footsteps. So where was he?

She dressed again, and went to look for him. She searched every room on the upper landing, including the bureaux and the closets. She even pulled down the ladder from the attic and looked up there, but all Mrs Gaylord had stored away was old pictures and a broken-down baby carriage. Up there, with her head through the attic door, she could hear the leaves rustling for miles around. She called: "Peter?" anxiously; but there was no reply, and so she climbed down the ladder again.

Eventually, she came to one of the sun rooms downstairs. Mrs Gaylord was sitting in a basketwork chair reading a newspaper and smoking a cigarette. The smoke fiddled and twisted in the dying light of the day. On the table beside her was a cup of coffee with a wrinkled skin forming on top of it.

"Hallo," said Mrs Gaylord, without looking around. "You're down early. I didn't expect you till later."

"Something's happened," said Jenny. She suddenly found that she was trying very hard not to cry.

Mrs Gaylord turned around. "I don't understand, my dear. Have you had an argument?"

"I don't know. But Peter's gone. He's just disappeared. I've looked all around the house and I can't find him anywhere."

Mrs Gaylord lowered her eyes. "I see. That's most unfortunate."

"Unfortunate? It's terrible! I'm so worried! I don't know whether I should call the police or not."

"The police? I hardly think that's necessary. He's probably gotten a case of cold feet, and he's gone out for a walk on his own. Men do feel like that sometimes, when they've just been wed. It's a common complaint."

171

"But I didn't even hear him leave. One second we were – well, one second we were resting on the bed together, and the next thing I knew he wasn't there."

Mrs Gaylord bit at her lips as if she was thinking.

"Are you sure you were on the bed?" she asked.

Jenny stared at her hotly, and blushed. "We are married, you know. We were married today."

"I didn't mean that," said Mrs Gaylord, abstractedly.

"Then I don't know what you *did* mean."

Mrs Gaylord looked up, and her momentary reverie was broken. She gave Jenny a reassuring smile, and reached out her hand.

"I'm sure it's nothing terrible," she said. "He must have decided to get himself a breath of fresh air, that's all. Nothing terrible at all."

Jenny snapped: "He didn't open the door, Mrs Gaylord! He just vanished!"

Mrs Gaylord frowned. "There's no need to bark at me, my dear. If you're having a few complications with your new husband, then it's most certainly not my fault!"

Jenny was about to shout back at her, but she put her hand over her mouth and turned away. It was no good getting hysterical. If Peter had simply walked out and left her, then she had to know why; and if he had mysteriously vanished, then the only sensible thing to do was search the house carefully until she found him. She felt panic deep inside her, and a feeling which she hadn't felt for a very long time – loneliness. But she stayed still with her hand against her mouth until the sensation had passed, and then she said quietly to Mrs Gaylord, without turning around: "I'm sorry. I was frightened, that's all. I can't think where he could have gone."

"Do you want to look around the house?" asked Mrs Gaylord. "You're very welcome."

172

"I think I'd like to. That's if you don't mind."

Mrs Gaylord stood up. "I'll even help you, my dear. I'm sure you must be feeling most upset."

They spent the next hour walking from room to room, opening and closing doors. But as darkness gathered over the grounds and the surrounding woods, and as the cold evening wind began to rise, they had to admit that wherever Peter was, he wasn't concealed or hiding in the house.

"Do you want to call the police?" asked Mrs Gaylord. They were standing in the gloomy living room now. The log fire in the antique hearth was nothing more than a heap of dusty white ashes. Outside, the wind whirled in the leaves, and rattled at the window frames.

"I think I'd better," said Jenny. She felt empty, shocked, and hardly capable of saying anything sensible. "I think I'd like to call some of my friends in New York, too, if that's okay."

"Go ahead. I'll start preparing dinner."

"I really don't want anything to eat. Not until I know about Peter."

Mrs Gaylord, her face half hidden in shadow, said softly: "If he's really gone, you're going to have to get used to it, my dear; and the best time to start is now."

Before Jenny could answer her, she had walked out of the living room door and along the corridor to the kitchen. Jenny saw an inlaid mahogany cigarette box on a side table, and for the first time in three years she took out a cigarette and lit it. It tasted flat and foul, but she took the smoke down, and held it, her eyes closed in anguish and isolation.

She called the police. They were courteous, helpful, and they promised to come out to see her in the morning if there was still no sign of Peter. They had to warn her,

173

though, that he was an adult, and free to go where he chose, even if it meant leaving her on her wedding night.

She thought of calling her mother, but after dialling the number and listening to it ring, she set the phone down again. The humiliation of Peter having left her was too much to share with her family or her close friends right now. She knew that if she heard her mother's sympathetic voice, she would only burst into tears. She crushed out the cigarette and tried to think who else to call.

The wind blew an upstairs door shut, and she jumped in nervous shock.

Mrs Gaylord came back after a while with a tray. Jenny was sitting in front of the dying fire, smoking her second cigarette and trying to keep back the tears.

"I've made some Philadelphia pepper soup, and grilled a couple of New York steaks," said Mrs Gaylord. "Would you like to eat them in front of the hearth? I'll build it up for you."

Throughout their impromptu dinner, Jenny was silent. She managed a little soup, but the steak caught in her throat, and she couldn't begin to swallow it. She wept for a few minutes, and Mrs Gaylord watched her carefully.

"I'm sorry," said Jenny, wiping her eyes.

"Don't be. I understand what you're going through only too well. I lost my own husband, remember."

Jenny nodded, dumbly.

"I think it would better if you moved to the small bedroom for tonight," suggested Mrs Gaylord. "You'll feel more comfortable there. It's a cosy little room, right at the back."

"Thank you," Jenny whispered. "I think I'd prefer that."

They sat in front of the fire until the fresh logs were burned down, and the longcase clock in the hallway began to strike two in the morning. Then Mrs Gaylord cleared away their plates, and they mounted the dark, creaking staircase to go to bed. They went into the bridal suite to collect Jenny's case, and for a moment she looked forlornly at Peter's case, and his clothes scattered where he had left them.

She suddenly said: "*His clothes*."

"What's that, my dear?"

She flustered: "I don't know why I didn't think about it before. If Peter's gone, then what's he wearing? His suitcase isn't open, and his clothes are lying right there where he left them. He was *naked*. He wouldn't go out on a cold night like this, naked. It's insane."

Mrs Gaylord lowered her gaze. "I'm sorry, my dear. We just don't know what's happened. We've looked all over the house, haven't we? Maybe he took a robe with him. There were some robes on the back of the door."

"But Peter wouldn't –"

Mrs Gaylord put her arm around her. "I'm afraid you can't say what Peter would or wouldn't do. He *has*. Whatever his motive, and wherever he's gone."

Jenny said quietly: "Yes. I suppose you're right."

"You'd better go get some sleep," said Mrs Gaylord. "Tomorrow, you're going to need all the energy you can muster."

Jenny picked up her case, paused for a moment, and then went sadly along the landing to the small back bedroom. Mrs Gaylord murmured: "Goodnight. I hope you sleep."

Jenny undressed, put on the frilly rose-patterned night-dress she had bought specially for the wedding night, and brushed her teeth at the small basin by the window. The bedroom was small, with a sloping ceiling, and there was a single bed with a colonial patchwork cover. On the pale

175

flowery wallpaper was a framed sampler, reading, "God Is With Us".

She climbed into bed and lay there for a while, staring up at the cracked plaster. She didn't know what to think about Peter any more. She listened to the old house creaking in the darkness. Then she switched off her bedside lamp and tried to sleep.

Soon after she heard the longcase clock strike four, she thought she detected the sound of someone crying. She sat up in bed and listened again, holding her breath. Outside her bedroom window the night was still utterly dark, and the leaves rattled like rain. She heard the crying noise again.

Carefully, she climbed out of bed and went to the door. She opened it a little way, and it groaned on its hinges. She paused, her ears straining for the crying sound, and it came again. It was like a cat yowling, or a child in pain. She stepped out of her room and tippy-toed halfway along the landing, until she reached the head of the stairs.

The old house was like a ship out at sea. The wind shook the doors and sighed between the shingles. The weathervane turned and grated on its mounting, with a sound like a knife being scraped on a plate. At every window, drapes stirred as if they were being touched by unseen hands.

Jenny stepped quietly along to the end of the landing. She heard the sound once more – a repressed mewling. There was no doubt in her mind now that it was coming from the bridal suite. She found she was biting at her tongue in nervous anxiety, and that her pulse rate was impossibly quick. She paused for just a moment to calm herself down, but she had to admit that she was afraid. The noise came again, clearer and louder this time.

She pressed her ear against the door of the bridal suite.

176

She thought she could hear rustling sounds, but that may have been the wind and the leaves. She knelt down and peered through the keyhole, although the draught made her eyes water. It was so dark in the bridal suite that she couldn't see anything at all.

She stood up. Her mouth was parched. If there was someone in there – who was it? There was so much rustling and stirring that it sounded as if there were two people there. Maybe some unexpected guests had called by while she was asleep; although she was pretty sure that she hadn't slept at all. Maybe it was Mrs Gaylord. But if it was her, then what was she doing, making all those terrifying noises?

Jenny knew that she had to open the door. She had to do it for her own sake and for Peter's sake. It might be nothing at all. It might be a stray cat playing around in there, or an odd downdraught from the chimney. It might even be latecoming guests and, if it was, then she would wind up embarrassed. But being embarrassed had to be better than not knowing. There was no way she could go back to her small bedroom and sleep soundly without finding out what those noises were.

She put her hand on the brass doorknob. She closed her eyes tight, and took a breath. Then she turned the knob and jerkily opened the door.

The noise in the room was horrifying. It was like the howl of the wind, only there was no wind. It was like standing on the edge of a clifftop at night, with a yawning chasm below, invisible and bottomless. It was like a nightmare come true. The whole bridal suite seemed to be possessed by some moaning, ancient sound; some cold magnetic gale. It was the sound and the feel of fear.

Jenny, shaking, turned her eyes towards the bed. At first, behind the twisted pillars and drapes, she couldn't make out what was happening. There was a figure there, a naked woman's figure, and she was writhing and whimpering and letting out sighs of strained delight. Jenny peered harder through the darkness, and she saw that it was Mrs Gaylord, as thin and nude as a dancer. She was lying on her back, her claw-like hands digging into the sheets, her eyes closed in ecstasy.

Jenny stepped into the bridal suite, and the wind gently blew the door shut behind her. She crossed the rug to the end of the bed, her mind chilled with fright, and stood there, looking down at Mrs Gaylord with a fixed and mesmerized stare. All around her, the room whispered and moaned and murmured, an asylum of spectres and apparitions.

With complete horror, Jenny saw why Mrs Gaylord was crying out in such pleasure. *The bed itself, the very sheets and under-blankets and mattress, had taken on the shape of a man's body, in white linen relief, and up between Mrs Gaylord's narrow thighs thrust an erection of living fabric. The whole bed rippled and shook with hideous spasms, and the man's shape seemed to shift and alter as Mrs Gaylord twisted around it.*

Jenny screamed. She didn't even realize that she'd done it until Mrs Gaylord opened her eyes and stared at her with wild malevolence. The bed's heaving suddenly subsided and faded, and Mrs Gaylord sat up, making no attempt to cover her scrawny breasts.

"*You!*" said Mrs Gaylord, hoarsely. "What are you doing here?"

Jenny opened her mouth but she couldn't speak.

"You came in here to spy, to pry on my private life, is that it?"

"I – I heard –"

Mrs Gaylord climbed off the bed, stooped, and picked

178

up a green silk wrap, which she loosely tied around herself. Her face was white and rigid with dislike.

"I suppose you think you're a clever girl," she said. "I suppose you think you've discovered something momentous."

"I don't even know what –"

Mrs Gaylord tossed her hair back impatiently. She didn't seem to be able to keep still, but kept on pacing around the bridal suite, loaded with tension. Jenny, after all, had interrupted her lovemaking, however weird it had been, and she was still frustrated. She gave a sound like a snarl, and paced back around the room again.

"I want to know what's happened to Peter," said Jenny. Her voice was shaky but for the first time since Peter's disappearance, her intention was firm.

"What do you think?" said Mrs Gaylord, in a caustic voice.

"I don't know what to think. That bed –"

"This bed has been here since this house was built. This bed is the whole reason this house was built. This bed is both a servant and a master. But more of a master."

"I don't understand it," said Jenny. "Is it some kind of mechanism? Some kind of trick?"

Mrs Gaylord gave a sharp, mocking laugh. "A trick?" she asked, fidgeting and pacing. "You think what you saw just now was a trick?"

"I just don't see how –"

Mrs Gaylord's face was sour with contempt. "I'll tell you how, you witless girl. This bed was owned by Dorman Pierce, who lived here in Sherman in the 1820s. He was an arrogant, dark, savage man, with tastes that were too strange for most people. He took a bride, an innocent girl called Faith Martin, and after they were married he led her up to his bridal suite and *this* bed."

Jenny heard the wind moaning again. The cold, old wind that stirred no drapes nor aroused any dust.

"What Dorman Pierce did to his new bride on this bed that first night – well, God only knows. But he used her cruelly and broke her will, and made her a shell of the girl she once was. Unfortunately for Dorman, though, the girl's godmother got to hear of what had happened, and it was said that she had connections with one of the most ancient of Connecticut magic circles. She may even have been a member herself. She paid for a curse to be put upon Dorman Pierce, and it was the curse of complete submission. In future, *he* would have to serve women, instead of women serving *him*."

Mrs Gaylord turned towards the bed, and touched it. Its sheets seemed to shift and wrinkle by themselves.

"He lay in this bed one night and the bed absorbed him. His spirit is in the bed even now. His spirit, or his lust, or his virility, or whatever it is."

Jenny frowned. "The bed did what? *Absorbed* him?"

"He sank into it like a man sinking into quicksand. He was never seen again. Faith Martin stayed in this house until she was old, and every night, or whenever she wished it, the bed had to serve her."

Mrs Gaylord pulled her wrap tighter. The bridal suite was growing very cold. "What nobody knew, though, was that the enchantment remained on the bed, even after Faith's death. The next young couple who moved here slept on this bed on their wedding night, and the bed again claimed the husband. And so it went on, whenever a man slept on it. Each time, that man was absorbed. My own husband, Frederick was – Well, he's in there, too."

Jenny could hardly stand to hear what Mrs Gaylord was going to say next.

She said: "And *Peter*?"

180

Mrs Gaylord touched her own face, as if to reassure herself that she was real. She said, ignoring Jenny's question: "The women who decided to stay in this house and sleep on this bed all made the same discovery. For each man who was absorbed, the bed's strength and virility grew that much greater. That's why I said that it's more of a master than a servant. Right now, with all the men that it has claimed, it is sexually powerful to an enormous degree."

She stroked the bed again, and it shuddered. "The more men it takes," she whispered, "the more demanding it becomes."

Jenny whispered: "Peter?"

Mrs Gaylord smiled vaguely, and nodded, her fingers still caressing the sheets.

Jenny said: "You knew what was going to happen, and you actually let it? You actually *let* my Peter –"

She was too shocked to go on. She said: "Oh, God. Oh, my God."

Mrs Gaylord turned to her. "You don't have to *lose* Peter, you know," she said, cajolingly. "We could both share this bed if you stayed here. We could share all of the men who have been taken by it. Dorman Pierce, Peter, Frederick, and all the dozens of others. Have you any idea what it's like to be taken by twenty men at once?"

Jenny, feeling nauseous, said: "Yesterday afternoon, when we –"

Mrs Gaylord bent forward and kissed the sheets. They were snaking and folding with feverish activity, and to Jenny's horror, they were beginning to rise again into the form of a huge, powerful man. It was like watching a mummified being rise from the dead; a body lifting itself out of a starched white shroud. The sheets became legs, arms and a broad chest, and the pillow rose into the form of a heavy-jawed masculine face. It wasn't Peter, it wasn't any man; it was the sum of *all* the men who had been caught by the curse of the bridal suite, and dragged into the dark heart of the bed.

Mrs Gaylord pulled open her wrap, and let it slither to the floor. She looked at Jenny with glittering eyes, and said: "He's here, your Peter. Peter and all his soulmates. Come and join him. Come and give yourself to him . . ."

Skinny and naked, Mrs Gaylord mounted the bed, and began to run her fingers over the white shape of the sheets. Jenny, with rising panic, crossed the room and tried the door handle, but the door seemed to be wedged firmly shut. The windless wind rose again, and an agonized moaning filled the room. Now Jenny knew what that moaning was. It was the cries of those men trapped for ever within the musty substance of the bridal bed, buried in its horsehair and its springs and its sheets, suffocatingly confined for the pleasure of a vengeful woman.

Mrs Gaylord seized the bed's rising member, and clutched it in her fist. "See this?" she shrieked. "See how strong it is? How proud it is? We could share it, you and I! Come share it!"

Jenny tugged and rattled at the door, but it still refused to open. In desperation she crossed the room again and tried to pull Mrs Gaylord off the bed.

"Get away!" screeched Mrs Gaylord. "Get away, you sow!"

There was a tumultuous heaving on the bed, and Jenny found herself struck by something as heavy and powerful as a man's arm. She caught her foot on the bed's trailing sheets, and fell. The room was filled with ear-splitting howls and bays of fury, and the whole house was shuddering and shaking. She tried to climb to her feet, but she was struck again, and she knocked her head against the floor.

Now Mrs Gaylord had mounted the hideous white figure on the bed, and was riding it furiously, screaming at the top of her voice. Jenny managed to pull herself up against a pine bureau, and seize an old glass kerosene lamp which was standing on top of it.

"*Peter!*" she shouted, and flung the lamp at Mrs Gaylord's naked back.

She never knew how the kerosene ignited. The whole of the bridal suite seemed to be charged with strange electricity, and maybe it was a spark or a discharge of supernatural power. Whatever it was, the lamp struck Mrs Gaylord on the side of the head and burst apart in a shower of fragments, and then there was a soft *woofff* sound, and both Mrs Gaylord and the white figure on the bed were smothered instantly in flames.

Mrs Gaylord screamed. She turned to Jenny with staring eyes and her hair was alight, frizzing into brownish fragments. Flames danced from her face and her shoulders and her breasts, shrivelling her skin like a burning magazine.

But it was the bed itself that was most horrifying. The blazing sheets struggled and twisted and churned, and out of the depths of the bed came an echoing agonized roar that was like a choir of demons. The roar was the voice of every man buried alive in the bed, as the fire consumed the material that had made their spirits into flesh. It was hideous, chaotic, unbearable and, most terrible of all, Jenny could distinguish Peter's voice, howling and groaning in pain.

The house burned throughout the rest of the night, and into the pale cold dawn. By mid-morning it was pretty much under control, and the local firemen trod through the charred timbers and wreckage, hosing down the smouldering furniture and collapsed staircases. Twenty or thirty people came to stare, and a CBS news crew made a short recording for television. One old Sherman citizen, with white hair and baggy pants, told the newsmen that he'd always believed the place was haunted, and it was better off burned down.

It wasn't until they moved the fallen ceiling of the main bedroom that they discovered the charred remains of seventeen men and one woman, all curled up as small as monkeys by the intense heat.

There had been another woman there, but at that moment she was sitting in the back of a taxi on the way to the railroad station, wrapped tightly in an overcoat, her salvaged suitcase resting on the seat beside her. Her eyes, as she watched the brown and yellow trees go past, were as dull as stones.

The Root of All Evil

Harlem, New York

"With notable exceptions, Harlem is emblematic of the failures of American society, and is of interest primarily to visiting sociologists," wrote Herbert Bailey Livesey, in his perspicacious guide to New York. Long since vanished is the romantic image of the Harlem of the 1920s – the days of the Cotton Club and Connie's Inn, the Savoy and the Lafayette Theater – the days of jazz and bootleg liquor and diamond rings and "high yaller gals who could uncork the meanest kind of cootching". While its residents are still proud and fiercely loyal to their families and their neighbourhood, the Harlem of today is a stew of substandard housing, drug addicts and the hopelessly unemployed.

All the same, I paid several visits to Harlem and found much to reward me. The restored Apollo Theater (of James Brown fame) is worth going to see; and so is the Schomburg Center for Research in Black Culture, where I discovered the roots for this story. If you're planning on doing the same, however, a guided tour is probably the safest option . . . and not just because of the thing that you're about to encounter.

In the early 1900s, Harlem was mostly open country,

a patchwork of farms and summer vacation homes. But just before World War One, tenements began to be built off Harlem's main streets, and they were quickly filled with black refugees from the southern states, trying to escape humiliating and oppressive segregation. Their lives improved very little. They were still critically poor. But they brought to Harlem the character that was immortalized by Duke Ellington and Bessie Smith and Fats Waller.

Harlem was not just a hotbed of "sizzling cafés, 'speaks', nightclubs and spiritual seances". It was a place where the roots of Afro-American culture were nurtured, and where those roots are still nurtured today.

Most of those roots were fine and strong; but there is always the root of all evil.

THE ROOT OF ALL EVIL

I wouldn't even have known about it if the traffic hadn't
been so goddamned clogged up on the Triboro Bridge that
night. It was a wet Friday in November, rush hour, and I
had to drive some fat, agitated Texan out to JFK. Like
most of them, he'd left Manhattan with no time to spare,
and after we'd spent twenty minutes creeping and nudging
our way along FDR Drive, with the rain drumming on
the roof of the cab and the meter clicking its way up to
twelve dollars, he was bobbing up and down in his seat
and cursing blue lightning.

I got him out to the airport in plenty of time to make
his connection to Dallas, but the fat slob only tipped me
a buck. As if it was *my* fault it was Friday. I drove around
to the front entrance of the TWA building to see if I could
pick up one of those nice courteous English people to take
back into the city. One of those who sit there and say,
"Dear me, what frightful weather you're having." I'd had
enough of Texans in a hurry.

As it happened, I got some tall black guy in a camel's
hair coat. Maybe a professor or something like that. Gucci
suitcases, and a very Harvard way of talking. He told me
to drive him to the Croydon, on East 86th Street, but first
of all to stop at an address in Harlem, 113th Street, so that
he could drop off a package.

Well, I kind of demurred at that. The last place I wanted

187

to be on a wet Friday night was 113th Street, but the black guy said, "You'll be okay. It's my old neighborhood. Everybody knows me," and so I shrugged and told him I'd do it.

The bridge was clearer on the way back, but the weather wasn't. It was raining like all hell, and when I turned off the bridge into the side streets of Harlem, the taxi was splashing and bouncing through flooded potholes and brimming gutters. The radio was playing, "We're not as smart as we like to think we are –"

I could see the black guy peering out of the window as we drove along East 113th. The tenements were narrow and dilapidated, and the rain was glistening on the corrugated iron that covered half the windows and most of the stores. A few black kids were standing on the corner of 113th and 3rd, sheltering themselves under plastic trash bags and hooded windbreakers.

"Okay, it's here. Stop here," he said. I drew in to the side of the road.

"I'll give you five minutes," I told him. "If you're not back by then, I'm leaving. Take this card. If I'm gone, you can pick up your cases at the cab company."

He hesitated. Then his black hand, heavily embellished with gold rings, came through the partition. It was holding a neatly folded twenty. "I may be longer than five minutes," he said politely.

I took the twenty and tucked it into my shirt pocket. "All right. But make it quick, please. Even twenty isn't worth a mugging."

"I know."

He turned up the collar of his camel's hair coat and climbed out of the cab. I locked all the doors immediately and switched on my emergency flashers. Through the rain-spotted window, I could see the guy hurry across the garbage-strewn sidewalk and into a peeling entrance. He pressed a bell and waited. I tapped my fingers on the steering wheel. Judy, my wife, would be back from school by now and starting to cook dinner. I'd been driving since eleven in the morning, and I could have eaten a radial tire, provided it had enough mustard on it.

The radio said, "This is WPAT, where everything is beautiful."

I thought, This is cab medallion no. 38603, where everything is tedious. I looked at the black-and-white mug shot on my license: a frowning twenty-nine-year-old with thinning hair, a droopy mustache, and heavy-rimmed glasses. Edmond Daniels. Architect, failed genius, and cab driver. Just another member of that tired, irritable brotherhood of old men, Puerto Ricans, Jews and Chinese, the people who drive our battered yellow taxis around and keep our city moving.

My reverie was startlingly interrupted by a loud bang on the roof of the cab. I looked up in fright. But it was only the guy in the camel's hair coat. He was twisting his hand around to indicate that I should let down my window. He looked kind of agitated about something.

I put the window down two inches. Even then, the rain came drifting in. "What's the matter?" I asked him. "Did you deliver your package yet? I have to get going."

"You have to come inside," he said. His voice was high and strained. His eyes were very wide.

I said, "Mister, I'm not coming anywhere. And I'm not leaving my cab on this street."

"You have to. I need a witness. You don't understand."

I checked my driving mirror. The rain was so heavy now that even the kids on the street corner had sloped off. There was nobody else around, either. Nobody

189

who looked like a potential car thief or a mugging artist.

"Okay," I agreed, wearily. "What is it you want me to see?"

I opened the taxi door and stepped out into the rain. He immediately seized my arm and led me across to the doorway. The door was open now, and he pulled me into the dark hallway before I could say anything.

It stank in there. Of decay and rats and kids' urine. But the black guy led me quickly up the first flight of sagging stairs to the landing, and then down to an apartment at the front of the house. The apartment door was ajar, with a faint triangle of orange light crossing the floor, and a sound that I thought at first was a cricket, but which I soon recognized as a record player at the end of its record. Click-*hissss*, click-*hissss*, click-*hissss* . . .

"In here," he said. He was so scared that his face was the color of the sports pages at the back of the *New York Post*.

"I'm not sure I feel like going along with this," I said reluctantly. "I mean, I just drive people."

"You're the only one," he insisted. "I have to have a witness, and you're the only one. You saw that I came from the airport. You know how long I was in here. And you can see that I'm completely clean."

"Clean? What do you mean?"

"Take a look. I'm sorry, but it's necessary."

I tentatively pushed at the door with my fingertips. It swung open a little wider, then creaked to a stop.

"I hope you're sure about this," I told him.

He nodded.

Cautiously, with my heart beating in slow, suppressed bumps, I put my head around the door. There was a narrow room with a single lamp burning. The light was faint and orange because somebody had draped a knotted handkerchief over the shade. Probably soaked in cologne or aftershave, to mask the smell of grass. On the walls were all kinds of African souvenirs, like grinning wooden masks, and spears, and zebra-skin shields. And there was some kind of ebony effigy of a tall dark figure with slanting eyes and teeth like a piranha.

There was so much African stuff in there that I didn't notice the girl at first. But when I looked down toward the rug and actually made sense of the shape that was lying there, oh, Jesus, my hair prickled up and I felt as cold as a Thanksgiving turkey in a supermarket freezer.

She had to be dead. I hoped, for her sake, that she was dead. And for my sake, too, because if she was still alive I would have to touch her, try to bring her back to life. And the way she was right then, I didn't feel like touching her, you know? I was just too squeamish.

She was a black girl, young, with one of those cornrow hairstyles, all plaited and tied up in beads. Somehow, with some kind of maniacal strength and dedication, someone had impaled her on one of those bentwood hatstands, the kind Kojak tosses his hat onto when he walks into the office. *Impaled* her, right through her back and right through her stomach, so that her body had slid right down to the base, but her liver and spleen and long loops of her pale white guts had been left festooned around the hooks. There was blood all over the floor. More blood than I had ever seen in my whole life.

I wasn't sick. I don't know why. I was numb, as if my dentist had injected me all over with novocaine. I stepped back out of the room, and the guy held my arm, and I didn't know what to say or what to do.

"I'm sorry," he said, hoarsely. "I had to show you, just to prove to the cops that I couldn't have done it myself.

I couldn't have done it, could I, not in three minutes, not without getting myself splashed all over with blood?"

"Who is she?" I whispered. "Was she someone you knew?"

He nodded. "Her name is Bella X. A very close friend. Or she was."

"A Black Muslim?"

"Yes."

I said, "We have to call the police."

"I know," he nodded. "That's why I needed a witness. My name's John Bososama, by the way. I work for Chase Manhattan Bank. African investments."

There was a telephone at the end of the hall, mercifully unvandalized. I dialed 911 and waited for the police to answer. John Bososama stood beside me, still upset, but much more together than he had been before. They put me through to the local precinct and I told the duty officer what had happened; he instructed me to wait where I was and not to touch anything.

I said, "If you could see this mess, you wouldn't even want to touch it."

"All right," said the duty officer tiredly.

I put down the phone. I was still trembling. I said to John Bososama, "I'm going to wait in the street. Screw the rain. If I stay here any longer, I'm going to barf."

"Okay," he nodded.

The street smelled fresh by comparison. I leaned across the roof of my cab, while the rain fell in sparkling drops all around me, and I smoked a soggy Kool.

John Bososama stood a few paces away, his hands in the pockets of his camel's hair coat, his shoulders soaked with damp. "I was afraid this would happen," he said. His voice was deep and there was genuine sorrow in it.

I glanced at him. "You mean you knew in advance?"

"Not exactly. But it was one of the reasons I returned to Zaïre. One of the reasons I came here tonight with this."

He held up the brown paper package he'd been taking up to the girl's apartment.

"What's that?" I asked him. "Grass?"

He smiled sadly and shook his head. "A few charms that might have saved her."

I sucked at my cigarette. I could hear a police siren whooping and warbling in the distance.

"You mean she was superstitious?" I queried.

"In a way."

"In what way? Superstitious enough to worry herself about getting stuck through with a hatstand?"

John Bososama laid his hand on my shoulder. "You don't really understand. And maybe it's better that you don't."

I stared at him coldly. "Mr Bososama, if I'm going to be your lonely and only witness, then I think I'm going to need to know what's going on here. I'm not about to swear anything until you fill me in."

The siren was louder now. Then, farther away, another siren joined in. An ambulance.

John Bososama bit his lip. He was silent for a moment, then he said, "You wouldn't believe me anyway. You're white."

"My great-grandmother was Cuban. Try me."

He cleared his throat. Then he said, "Very well. What you have seen tonight, as far as anyone can tell, is the work of Iblis."

"Iblis? What the hell's Iblis?"

"Just listen. The police will be here in a minute. Iblis is the most terrible of Islamic devils. Now, I don't care right this moment whether you believe in devils or not. Just think of what you've seen tonight and try to understand."

I flipped my cigarette into the flooded gutter. "Come on," I said. "I'm listening."

"Listening sympathetically, or listening skeptically?"

"What does it matter? I'm listening."

"Very well," said John Bososama. "In the culture of Islam, the legend goes that when Allah created man, he required all His angels to bow down before His new creation. The angel Iblis alone refused, saying that he despised man because man was made of nothing more than dust. So Allah cursed Iblis, and dismissed him from heaven.

"Iblis, however, persuaded Allah to postpone his final punishment until the Day of Judgment and to grant him freedom to roam the earth and lead astray all those who are not true servants of Allah. It was Iblis, concealed in the mouth of a serpent, who tempted Eve."

"What was this Iblis like?" I asked. I could see the red and white flashing lights of the blue and white police car, only three blocks away. The rain, softer now, prickled on my face.

"Hunched, cloaked, with a head like a camel, only with rows and rows of teeth. Legs and claws like a vulture. A creature without any kind of mercy or feeling."

"And you think what happened tonight . . .?"

"You can believe me or not. But it was the work of Iblis."

I sniffed. "As a matter of fact, I don't believe you. You didn't really expect me to, did you?"

"No, I suppose I didn't," said John Bososama. He rubbed the glittering rain from his close-cropped hair. Then he added, almost sadly, "No, I guess not."

"I mean – how did he get here . . . to New York? This Iblis?"

John Bososama shrugged. "As far as I've ever been able

194

to find out, a long time ago. In the days of the slave trade. The slave ship *African Galley* sailed to New Callebarr in the winter of 1700, looking for slaves and teeth. Among the slaves the ship took on board was a young man called Bongoumba, who was unnaturally strong and said to be mad, or possessed. He was brought over to the New World and sold, although his madness made it necessary for him to be kept in shackles twenty-four hours a day. One day, however, he broke out of his chains and raped a young black girl slave, who became pregnant from his assault. She bore a son, and the line of Bongoumba has descended through to the present day.

"It was only when present-day blacks started to become aware of their roots, however, that the inherited possession of the Bongoumbas began to express its true strength. And when the blacks turned to the religion most suited to them, Islam – well, it was then that the spirit of Iblis, which had remained dormant through all these generations, was regenerated. It was like defrosting a body from a cryogenic chamber."

"So where do you come into this?" I wanted to know. The police car was just pulling in to the curb and we didn't have any more time to talk.

John Bososama looked at me. There were glistening drops under his eyes that could have been rain, or tears. "There was a young man called Duke Jones. His hereditary name, his African name, was Bongoumba. He lived here, in this apartment, and that young girl you saw tonight was his wife. Bongoumba had felt the dark power of something terrible inside him ever since he joined the muslims. Something evil and vengeful and strange. Something that threatened to take him over completely.

"That was why I was bringing him this package. On a business trip to Saudi Arabia, I detoured to Zaïre, and acquired all the magic artifacts which the old-time juju doctors used to dismiss the spirit of Iblis. Magic tokens, lion's hair, charmed bones."

"Kind of primitive, isn't it?" I asked him.

He nodded, almost smiled. "Sure. But we're dealing with a very primitive devil. An evil spirit from way, way back. You see, I think we're learning that every religion has its demons, and that when you embrace a religion as ancient as Islam, you have to cope with its ancient perils as well."

"And you still believe in Allah and Mohammed?"

"More than ever. The more evidence I find of the existence of Iblis, the more I believe in the greatness and the power of Allah and His holy messenger. Doesn't Satan prove beyond any reasonable doubt the true existence of God?"

A cop in a leather windbreaker came up and said, "Are you the people who called the police? Something about a homicide?"

John Bososama nodded. "She's upstairs," he said gravely. "I'm afraid she's been dead for a long time."

I went through the whole routine of a police interrogation, and hours of hanging around the station house, but eventually the detectives let me go home, and I tiredly ate a plate of congealed lasagna and watched the late-night news before I went to bed. Judy was kind of pissed, but when I told her what had happened, she was very calm and sympathetic about it and she mixed me a strong old-fashioned to help me sleep.

I didn't tell her about any of that Iblis stuff. Apart from the fact that I didn't believe it myself, I didn't want to give her nightmares. It was bad enough thinking about that black girl's looped-up intestines without thinking some kind of multifanged camel-headed creature might have done it. I woke up two or three times in the night, listening to the sound of sirens along 12th Street, where we lived, and wondering what the hell this world was really all about. Was there a dark and frightening underworld, populated by devils and demons, or was it nothing more than a bad dream? I heard a scratching noise in the darkness, and I hoped to hell it was nothing worse than mice.

For two or three weeks, everything ran as usual. I woke up mid-morning, took the subway to taxi headquarters, picked up my hack and drove my tour of duty. I picked up businessmen, shoppers, old ladies with tired blood, executives, models, hookers and tourists. I drove uptown, downtown and across town. I waited in jams in Herald Square. I edged my way up Sixth Avenue. I drove to the airport and back. I wended my way through the falling leaves of Central Park. It was cold and snappy and there was always the smell of burned pretzels in the air.

Then, one morning, I checked in for work and my boss came out of that little overheated shack of his with pin-ups of Chesty Morgan on the walls and handed me a package.

"This is for you," he said. "Some black guy brought it around. I said you wouldn't be long but he didn't want to wait."

"A black guy?" I asked, feeling the package. Feeling softness and hardness and unwelcome lumps. "Tall, speaks like a professor? Camel-color coat?"

"That's the one. Looked sick."

"Okay," I said, uncertainly. "Thanks."

I sat in my vehicle and opened up the package. I peered inside and saw a loop of silvery-black hair, tied with raffia, two brownish bones and a small figure of a man made up of discs of copper, all wired together and painted. There was a short letter in the package, too. I unfolded it and scanned it quickly.

Dear Mr Daniels,

You know that I wouldn't have passed this package to you unless it was a matter of life or death. But whether you believed what I told you or not, the spirit of Iblis has come alive again in Manhattan, and it is taking its revenge on "the sons of dust", those Muslims whose lapses in the observance of their religion makes them easy and legitimate prey.

I fear that it is after me, too, and that it has been tracking my movements. So all I can do is to pass this package to you and ask that if you read in the newspapers of my death, you *immediately* come to the morgue where my body is kept and perform with these enclosed artifacts the short ritual I have written down below. I know you are not a Muslim yourself, nor even black, but it is for that reason that Iblis will not suspect you at first and may allow you to approach my body unharmed.

For the sake of all those black people who were brought to this country in slavery – for the sake of Allah – please do what you can.

I remain your friend,
John Bososama

I tucked the letter back in the package. Your friend, huh. With friends like that, you wouldn't need enemies. You wouldn't even need crime on the streets. I started the cab's motor, and with an uneasy feeling of alarm and dread I drove out onto the streets. All that day, I avoided picking up black people. Even Chinese. Who the hell knew what kind of demons the Chinese had up their sleeves?

I slept badly for two or three nights. Judy was real worried and wanted me to call the doctor. But I didn't need to spend forty dollars to know what was wrong with me. I kept remembering the impaled girl on 113th Street, and the tall black guy in the camel's hair coat, and his stories about an ancient Islamic demon. It was nuts, I know. But there's something about driving through Manhattan day after day that makes you ready to believe anything. Do you know that one day in Queens I saw a girl sit in the roadway and set herself afire with gasoline? And the way people stood around and watched her, so casual and curious, I was only surprised that nobody came up with a wiener on a stick.

Then, the day before Thanksgiving, I got the word. Not in the newspaper, but over the radio when I was driving some insurance salesman home to Yonkers. "An official from the Chase Manhattan Bank has been found brutally murdered under the ramp where the southbound lane of Park Avenue joins 40th Street. Credit cards found on the body identified the corpse as John Bososama. The deceased was only a few blocks away from the Lexington Avenue branch of his bank. Police and bank officials say he was carrying no money and that the motive of the homicide was 'probably not robbery'. Bososama's head was jammed into a car door, and then his body was twisted around until his neck broke. His body was also slashed until, in the words of Detective Ernest Saparelli, 'it looked like hamburger'."

I felt nauseated. My driving began to waver and my fare said, "Watch it, fella. I want to get home safe, if you don't mind." I managed to steer the cab straight until I dropped my passenger off, and then I sat behind the wheel and thought and thought and didn't know what in all hell to do.

I mean, why should I care about a bunch of Black Muslims? They'd never meant anything to me and as far as I was concerned, they were nothing but trouble. Look at all the sweat they'd given us over Iran. Look at that loudmouth Muhammad Ali. Look at Malcolm X, and all that stuff. If their devil had caught up with them at last, what business was it of mine? Especially if there was genuine danger involved.

Yet, in a way that I can hardly even tell you about, I felt guilty. So the blacks had their problems. But *why?* Because they'd newly discovered their true religion and were trying to fight their way back to their own personal and religious identities. And why were they having to do that? Because they'd been denied their birthright for so long by the whites. Because, for centuries, they hadn't been allowed to know either the joys or the dangers of their beliefs.

I drove to the morgue. Don't ask me why. If I was in the same position again, I'd drive anyplace else but. Up to Buffalo maybe, or clear across to Cleveland. Anywhere but the midtown police morgue to look at some mutilated stiff.

Surprisingly, I didn't have much trouble getting in. I said that John Bososama had been an acquaintance of mine and that maybe I could help identify him. They took me along a narrow brown-tiled corridor until we reached the cold room. Then the morgue assistant slid out a drawer, and there he was, swathed up to the neck in a white sheet. The morgue assistant chewed gum and occasionally blew a green bubble.

200

"He wanted me to say a few words over the body," I said. "Do you think that's okay?"

"What kind of words?"

"He was a Black Muslim. Some kind of special ritual, you know?"

The morgue assistant turned to the uniformed cop who had accompanied me down there. The cop shrugged, and said, "Okay by me. Long as you don't take all night."

The two of them watched me as I fumbled with my brown paper package. I knelt on the cold wax-polished floor and took out all the magic artifacts: the hair, the bones, the little copper figure. The morgue assistant popped a bubble and shrugged at the cop in bafflement.

I spread out the paper that John Bososama had written out for me. The hair had to be arranged like the rays of the sun. The two bones had to point north and south. The little copper man represented human hope and had to be set down in the center of the hair.

I cleared my throat. It was totally silent in the morgue except for the uneven whirring of the cooling system. To tell you the truth, I felt like a real fool at that moment and I couldn't stop myself from blushing. But I'd decided to do it, so I went ahead with it.

"Iblis," I said, "evil angel of Islam, I recognize you."

The cop sniffed.

"Iblis," I repeated. "Evil angel of Islam, I recognize you and I am here to cast you out of this body and out of this world."

I stood up now, holding John Bososama's paper in front of me so that I could read it.

"You are to leave this true servant of Allah, and to continue your wanderings elsewhere. Yes, even unto the Day of Judgment itself. And you shall allow this servant of Allah to take his place in heaven, and you shall let him be."

The morgue lights, three fluorescent tubes, began to flicker. Then one of them dimmed and almost went out. The morgue attendant raised his head and looked around uneasily.

"Busted fuse?" suggested the cop.

"Iblis, I cast you out from this earthly body, and I expel you," I said, louder this time, maybe because I was getting a little scared. "I call upon all of your former brothers in Allah's heaven to lock you out."

The morgue was suddenly pitched into complete darkness. And then a wind blew up, a harsh, moaning wind. A wind that was not only abrasive and fierce, but *hot*, like a wind across the desert. I heard the cop say something indistinguishable, and the attendant say, "The lights, what happened to the goddamned lights?"

"Go, Iblis!" I shouted. "Go! Walk no more among these abandoned brothers of Africa! Let them be! Leave them to find their own way back to the true religion of Islam, untempted and untrammeled by your mischief! Go!"

A dim, pulsating glow lit the morgue. Only just enough for me to be able to distinguish the banks of drawers where the bodies lay stored. Only just enough for me to be able to see the face of John Bososama. His face glistened, as if he were sweating, and his eyes were wide open.

There was a sudden, terrifying bang. One of the upper drawers had slid open by itself. The morgue attendant said "Jesus" and his jaw dropped. The cop had his revolver out, but there didn't seem to be anything to shoot at. Just the wind and the darkness and the terrible moaning sound of a distant and ancient desert.

Then there was fire. Drawer after drawer banged open by itself and out of each drawer rose a corpse, sitting up as if it were alive. Gray-green corpses that had been dragged out of the East River, their flesh puffy with gas. White corpses that had bled to death in unknown doorways on Eighth Avenue. Corpses that were mauve from heart attacks, and corpses that were dark red with post-mortem lividity. Each one, as it rose out of its drawer, burst into flames. Spontaneous combustion. I saw their hair frizzle and their skin sizzle and smoke that was heavy with the smell of charred humanity filled the room like a fatty mist.

"*Jesus,*" gibbered the cop. "Jesus *Christ.*"

But this horror didn't respond to appeals to Jesus, nor to any Christian God. And out of the dark and wind-blown smoke, impossibly tall and black as some kind of tattered crow, came the apparition of Iblis.

His head was more like that of a skeletal horse than a camel, and when he bared his teeth, I saw row upon row of dripping incisors. He was gigantic, hideous, terrifying. His eyes gleamed in the smoky gloom like the headlights of some dark and unstoppable truck. He roared, but it was more like a harmonic vibration than a roar. A sensation more than a sound. It set my teeth on edge and went right through my bones to my balls.

"*Iblis!*" I screamed. "*I expel you!*"

By the unsteady light of this roomful of blazing corpses, the devil twisted its head around in a gesture of contemptuous superiority.

"*You cannot expel me, you fool,*" it roared, in that same subaudible rumble. "*Only those who think they believe in Allah can expel me. Only those who heed the word of the prophet Muhammad.*"

"I act on behalf of such a man," I shouted. My voice was taut with fear. "This man here. John Bososama. He deputized me."

Iblis laughed. It was more like a subway train falling down a bottomless well than a laugh.

"*You are not of his kind*," he mocked me. "*You can do nothing.*"

I stood my ground. Don't ask me why. But it seemed, just for a moment, that I had something to believe in. I could see at last, right in front of my eyes, the kind of evil that really made the world what it was. Iblis, like Satan, was a sham and a shyster, a trickster dealing in uncertainty and fear.

"I can do *everything*!" I screeched. "I can expel you because I respect my black brothers' belief in Allah and the prophet Muhammad! I can expel you because all men are equal, and because this country guarantees it so! I can expel you because I came to help this man John Bososama for no reason at all except his people ought to be free! I can expel you because I accept the responsibility for what the white people did to his people, and because both of our races have come to terms with history, and with what we are, and our religious and magical roots!"

I paused for breath. I was mad with rage and fear. "*Get out!*" I yelled. "Go! And leave our brothers alone!"

There was a moment when the air itself seemed to be under intolerable stress. When vision wavered, and an unbearable droning crowded the morgue.

Then the fiery bodies exploded. Chunks of blazing torso were hurled over my head. Skulls with eyes of fire. Hands that were heat-twisted claws. I dropped to the floor and kept my eyes shut tight, and prayed to God that this wasn't the end.

It was a long time, minutes, before I opened my eyes. Iblis had vanished. The morgue was blackened with smoke, choking, but more or less intact. Fragments of body were strewn all around. The cop got up from the floor, brushing human ashes from his clothes, and he seemed incapable of saying anything. The morgue attendant was still lying on the floor, concussed.

Eventually, the cop said, "What the hell happened?"

I shook my head. My throat was dry and constricted. "I don't know. I think we won."

I looked down at John Bososama and his eyes were closed. He seemed to be peaceful enough.

I never heard any more about Iblis or the Black Muslims. Sometimes, in my cab, I pick up young black ladies with cornrow hairstyles, and I don't shy away from talking to them about their religion. It usually seems like they are happy and content and finding all kinds of exciting new openings in their lives. It seems like ill luck is leaving them alone.

I don't mix with black people any more than I used to. I don't even pretend to understand what they really want out of life, or out of society, or out of anything. But that experience with John Bososama and his Islamic devil taught me more than any other kind of experience could have that we're more than brothers under the skin. We're all Americans, we're all ordinary people, and we all have the obligation to stand up for each other when danger threatens, or when the ground starts falling away from under our feet.

You think I'm a sentimentalist? Judy thinks I am. But she and you can think what you like. As far as I'm concerned, there's a motto under our country's crest that reads E PLURIBUS UNUM, and it's practical enough to beat devils as well as men.

Someplace out there, in space or in time, there's a banished black devil called Iblis to prove it.

Will

London, England

On the south bank of the River Thames, Sam Wanamaker's replica of the Globe Theatre has risen from the mud, to recreate the days when Midsummer Night's Dream *and* Romeo and Juliet *were first played out in front of an enraptured Elizabethan audience.*

But great men leave more behind them than the plays they wrote; or the words they spoke. They leave behind them the legacy of what it was that made them famous, whether it was good or whether it was evil.

Will *was written as a tribute to H.P. Lovecraft, the creator of the Cthulhu Mythos – a collection of novels and stories which argued that the world had once been dominated by the Great Old Ones, mythical creatures from a region far beyond time and space.*

But it was also written as a tribute to England's greatest storyteller; and to show that, wherever you go, fame and fortune have their price.

As Shakespeare himself would have put it, "The world is still deceived by ornament. In law, what plea so tainted or corrupt, but, being seasoned with a gracious voice, obscures the show of evil?"

Turn the page, and start the show of evil.

WILL

Holman sounded uncharacteristically excited on the phone, almost hysterical. "Dan, get down here," he said. "We've dug up something terrible."

"Terrible?" Dan queried. He was trying to sort his way through four hundred black-and-white photographs, and his desk was so heaped up with them that he had lost his mug of coffee. Dan didn't work well without coffee. Instant, espresso, mocha, arabica, it didn't matter. All he needed was that sharp jolt of caffeine to get him started.

Holman said, "Rita came across it this morning, about twenty yards away from the east wall. I can't tell you anything else; not over the blower."

"Holman," Dan told him, "I'm far too busy to come over now. I have to have these goddamned preliminary site photographs ready for the goddamned Department of the Environment by nine o'clock tomorrow morning. So far they all look like mud, mud and more mud."

"Dan, you'll have to come over," Holman urged him.

"You mean it's so terrible that it can't wait until tomorrow afternoon."

"Dan, believe me, it's terrible. It could hold us up for months, especially if the police want to investigate. And you know what the hell *they're* like, trampling all over the shop in their size twelves."

Dan found his coffee, in a red mug with the slogan *I*

Dig Archeology printed on it. The corner of one of the photographs had fallen into it, and it was scummy and cold. He drank it all the same.

"Holman," he said, wiping his mouth with the back of his hand, "I simply can't make it."

"It's a body," said Holman.

The rain had eased off less than an hour before, and the greasy blue-gray clay was slick and shining under the soles of his green Harrods wellies. A watery sun floated over Southwark, glancing occasionally off gray-slated Victorian rooftops or distant sash windows; or the wide green curve of the Thames. There was a smell of impending winter in the air, a sore-throaty rawness that Dan had forgotten from his last excavation in England. In San Antonio, it was easy to forget that something called cold had ever existed.

Holman was standing on the far side of the low east wall, next to a makeshift screen made of canvas and old front doors. He was very tall and stooped in his mud-spattered duffle coat, with loose horn-rimmed glasses which he constantly pushed back onto his fleshy nose. He was trying to grow a beard, not very successfully. It wouldn't have been hard to mistake him for one of those ferret-eyed men who spend their nights in cardboard boxes, rather than Manchester University's most admired excavator of difficult historical sites. By comparison, Dan was shorter, but much more athletically built, with the kind of wavy-haired leonine looks that reminded women of Richard Burton. He was always dressed casually but expensively. Holman called him Dapper Dan the Sartorial Archeologist.

He reached out a long arm as Dan approached, and shook his hand. "There he is," he announced, without

210

any further preliminaries. "The man who never left the theatre."

Dan drew aside the canvas, and saw a mud-gray figure lying on its left side in the mud; a small bald monkey of a man with his legs drawn up into the foetal position. He appeared to have been wearing doublet and hose when he died, although his clothes were less well preserved than his skin, and they were so stained with mud that it was impossible to tell what colour they might have been.

Watched closely by Holman, Dan leaned over the body and examined it with care. A thin-faced man, with a few wisps remaining of a pointed goatee, and lips drawn back in a hideously tight grimace, exposing broken and rotted teeth. His eyes were as milky as a boiled cod's.

"How long ago did he die?" asked Dan.

Holman shrugged. "Difficult to say. He's like the bog people they found in Jutland and Schleswig-Holstein, perfectly preserved by the clay. The bog people were carbon-dated as being anywhere between sixteen hundred and two thousand years old. But obviously *this* fellow isn't anything like as old as that."

Dan hunkered down beside the shining gray body and stared into the face. "He looks as if he could've died yesterday, doesn't he? Did you call the police, just in case?"

Holman shook his head.

"Well, you have to," Dan insisted. He stood up. "This is probably exactly what it looks like, which is a mummified Jacobean. But you never know. Somebody might have been devious enough to murder his wife's lover, dress him up in a rented costume, and bury him right here, on the site of the Globe Theatre, where everybody would *think* he was Jacobean."

"That, Dan, with all due respect, is about the most

far-fetched theory I have ever heard in my life," Holman replied. "Apart from which, the clay around the body was compacted hard, exactly like the clay around the remains of the theatre walls. If it had been buried recently, the disturbance in the clay would have been quite obvious."

He held up a small age-darkened piece of wood. "Look what we found tied around his neck. An actor's gag. The piece of wood they put in their mouth to exercise their tongues. That's where we got the phrase 'telling gags' from. Definitely Jacobean."

"We still have to call the police. It's the law."

"Very well," Holman agreed, impatiently, flapping his arms. "But can we delay it please for forty-eight hours? In fact, can we not tell *anyone* about it for forty-eight hours? I just want to carry out some preliminary tests without hundreds of sightseers. I want to be alone with him."

Holman stood up straight and looked around the muddy sun-glistening trenches, and then back down at the body. "Do you realize, Dan, this man probably witnessed a live performance of a play by William Shakespeare? One morning in the early 1600s he dressed in these clothes and left his house and went to the Globe, and died there. Maybe he was caught in the fire in 1613, when the Globe burned down."

"Well, let's hope so," Dan remarked. "The last thing we want right now is a full-scale murder inquiry, right in the middle of the dig. It's going to be bad enough when the Press get to hear about this anyway."

They were still talking when a girl of about twenty came walking towards them across the site. She wore a yellow safety helmet and a ballooning green anorak. A long wisp of blonde hair curled down one side of her face. She was hardly more than five-foot-three, and exceptionally pretty in a dolly-eyed snub-nosed way. But apart from the fact that she was an excellent archeologist, which both men respected, she was seriously engaged to a broad-shouldered professional tennis player called Roger, and Roger combined a short temper with a ferociously jealous nature, so most of her fellow archeologists kept well away.

"Hallo, Dr Essex," she said, as she approached. "What do you think of him? I've decided to call him Timon. Just like *Timon of Athens*, you see, Shakespeare's worst play – he died a death."

"How're you doing, Rita?" Dan asked her. "Congratulations. This is quite some find, if he's the genuine article."

"Well, of *course* he's the genuine article," said Rita, kneeling in the mud beside him. "He must have been trapped in some kind of cellar, poor man. I found him underneath all of that solid oak boarding. We had to use the JCB to lift it off."

She meticulously brushed more clay away from Timon's chest. "I want to get him out of here as quickly as possible, and into a controlled environment. There's no telling what might happen to him once he's exposed to the air. We could lose him in two or three days, maybe sooner. Look at these buttons he's wearing! Beautiful, mother-of-pearl, all hand-carved."

"This is really something, you know, Dan," said Holman. "This is history, right before your very eyes."

Dan lifted his hands in surrender. "All right. You've got your extra time. I'll have a word with Dunstan & Malling, too, to see if they can beef up their security. Of course I won't tell them why." Dunstan & Malling were the property developers who had first revealed the ruins of Shakespeare's 17th-century Globe Theatre, three days after they had begun to excavate the foundations for a

213

twenty-two-storey headquarters, Globe House. Publicly, their directors had talked about "protecting England's cultural heritage". Privately, they had been infuriated by the delay while Dan and his team had been called in by the Department of the Environment to excavate the site, and to suggest feasible ways of preserving it as a tourist attraction.

Buttoning up his coat against the wind, Dan turned to go. As he did so, however, Rita called out, "Wait, Dan! Look!"

Dan found dead bodies particularly unappealing, even three-hundred-year-old dead bodies whom he didn't know. But he turned and came back to the canvas screen where Rita was working.

"Look," said Rita. "He wasn't killed in a fire, or anything like that. Look at his chest."

She had turned him over slightly so he was staring sightlessly but accusingly over her right shoulder. Then she stepped away, and stood up, so that Dan could see the enormity of what had happened to Timon for himself. From his groin to his breastbone, the left side of his body had been torn right open, as if a huge and maddened beast had attacked him. His body cavity was filled with wet clay, but it was still possible to see that most of his internal organs must have been ripped out of him.

"Jesus," said Dan, and approached Timon with awe. "What the hell could have happened to him?"

"I don't know. Maybe he was impaled by a piece of falling timber, when the theatre burned down," Holman suggested.

"It looks more like he was attacked by a wild animal," Dan remarked.

"Maybe he was attacked by a bear," said Rita. "They

used to bring in bears sometimes, to entertain the audience. If there was a fire, the bear could have gone berserk."

"That's a bit over-inventive," said Holman.

"I don't know," said Dan. "I don't care for this at all. It definitely looks to me like something *bit* him, something very big and something very mean. Look at the way his shirt's been ripped. A bear didn't do that. A bear plays with you, claws at you. Whatever did this, it took one long look and then it went *nyyunngg!*"

"*Nyyunngg?*" queried Holman. "What on earth did they have in Jacobean London that could have gone '*nyyunngg!*'?"

"Well . . . maybe that's a little too fanciful," Dan agreed. "But maybe I could check up on the day the Globe burned down, and see if there's any contemporary mention of casualties, and how they died."

Holman clapped him on the back. "Good luck, then," he said. "And . . . well, thanks for the extra time. I know it isn't all that easy, with the Government and the developers and the Press all climbing all over you. Not to mention Rita and me."

Dan wiped his nose. "Deal with our friend here as quick as you can, okay?"

Holman took a long look at the greasy gray remains of the man called Timon. "If all goes well, Dan, this chappie's going to make us famous. The Essex-Holman Man. But before anybody else gets their sticky fingers on him, I want to do my best to find out who he was, and how he died."

"I wish I could give you longer," said Dan.

"That's okay. I'll stay here all night; and all tomorrow night, too, if I need to."

"Christ, you'll get cold."

215

"I'm used to the cold. I was brought up in Yorkshire, remember."

Dan checked his watch. He had a lunch date with Fiona Blessing, the triangular-shaped power-dressed lady executive from British Fuels, who were interested in financing something cultural with a capital "C" and tax-deductible with a capital "T". Then he had to take the bus to Chiswick to pick up his Renault, which was being repaired for the third time this year. He would have liked to have stayed and watched Rita painstakingly excavating Timon from the mud. But he had to keep this dig going in any way he could, especially with funds so low and the developers hovering over his head like a giant black anvil out of "Roadrunner". He shook Holman's hand, waved to Rita, and returned to the taxi that was waiting for him.

The cab driver said, "What's that, then? Looks like a bleeding graveyard."

"A dig," Dan replied, patiently. "An archeological dig. By the time we're finished, we should have a pretty clear idea of what the Globe Theatre looked like."

"Oh, yeah?" asked the cab driver, as they jostled through the lunchtime traffic. "What you want to know that for, then?"

For the first time, Dan couldn't think what to say. Maybe there was no reason. Maybe he was searching for nothing more than the living proof that the past really existed; and that men knew things then which they will never know again, not unless they seek them out.

He couldn't sleep. He kept dreaming that he was lying on his side in gray shining mud. He was cold, but he couldn't think how to get warm again, and somebody kept calling his name.

He sat up and switched on the bedside light. As usual,

the other side of the bed was empty. Margaret hadn't wanted to join him in London; she hated London. He didn't really blame her. At this time of the year it was damp and expensive and derelict, the dark capital of a grim, worn-out culture. Everywhere he walked, there were black bronze statues of stern, eccentric and long-dead men.

He read for a while, from some of the books that he had been able to find in the Kensington Library. *Shakespeare's Life And Art* by P. Alexander; *Shakespeare at the Globe* by Nigel Frost; and a fascinating monograph called *The Sharer* by Dudley Manfield. By 1598, when the new Globe Theatre had been built, Shakespeare had already become one of the most prosperous actor-playwrights in the country, and he was one of the theatre's "sharers" or shareholders.

There was something about Manfield's account that Dan found strange and intriguing. It referred again and again to Shakespeare's twin children, Hamnet and Judith, and how Hamnet had died in 1596 at the age of 11, a tragedy which Shakespeare had called "my Payment". At the same time, Manfield frequently referred to "Shakespeare's Debt", as if Shakespeare had somehow made a promise to somebody, or borrowed money from them. One passage from the diary of a fellow actor at the Globe Theatre, Ben Fielding, made repeated mention of it.

In this ye sommer of 1611 we perform'd for the firste time The Tempeste which drama Will declar'd to me was the nearest he dar'd to speak of the Great Olde One to whom he had made his Pledge. He said it was a Debt which No Man could honour & that he woulde have given all his wealthe never to have made it. For the time cometh alwayes when a Debt must be redemed.

So it appeared that for some reason, Shakespeare had entered into a binding commitment with "the Great Olde One". whoever that was. Dan got out of bed and went through to his living room to find his paperback collection of Shakespeare's plays. He leafed through to *The Tempest*, and read passages from it at random, but he could find no indication of what Shakespeare might have been trying to say about his Debt.

One phrase did catch his eyes, however. *"He that dies pays all debts."*

He returned to Manfield's book. By 1613, the year that the Globe burned down, Shakespeare had retired almost permanently to his house in Stratford. But Ben Fielding had written,

> Will confided in me then that his Debt had given him no peace; and that it must at last be settl'd by Hee himself, whate'er the coste. He must needs return to Southwarke there to face his Tormentor & to make his peace. All of which he spake he also writ, and lodged with John Heminge.

That was the last entry in Ben Fielding's diary. According to Manfield, Fielding had disappeared on the night that the Globe caught fire, and had been presumed burned.

Dan read and reread Fielding's words, and then switched the light off again and tried to sleep. But all the time he had the strangest feeling that something was badly wrong; as if the world had silently decided to start turning backwards.

He arrived at the Globe site a few minutes after seven the next morning. It was cold and foggy but the rain had stayed away. He unlocked the gates and plodded across the clay to Holman's site hut, his hands thrust into his coat pockets.

Unusually, there was no smoke pouring from the hut's tin chimney. At this time of the morning, Holman was usually brewing up tea and cooking his breakfast. Even more unusually, the site hut door was ajar. Dan climbed the gritty wooden steps and put his head around it.

"Holman?" he called. "Holman? Are you there?"

The inside of the hut was chilly and dark. Holman's untidy cot was empty; site drawings and blueprints rustled on the notice board like the whispering of mourners in a shadowy chapel. The stove was cold, the kettle lidless and unfilled.

"Holman?" Dan repeated.

He left the hut and made his way across the muddy site toward the screen of canvas and old doors where the body had been found. Maybe Holman had decided to make an especially early start, and have his breakfast later. A fine drizzle was falling across Southwark, and a barge hooted dolefully on the river.

He shifted aside one of the old front doors. "Holman?" he called; and then he saw why Holman hadn't replied; and he stopped where he was, breathing in quick, shallow gasps, as if he had been running. At first, he could scarcely understand what he was looking at, but gradually the intricate loops and tangles of scarlet and gray became clear. His throat tightened, and his mouth suddenly filled with bile and tepid coffee.

Holman had somehow been torn apart; ripped to pieces and dragged around the site in long strings of entrails and glistening muscle. His ribcage lay on the far side of the excavation like the parts of an abandoned car. Part of his flattened face stared up from the mud close to Dan's right foot. One eye, half a blood-clotted beard, no jaw. His spectacles lay nearby, both lenses blinded with sticky blood.

Shaking with cold and fear, Dan crossed to the centre of the site where Rita had discovered the mummified body. It was still there, but it had been thrown to one side, and one of its legs was sticking out from underneath it at an impossible angle. Next to it, the clay looked as if it had been churned up by their mechanical digger. God knows what had happened here. Holman would never have done anything like this, not to such an important archeological find. And what had happened to Holman?

Dan sniffed the morning air. Sharp and cold as glass paper. And there was a smell to it, too, which wasn't just the smell of a ripped-apart human body. It was a musty, fetid smell; like a roomful of hymn books which has been closed for too long. A closed smell. An airless smell. An *old* smell.

Dan circled the muddy site with legs that felt like lead and didn't know what to do. He stood still for a while, with his hand pressed over his mouth, trying to decide if he needed to vomit. But it was then that he heard a whimpering noise, like a run-over cat. He frowned, turned; and for the first time saw Rita crouched behind one of the doors. She was smothered in clay from head to foot, and her eyes were bloodshot and staring.

He knelt down beside her and took hold of her clay-slimy hand.

"Rita? Rita, it's Dan."

She stared at him wildly. She was shuddering all over, and she kept jerking and nodding her head like a mad-woman.

"Rita, for God's sake what happened?"

"It came out," she whispered, through mud-gray lips.

"We turned him over; and the ground looked as if it was boiling. *And it came out!*"

"What came out? Rita, what was it?"

She shook her head furiously from side to side. "There was a wind . . . a wind that came *downwards*. And then the ground was boiling. And then Holman was screaming because it was black with tentacles and it kept changing shape and it tore him to pieces."

Dan held her close while she shuddered and rocked and shook her head. At last he wiped the grit from her forehead and said, "It's all right. It's all right now. I'll call for an ambulance."

He went to visit her two weeks later. She was staying at Ettington Park, a huge Gothic hotel of cream and gray stone, set deep in the Warwickshire countryside just south of Stratford-on-Avon, amongst rook-clotted elms, beside a slow-moving river.

They walked through the grounds and the cold afternoon was quite silent except for the occasional cawing of rooks. She said, "What are they going to do about the dig?"

Dan lit a cigarette and blew out smoke. "The plan so far is to fill it with sharp sand, to preserve what we've excavated already, then build the office block's foundations on top of it. Nobody will get to see it again till they knock their damned office block down."

Rita said, "It's nice here. Really quiet. They've got a library and lots of open fires and an indoor swimming pool."

"Have you managed to remember what happened?" Dan asked her; watching her closely.

She looked away, her eyes stony. "Only what I told you. The wind came down and the ground boiled and

221

out it came. The police said it was probably an explosion of marsh gas; some freaky accident like that. Will-o'-the-wisp to the nth power."

Dan took hold of her hand, and squeezed it. "Be lucky," he told her, and left.

Under a dour sky he drove to Stratford-on-Avon and visited the Shakespeare Library next to the Memorial Theatre. For the rest of the afternoon he sat at a small desk in the corner, under a window, not reading the works of Shakespeare, but of Shakespeare's fellow player at the Globe Theatre, John Heminge, who had helped to compile the First Folio of Shakespeare's works.

It was almost dark when he found the letter, and the library's fluorescent lights were flickering on. He found it almost as if it had been waiting for him, bound into a volume of John Heminge's diaries. Part of it was illegible; and nobody who hadn't seen Holman's body would have understood what it really meant, or have realized that Shakespeare himself had written it. It was dated 1613, three years before Shakespeare's death, and ten years before Heminge had put together the first collection of Shakespeare's works.

&, John, this is an errand from which I shall never return. I offered him my life in return for my success; but never did I think that he would demand my poor child's life. I realize now that such an arrangement was not mine to make, nor any man's. Only God can decide one's fortune, not this creature from times when God was not, & places where God had no dominion. I have enjoyed my good fortune, but I have grieved much, and now the price must be paid. Poor Hamnet, please forgive me.

Be warned, John, of the Great Old Ones, who

came from Outside. They have the power to give all that a man could desire; and the power to exact a punishment beyond all reason. Be warned most of all of Y'g Southothe, who came from beyond the very bounds of space and time, but who dwells now beneath the cellars of the Globe.

The Globe was built in such a shape in order to give him a Hiding-Place; so now must the Globe be razed; and the cellars fill'd & boarded; and I with them; in order that Hamnet may live again.

Later that evening, Dan went for a long walk beside the Avon; finally arriving beside the memorial statue of the Bard. The sodium street lights were strident and orange; they made the statue look as if it had been cast out of some strangely unearthly metal. Dan was beginning to form an idea about what had happened, although he couldn't completely understand it. From his letter to John Heminge, it seemed as if Shakespeare had achieved his huge success as a playwright by striking a bargain with "Y'g Southothe", which was some kind of primeval life-force *"from a time when God was not"*. Dan could only guess that this life-force had for some reason demanded Hamnet's life. Perhaps as insurance? Perhaps to force Shakespeare to build him a "Hiding-Place" on earth, by demolishing the old theatre and building the Globe on the same site?

Nobody would ever know what had really happened. But from the letter he had written to John Heminge, it appeared that in 1613 Shakespeare had been able to bear the guilt of Hamnet's death no longer, and had travelled to London to burn down the Globe, and to destroy this "Y'g Southothe" for ever.

There had been one clue which had survived down

all these centuries. In Shakespeare's letter, he had concluded,

> I shall carry with me the gag that Hamnet gave me when he was just ten years old – the gag which he had whittled himself, and which I could never use because of its discomfort. It shall be the token of my craft and the token of my love for the son which I have loste.

Dan returned to London early the following morning. The archeological dig was foggy and abandoned. Strings of red warning pennants hung in the airless chill, and there were Metropolitan Police signs everywhere, warning Danger: Inflammable Gas.

He climbed awkwardly across the muddy ruts and jumped over the half-finished trenches. The body had been covered by an aluminum-framed tent of heavy-duty builder's polythene, and a full-time security guard now occupied Holman's hut. He waved to Dan from the front steps as he emptied a potful of used teabags on to the clay. "Morning, Mr Essex! Brass monkeys this morning, ain't it?"

Dan lifted aside the fog-moistened polythene. The gray mummified body was lying where it had been flung on the night that Holman had died: untouched, but much more sunken looking now. Nobody had been able to decided who it belonged to; or who it was; or whether it should be touched at all.

Dan stood looking at the body for a long time, smoking. Then he knelt closer, and said, "Will Shakespeare. In the flesh. So who's that buried in the chancel of the Holy Trinity, at Stratford, next to Anne Hathaway?"

The mummified face grinned sightlessly back at him. Now that he was sure who he was, Dan could see the strong resemblance to Martin Droeshout's portrait in the First Folio. He reached out and touched the bald domed forehead, beneath which there had once been the brain which had created Macbeth and Hamlet and Othello.

"He that dies pays all debts."

Dan felt the ground shudder and churn. There was a slow sucking noise, like thick cement being drawn down a metal chute. He hesitated; but then he smelled that decayed hymn book smell, that *old* smell; and he backed out of the tent and across the site, to the corner where the bright yellow mechanical digger was parked.

He managed to start the JCB after three tries. The engine bellowed, black diesel smoke blurted into the morning air. Then, steering with jerky, awkward movements, he manoeuvred it over to the polythene-covered tent.

The security guard, his hands in his pockets, came out to watch. Dan gave him a salute and he saluted back. *Poor sucker*, thought Dan. *Wait till he sees what I'm going to do.*

Dan lowered the vehicle's shovel-blade, and began to drive it slowly forward, scraping up huge carpet-like lumps of solid gray clay as well as timber shoring and tools and old doors and debris. He forced the whole shovelful into the tent, which immediately collapsed. Then he backed up and dug up even more mud.

He thought for a moment that he might have gotten away with it – that he might have reburied Y'g Southothe without any more trouble. But as he was backing up the JCB for a third time, the mud suddenly erupted and splattered the vehicle's windshield like black blood.

Dan wrestled with the digger's gears. But then the

engine stalled, and there was nothing he could do but to watch the ground boil up in front of him a huge thrashing mountain of liquefied clay.

Timber and tools were hurtled in all directions. A blizzard of debris clattered against the digger's cab.

Then the mud itself opened up like a grisly maw, turning faster and deeper. Dan smelled a sickening cold slaughter-house smell, a smell which came from somewhere *outside* of the world, rather than within it. And out of the mud, brighter than the sun, rose globe after globe of shuddering light – globes which broke apart and disgorged a glistening black tentacled protoplasm. *Y'g Southothe, the Elder God, from a time so far back that it was unimaginable; the lord of the primal slime.*

He didn't hear himself screaming. All he heard was the bellowing of the JCB's restarted diesel, and the protesting whinny of its transmission. Then he was forcing heaps of raw clay into the open maw, and backing up, and pushing in more clay, while the site glittered and shuddered with the awful power of Y'g Southothe.

A devastating explosion split the morning air. A crack that was felt as far away as Croydon, seventeen miles away. A feeling that the very substance of the world had broken; which it had.

The security guard saw the JCB dissolve into dazzling white light; and then the site was empty; and there was nobody there. No light, no shuddering globes. Only the fog and the flags and the mournful unseen barges on the early-morning Thames.

It was almost a month before Rita received the scribbled notes that Dan had sent her. She had left Ettington Park and gone to stay with her parents in Wiltshire. Most of the notes she couldn't understand. But the very last note,

226

torn from a springback reporter's notebook, had a terrible logic that almost turned her senses.

I am sure now that Y'g Southothe forced Shakespeare to build the Globe Theatre by taking his son Hamnet; and that it hid there and dominated life in Jacobean London for years. I am also convinced that Shakespeare burned down the Globe himself; losing his own life but releasing Hamnet at last from Y'g Southothe. The man who tried to write Shakespeare's last play, *The Two Noble Kinsmen*, was not Shakespeare himself but his son Hamnet, reincarnated, or released, whichever you can believe most easily. According to contemporary records, Hamnet 'had the looke of his Parente', and after fifteen years in the guardianship of this Y'g Southothe he probably looked almost as old. I am convinced that this is the truth of what happened to Shakespeare. Remember that "Will Shakespeare" couldn't finish *The Two Noble Kinsmen* and that it was necessary for John Fletcher to write Acts II, III and IV.

I don't yet understand what this Y'g Southothe actually is; but what it did to Holman shows that it is infinitely dangerous. It was I who initiated the project which led to its being dug up. It is up to me to bury it again. I am sending you these notes in the unlikely event of something going wrong.

Three days later, Rita drove to Stratford-on-Avon in her father's car, and laid a small old-fashioned posy on the tomb in the Holy Trinity which was supposed to contain the remains of Will Shakespeare. The message on the posy read, "For Hamnet; At Long Last; From the Father Who Loved You More Than Life."

The Heart of Helen Day

Tumbleton, Alabama

Alabama is special to the heart of anybody who has ever visited it, especially the south of Alabama, close to the Gulf, which is low lying and heavily wooded and has a dream character all of its own. Alabama was named after a Native American tribe which used to inhabit it, before the white men came. In 1763, the French ceded Alabama to Great Britain by the peace of Paris, but at the close of the 18th century, it was ceded by Great Britain to the USA. In 1819, it was admitted to the Union – although it seceded in 1860, along with other cotton states – and sent most of its white male population to fight in the Civil War.

After the war, with the white population decimated, the black population gained the ascendancy, but for over a hundred years life has remained politically and racially difficult in Alabama, and there is still a long way to go.

All the same, Alabama is warm and welcoming and alluring. Visitors are treated with courtesy and great respect, especially if they visit the Sweet Gum Motor Court, which is where you are headed for now.

THE HEART OF HELEN DAY

A huge electric storm brewed up as Martin drove out of Tumbleton, in Henry County, Alabama, and fat warm raindrops began to patter onto the windshield of his rented Pontiac. Over to the east, above the Chattahoochee valley, the sky was so dark that it was purple, and snakes' tongues of lightning licked the distant hills.

Behind him, to the west, the sky was still clear and serene, and Martin was tempted to U-turn and drive back. But he was expected in Eufaula this evening at six, and he still had a hell of a haul; and he doubted in any case if he could outrun the approaching rainclouds. The wind was rising, and already the bright green sunlit trees were beginning to thrash and dip like panicky women.

He switched on the Pontiac's radio, and pressed "seek". Maybe he could find a local weather forecast. But all he could hear was fuzzy voices. One of them sounded just like his ex-wife nagging. Over and over, "you bastard, you bastard." He pressed "seek" again and picked up "*O-R-C-E becomes final today.*"

"Divorce" – shit. That was all he wanted to hear. If he hadn't gone to that sales seminar in Atlanta last April . . . if he hadn't picked up that girl in the hotel bar . . . if Marnie hadn't flown to Atlanta to surprise him . . . if life wasn't always so damned grisly and so damned absurdly predictable.

Marnie had always told him that it would only take one act of infidelity to destroy her trust in him; and it had.

She and her lawyers had systematically dismantled his life. She had taken the house, the cars, the paintings, the silver, the savings. She hadn't taken Ruff, his retriever, but the day after the divorce became final, Ruff had slipped the dog-sitter's leash and been fatally injured under the wheels of a van.

Martin was now reduced to old-fashioned town-to-town travelling, the Alabama and Louisiana representative of Confederate Insurance, selling packages of cut-price business cover to one fat sweaty redneck after another. He could sum up the majority of his customers in just a few words: bald, bigoted, with appalling taste in neckties. But he wasn't complaining. It had been his own choice to travel. He had the experience and the references to find himself a much better job, but (for a while, anyway) he felt like letting the days go by without name or number, and he felt like exploring the south. Days of steamy heat and sassafras; days of rain and bayous and girder bridges; days of small towns melting under dust-beige skies; and deputy sheriffs with mirror-blind eyes.

The rain lashed harder and harder. Martin flicked the windshield wipers to HI, but even when the wipers were flinging themselves from side to side at top speed, they were scarcely able to cope. The evening grew suddenly so dark that Martin felt as if the highway had been overshadowed by the wing of a giant crow. *Just then flew down a monstrous crow, as black as a tar-barrel . . .*

He kept driving, hoping that the storm would ease. But after nearly an hour the rain was just as furious, and lightning was crackling all around him like a plantation of tall electrified trees. He had to drive slower and slower, down to 20 mph, simply because he couldn't see where he was going. The ditches at the sides of the highway were gorged with sewage-brown water and the water suddenly began to flood across the blacktop. The Pontiac's air-conditioning worked only intermittently, and he had to keep wiping the inside of the windshield with his crumpled-up handkerchief. He was terrified that a truck was going to come cannonballing out of the rain and collide with him head on. Or – almost as bad – that another truck would rear-end him. He had seen that happen only two days ago, on Highway 331 just a few miles north of Opp. A whole family had been sent careening in their Chevy Blazer right off a bridge and down a steep embankment, where they had lain in individual depressions in the lush green weeds, bleeding, broken, screaming for help.

He had woken up in his motel room the same night and he could still hear them screaming.

Lightning crackled again; followed almost at once by a catastrophic rumble of thunder, real heaven-splitting stuff. If it were possible, the rain cascaded down harder, and the floodwaters spurted and bellowed against the Pontiac's floor-pan. Martin smeared the windshield with his handkerchief and strained his eyes and prayed for some kind of a turn-off where he could wait for the storm to pass over.

Then, through the rain and the spray and the misted-up glass of his windshield, he saw a pale illuminated blur. A light. No – a sign, of some kind. A green neon sign that (as he slowed and approached it) said Sweet Gum Motor Court. And, underneath, flickering dully, the word *acancies*.

O Lord I thank Thee for all Thy many favors, and in particular for the Sweet Gum Motor Court in Henry County, Alabama, with its acancies.

233

Martin turned off the highway and down a sloping driveway that, in this weather, was almost a waterfall. Then ahead of him he saw an L-shaped arrangement of cabins with wooden verandahs and corrugated-iron roofing, and (on one side) an oddly proportioned clapboard house which at first appeared to be gray, but in the sweeping light of his headlights turned out to be pale green. There were lights inside the house, and he could see a white-haired man in a red plaid shirt and suspenders, and (O Lord I really do thank Thee) the smell of hamburgers in the air.

He parked as close to the house as he could, then wrenched open the Pontiac's door and hurried with his coat tugged in a peak over his head to the brightly lit front verandah. Even though the highway had been flooded and his wipers had struggled to keep his windshield clear, he hadn't realized how torrential this rainstorm was. In the few seconds it took him to cross from his car to the house, he was soaked through, and the new light tan Oxfords that he had bought in Dothan were reduced to the consistency of blackened cardboard.

He opened the screen door but the main door was locked, and he jarred his wrist trying to pull it open. He rattled the door handle and then knocked with his wedding band on the glass. Yes, he still wore his wedding band. It gave him a ready-made excuse when pink-lipsticked strumpets slid up onto bar stools next to him and asked him in those cheap husky accents if he needed a little friendship.

He didn't need friendship. He needed hot timeless days, and miniscule communities where it was interesting to watch flies walking up a window, and electric storms like this; the catharsis of being unimportant, and adrift.

The white-haired man in the red plaid shirt came to the

door and somehow he was uglier and less welcoming than he had appeared through the rain. He had a face that would have looked better the other way up, chin-side up, like Old Man Muffaroo. Dull brown suspicious eyes, like olives left on a lunch-counter too long.

"What do you want?" he shouted through the glass.

"What do you think I want?" Martin shouted back. "Look at me! I'm soaked! I need a room!"

The white-haired man stared at him without answering as if he had spoken a foreign language. Then a big henna-haired woman in a green dress appeared behind him, and Martin could hear her say, "What the hell's going on here, Vernon?"

"Fellow wants a room."

"A room?"

"That's what he said."

"Well, for God's sake, Vernon, if the fellow wants a room, then for God's sake open up that door and give him a room. You don't get any damned better, do you? You really don't."

She unlocked the door and held it wide so that Martin could step inside. As he passed her he smelled frying hamburgers and sour armpit and Avon scent.

"Hell of a storm," she said, closing and locking the door behind him. "Come through to the office, I'll fix you up."

Martin followed her along a red-lino corridor flanked with damp-stained posters for Martz Airlines "Safe Scenic Swift Service" and vacations in Bermuda. In the office there was an untidy desk, a whirring electric fan, and a pegboard with rows of keys hanging on it. There were no keys missing, so Martin assumed that he was the only guest. Not surprising, the reception that would-be customers were given by old upside-down-face Vernon.

A ragged-looking brown dog was slumbering on the floor. "Just for the night?" asked the woman, stepping over it.

"That's right," Martin told her. "I was supposed to meet somebody in Eufaula at six, but there's no hope of my getting there now." As if to reassure him that he had made the right decision by stopping here, the rain rattled noisily against the window, and the dog stirred in its sleep. Dreaming of quail, maybe; or hamburgers.

Vernon was standing just outside the office, scratching the eczema on his elbow. "You'll find plenty of peace here, mister. You won't be disturbed."

Martin signed his name in the register. The pages were deckled with damp. "Anyplace I can get something to eat?"

The woman peered at his signature. Then she said, "Used to be a diner down the road about a half-mile did good ribs but that closed. Owner blew his head clear off with a shotgun. Business being so bad and all."

She looked up at him, aware that she hadn't yet answered his question. "But I can rustle you some eggs'n'bacon or cornbeef hash or something of that nature."

"Maybe some eggs and bacon," said Martin. "Now . . . maybe I can get myself dried off and use the telephone."

The woman unhooked one of the keys and handed it to Vernon. "Number Two'll do best. It's closer to the office and the bed's new."

She unlocked the front door and Vernon led him out into the rain again. The concrete parking lot was awash with floodwater and bright brown silt. Martin heaved his overnight case out of the trunk of the Pontiac, and then followed Vernon across to the first row of cabins. Vernon stood hunched in front of the door with his white hair

236

dripping, trying to find the right way to turn the key. At last he managed to open up, and switch on the light.

Number Two was a drab room, with a sculptured red carpet and a mustard-colored bedspread. There were two dimly-shaded lamps beside the bed, and another on the cheap varnished desk. Martin put down his case and offered Vernon a dollar bill, but Vernon waved it away. "That's not necessary, mister; not here, on a night like this. So long as you pay before you go." It occurred to Martin that – almost uniquely, for these days – the woman hadn't taken an impression of his credit card.

"Food won't be long," said Vernon. "You want any drinks or anything? Beer maybe?"

"A couple of lites would go down well."

Vernon frowned around the room. "These lights ain't sufficient?"

"No, no. I mean 'lites' like in 'lite beer'."

"Lite beer," Vernon repeated, as if Martin had said something totally mysterious, but he was too polite to ask what it meant.

"Miller Lite, Coors Lite, anything."

"Coors Lite," Vernon repeated, in the same baffled way.

He left, closing the door firmly behind him. It had swollen slightly in the downpour, and needed to be tugged. With a loud, elaborate, extended sigh, Martin raked back his wet hair with his fingers, lifted off his dark-shouldered coat, and loosened his wet necktie with a squeak that set his teeth on edge almost as much as fingernails on slate.

He pushed open the door to the bathroom and found dismal green-painted walls and a shower curtain decorated with faded tropical fish. But there were four large towels folded up on the shelf, three of them marked "Holiday Inn" and the fourth marked "Tropicana Hotel, Key

Largo". He stripped and dried himself, and then dressed in clean pyjamas and a blue silk bathrobe, and combed his hair. He wished that Vernon would hurry up with that beer: his throat was dry and he felt that he might be catching a cold.

He looked around for the TV. Maybe there was a cable movie he could watch tonight. But to his surprise there was no TV. He couldn't believe it. What kind of a motel had rooms with no TV? The only entertainment available was a pack of sexy playing cards and an old Zenith radio. Shit.

He pulled open the cabin door and looked outside. The rain was still thundering down. A water butt under the next row of cabins was noisily overflowing, and somewhere a broken gutter was splattering. No sign of Vernon. No sign of anything but this shabby huddle of cabins and the dim green light that said 'acancies'.

He wedged the door shut. He thought of all the times that he has cursed Howard Johnson's for their sameness and their lack of luxury. But a Howard Johnson's would have been paradise compared with the Sweet Gum Motor Court. All it was doing was keeping him safely off the highway and the rain off his head.

He sat down at the desk and picked up the telephone. After a long crackling pause, the voice of the henna-haired woman said, "You want something, mister?"

"Yes, I do. I want to place a call to a number in Eufaula – Chattahoochee Moldings, Inc. Person-to-person to Mr Dick Bogdanovich."

"I'm frying your eggs'n'bacon. What do you want first, your call or your eggs'n'bacon?"

"Well . . . I really need to make this call. He usually leaves the office at seven-thirty."

"Eggs'll spoil, if they haven't already."

"Can't I dial the number myself?"

"'Fraid not, not from the cabins. Otherwise we'd have guests calling their long-lost sweethearts in Athens, Georgia, and chewing the fat for an hour at a time with their folks back in Wolf Point, Montana, wouldn't we, and the profit in this business is too tight for that."

"Ma'am, all I want to do is make a single fifteen-second telephone call to Eufaula, to inform my client that I shan't be able to make our meeting this evening. That's a little different from an hour-long call to – Wolf Point, Montana?" Thinking: what on earth had inspired her to say "Wolf Point, Montana"?

"I'm sorry, you can't dial direct from the cabins; and I can smell egg-white burning."

The phone clicked, and then he heard nothing but a sizzling sound. It could have been static, it could have been frying. It didn't much matter. Frying and static were equally useless to him.

His eggs and bacon eventually arrived at a quarter after eight. Vernon brought them across from the office building under a rain-beaded aluminum dishcover. Vernon himself was covered by an Army surplus parka, dark khaki with wet.

"Rain, rain, goddamned rain," said Vernon. He set the plate down on the desk.

"No knife and fork," said Martin. "No beer."

"Oh, I got it all here," Vernon told him, and fumbled in the pockets of his parka. He produced knife, fork, paper napkins, salt, pepper, catsup, and three chilled bottles of Big 6 Beer.

"Denise fried the eggs over, on account of them being burned."

Martin raised the aluminum cover. The eggs and bacon

looked remarkably good: heaps of thin crisp rashers, three big farm eggs, sunnyside up; toast, fried tomatoes, and hash browns; and lots of crispy bits. "Tell her thanks."

"She'll charge you for them, the extra eggs."

"That's okay. Tell her thanks."

After Vernon had gone, wedging the door shut yet again, Martin propped himself up in bed with his supper balanced in his lap, and switched on the radio. It took a few moments for the radio to warm up: then the dial began to glow, and he smelled that extraordinary nostalgic smell of hot dust that his grandmother's Zenith had always given off whenever it heated up.

He twisted the brown bakelite tuning knob, but most of the dial produced nothing but weird alien whistlings and whoopings, or a fierce sizzling noise, or voices that were so blippy and blotchy that it was impossible to understand what they were saying. As he prodded his fork into his second egg, however, he suddenly picked up a voice that was comparatively crisp.

". . . *Eight-thirty, Eastern Time . . . and this is the Song O' The South Soda Hour . . . coming to you from the Dauphin Street Studios in Mobile, Alabama . . . continuing our dramatization of . . . 'The Heart of Helen Day' . . . with Randy Pressburger . . . John McLaren . . . Susan Medici . . . and starring as Helen Day . . . Andrea Lawrence . . .*"

Martin turned the dial further, but all he could find were more fizzes, more pops, and a very faint jazz rendition of the old Negro ballad *Will The Circle Be Unbroken*.

". . . *in the same old window, on a cold and cloudy day . . . I seen them hearse wheels rolling . . . they was taking Chief Jolly away . . .*"

He decided that he could do without a funeral dirge, so he turned back to *The Heart of Helen Day*. This turned

240

out to be a chatty romantic radio-soap about a busybody girl who who worked for a tough-talking private detective and kept losing her heart to his clients, even though the tough-talking private detective really loved her more than anybody else.

Martin finished his supper and drank two bottles of beer and listened to the serial in amusement. It sounded incredibly 1930s, with all the actors talking in brisk, clipped voices like *One Man's Family* or the *Chase & Sanborn Hour*.

"But he's not guilty, I tell you. I just know he's not guilty."

"How can you know? You don't have any proof."

"I searched his eyes, that's all."

"You searched his eyes but I searched his hotel room."

"Oh, Mickey. I looked in his face and all I saw was innocence."

"You looked in his face? That's unusual. I never knew you look any higher than a man's wallet."

This week's episode concerned a famous bandleader who had been accused of throwing a beautiful but faithless singer out of the 7th floor window of a downtown hotel. The band leader's alibi was that he had been conducting a recording session at the time. But Helen Day suspected that he had used a stand-in.

Martin got up off the bed and went to the door, and opened it. The room was becoming stuffy, and smelled of food. He put his plate out on the boardwalk, where it rapidly filled with rain and circles of grease.

"It couldn't have been Philip, Philip always taps the rostrum three times with his baton before he starts to conduct . . . and in this recording the conductor doesn't tap the rostrum at all."

Martin stayed by the door, leaning against the jamb,

watching the rain barrel overflow and the silty mud forming a Mississipi delta in the parking lot, and the distant dancing of the lightning. Behind him the radio chattered, with occasional melodramatic bursts of music, and interruptions for commercials.

"'The Heart of Helen Day' is brought to you by Song O' The South Soda . . . the fruiter, more refreshing soda that makes the whole South sing . . ."

Then it was back to Helen Day. She was talking at a cocktail party about her success in solving the case of Philip the rostrum-tapping bandleader. Martin drank his third and last beer out of the bottle, and wondered why the radio station had even considered broadcasting such a stilted, outdated radio soap, when there was *Get A Life* and *The Simpsons* on TV, and wall-to-wall FM. Everyplace except here, of course, the Sweet Gum Motor Court, in Henry County, Alabama, in the rain.

"He was so handsome. Yet I knew that he was wicked, underneath."

Suddenly, there was the sound of a door banging in the background. Then the clatter of something falling over. A muffled voice said, "Get out here, you can't come in here, we're on air!" Then another shout, and a blurt of thick static, as if somebody had knocked the microphone.

At first, Martin thought that this must be part of the plot. But the shouting and struggling were so indistinct that he quickly realized that there must be an intruder in the radio studio, a real intruder, and that the actors and technicians were trying to subdue him. There was another jumble of sound, and then an extraordinary long drawn-out scream, rising higher and higher, increasingly hysterical.

Then the most terrible thing that Martin had ever heard in his life. He turned away from the open door and stared at the radio with his eyes wide and his scalp prickling with horror.

"Oh God! Oh God! John! John! Oh God help me! He's cut me open! Oh God! My stomach's falling out!"

A noise like somebody dropping a sodden bath towel. Then more shouts, and more thumps. A nasal, panicky voice shouting, "Ambulance! For Christ's sake, Jeff! Get an ambulance!" Then a sharp blip, and the program was cut off.

Martin sat on the bed beside the radio waiting for the program to come back on air, or some kind of announcement by the radio station. But there was nothing but white noise, which went on and on and on, like a bus journey along an endless and unfamiliar highway, through thick fog.

He tried returning the radio, but all he got were the same old crackles as before, or those distant foggy Negroes singing. *"I saw the . . . hearse wheels rolling . . . they were taking my . . . mother away . . ."* Did they always sing the same dirge?

Sometime after eleven o'clock he switched off the radio, washed his teeth, and climbed into bed. But all night he lay listening to the rain and thinking of *The Heart of Helen Day*. He guessed if an actress had really been attacked in a radio studio, he would hear about it on tomorrow's news. Maybe it had all been part of the soap. But – up until that moment – it had all sounded so normal and so correct, even if it had been ridiculously dated. Maybe it had been one of those *War of the Worlds*-type gimmicks, to frighten the listeners.

Or maybe it had actually happened, and *Helen Day* had really had her heart cut out.

He was woken at seven o'clock by Vernon tapping at the

243

door. Outside it was lighter but still raining, although not so heavily. Vernon had brought pancakes and syrup and hot coffee. He set them down on the desk and sniffed.

"Thanks," said Martin, smearing his face with his hands.

"Don't mention it."

"Hey . . . before you go . . . did you watch the news this morning?"

"The news?"

"The TV news . . . you know, like what's happening in the world."

Vernon shook his head, suspiciously.

"Well . . . did you hear about any radio actress being murdered, live on radio?"

Vernon said, "No . . . I didn't hear anything like that. But what I did hear, the highway's all washed out, between here and Eufaula, and 54 between Lawrenceville and Edwin's washed out, too. So you'll have to double back to Graball, and take 51 through Clio. That's if you're still inclined to go to Eufaula; can't stick the place myself."

"No . . ." said Martin, sipping coffee. "I don't think I can, either."

When he had finished his breakfast, Martin packed his travelling bag and looked around the room to make sure that he hadn't left anything behind. He stood by the open door listening to the rain clattering from the gutters and stared at the radio. Had he dreamed it? Maybe would never know.

He put down his bag, walked across to the radio and switched it on. After it had warmed up, he heard a stream of static; but then – so abruptly that it made him jump – an announcer's voice say, " – *of Helen Day,' brought to you by Song O' The South Soda . . .*"

He listened raptly, standing in the middle of the room with the door still open. It was the same episode as last night, the story of the bandleader who didn't tap the rostrum. Then, the same words, *"He was so handsome. Yet I knew that he was wicked, underneath."*

Then again, the door opening. The shouts. The microphone knocked. Scuffles, screams. And that terrible, terrible cry of agony, *"Oh God! Oh God! John! John! God help me! He's cut me open! Oh God! My stomach's falling out!"*

Then nothing. Only crackling and shushing and occasional spits of static.

Martin swallowed dryly. Was that a repeat? Was it the news? If it was the news, how come there was no commentary? He stood with his hand over his mouth wondering what to do. He drove into Mobile late that evening. The sky was purple, and there was still a strong feeling of electricity in the air. That day, he had driven on Highway 10 all the way across north Florida, and as he made the final crossing of Polecat Bay toward the glittering water-distorted lights of the docks, he felt stiff and cramped and ready for nothing but a stiff drink and a night of undisturbed sleep. But first of all he was determined to find the Dauphin Street radio studios.

It took him over an hour. The Dauphin Street Studios weren't in the phone book. Two cops he stopped hadn't heard of it, either, although they asked in a tight, suspicious drawl to look at his driver's license and insurance. Eventually, however, he stopped at a bar called the Cat's Pyjamas, a noisy, crowded place close to the intersection with Florida Street, and asked the bartender, whose bald head shone oddly blue in the light from the shelves, as if he were an alien.

"Dauphin Street Studios closed down before the war.

Nineteen forty-one, maybe nineteen forty-two. But ask Harry. He used to work there when he was younger, Studio technician or something. There he is, second booth along."

Harry turned out to be a neat, retired character with cropped white hair and a sallow face and a whispery way of talking. Martin sat down opposite him and said, "Understand you worked at the Dauphin Street Studios?"

Harry looked at him oddly. "What kind of a question is that?"

"I'm interested in something that might have happened there."

"Well . . . the last broadcast that went out from the Dauphin Street Studios was March 7, 1941, that was when WMOB went bust. That was a lifetime ago."

"Do you want a drink?" Martin asked him.

"So long as you're buying. Wild Turkey, on the rocks."

"Do you remember a soap called *The Heart of Helen Day*?"

There was a long silence. Then Harry said, "Sure I do. Everybody remembers *The Heart of Helen Day*. That program was part of the reason that WMOB had to close down."

"Tell me."

Harry shrugged. "Not much to tell. The girl who played Helen Day was real pretty . . . I never saw a girl so pretty before or since. Andrea Lawrence. Blonde, bright. I was in love with her; but then so was everybody else. She used to get all kinds of weird mail and phone calls. In those days, you could still be a radio star, and of course you got all the crank stuff that went with being a star. One day, Andrea started getting death threats. Very sick phone calls that said things like, 'I'm going to gut you, live on air', and stuff like that."

Martin said, "It really happened, then? She really was murdered in the studio?"

"Most horrible thing I ever saw in my life. I was only a kid . . . well, nineteen. I had nightmares about it for years afterward. A guy burst into the studio. I never even saw the knife, although the cops said that it was huge . . . a real hog-butchering knife. He stuck it in her lower abdomen and whipped it upwards – so quick that I thought that he was punching her. Then her entire insides came out, all over the studio floor. Just like that. I had nightmares about it for years."

Martin licked his lips. He didn't seem to have any saliva at all. "Did they ever catch him? The guy who killed her?"

Harry shook his head. "There was too much confusion. Everybody was too shocked. Before we knew what had happened, he was gone. The cops went through the city with a nit comb, but they never found him. *The Heart of Helen Day* was canceled, of course, and after that WMOB gradually fell apart and went out of business. Not that television wasn't slowly killing it already."

"Was there a recording of that broadcast?" asked Martin.

Harry said, "Sure. We recorded everything."

"Do you think that somebody could be transmitting it again?"

"What?"

"I've heard it. I've heard the episode where she gets murdered. I've heard the whole thing . . . even when says 'Oh God, he's cut my stomach open'."

"That's impossible."

"I heard it. Not just once, but twice."

Harry stared at Martin as if he were mad. "That's totally impossible. For one thing, there was only one recording,

247

and that was my master tape; and my master tape was destroyed in a fire along with all of WMOB's other tapes, in January, 1942. I saw the burned spool myself.

"For another thing, I jumped up as soon as the guy came into the studio, and accidentally switched off the tape recorder. The actual killing was never recorded. If you heard it, my friend, you were hearing ghosts."

"Ghosts? I don't think so. I heard it clear as day."

"Well . . . you're not the only one who's heard stuff from the past. I was reading the other day some guy in Montana picked up his dead mother arguing with his dead father on his car radio, whenever it thundered."

Martin had been ready to leave, but now he leaned forward and said to Harry, "Whenever it *thundered*? How?"

"I don't know. It sounds far-fetched. But the theory is that the human brain records things it hears as electrical impulses, right? Normally it *keeps* them stored. But in certain atmospheric conditions, it *discharges* those impulses . . . so strongly that they can get picked up by a radio receiver. In this case, the guy's car radio. But apparently they have to be real close. Seventy or eighty feet away, not much more."

Seventy or eighty feet away. Who had been seventy or eighty feet away from that old Zenith radio when it thundered? Who had been old enough and crazy enough to have attacked Andrea Lawrence, all those years ago in the Dauphin Street Studios? Who wouldn't have been found in the city because, maybe, he didn't actually live in the city?

There was no proof. No proof at all. But apart from the actors and the radio technicians, only the killer would have heard Andrea Lawrence's last words . . . only the killer would have remembered them. So that one thundery night, nearly forty years later, his memory would have come crackling out on an old-fashioned radio set.

It was late in the afternoon and unbearably steamy when Martin drove his mud-splattered Pontiac back to the Sweet Gum Motor Court. There was a strong smell of drying mud and chicken-feed in the air. He parked, and wearily climbed out.

He knocked at the screen door. He had to wait for a long time before anybody answered. The ragged tan dog sat not far away, and watched him, and panted. Eventually Vernon appeared, and unlocked the door.

"You again," he said, suspiciously.

"Is Denise around?"

"What do you want her for?"

"To tell you the truth, it's you I wanted."

"Oh, yeah?"

"I just wanted to ask you a couple of questions about Andrea Lawrence. You ever heard of Andrea Lawrence? She played Helen Day, in *The Heart of Helen Day*."

Long silence. Eyes glittering behind the reflective glass. Then the key turning in the lock. "You'd best come on in. Go in the office. I won't keep you more'n a couple of minutes."

The tired-looking woman took the barrettes out of her hair and shook it loose. On the desk, the remains of her evening meal had attracted the attention of two persistent flies. She picked up the whisky glass and swallowed, and coughed.

She couldn't believe there was no TV here. If it hadn't been such a stormy night, she would have driven further, to someplace decent. But half the roads were flooded out, and she was frightened of lightning.

She switched on the radio. Fuzzy jazz, dance music, some kind of black funeral song. Then two voices in what sounded like a radio play. She lay back on the bed and closed her eyes and listened. If only her husband could see her now.

"*You again.*"

"*Is Denise around?*"

"*What do you want her for?*"

"*To tell you the truth, it's you I wanted.*"

The woman sipped more whisky. Outside, the thunder grumpily banged, and the rain started to gush down more heavily.

"*I heard something pretty curious on my radio last night.*"

"*Oh yeah?*"

"*I heard – hey, what are you doing? What the hell do you think you're doing? Get away from – aahh! Jesus Christ! Aaaaggggh! Jesus Christ! You've cut me! Oh Jesus Christ you've cut me open!*"

Muffled knocks. A sound like a chair falling over. A thick, indescribable splattering. Then an awful gasping.

"*Help me, for Christ's sake. Help me!*"

"*Help you what? Help you get me and Denise put away for murder? Or a nuthouse or something?*"

"*Help me, Jesus, it hurts so much!*"

"*And didn't it hurt Denise, to listen to that Helen Day every single week, and how Helen Day got men just by winking her eye, and Denise's only fiancé left her high and dry for a girl like that? Don't you think that hurt?*"

"*Help me, Vernon.*"

"*Help you nothing. You're all the same. Leaving Denise for your fancy-women . . .*"

There was a cry like an owl being dismembered alive by a coyote. Then nothing but white noise, on and on and on.

The woman was already asleep. The white noise continued as she slept, like an endless bus journey along an unfamiliar highway, through thick fog. At a few minutes after 3 a.m., the door of her cabin softly clicked open, and a shadow fell into the room, but all she did was mutter and turn over.

The Jajouka Scarab

Fes, Morocco

I was introduced to Morocco by the late Brion Gysin, whose mystical novel The Process *was an extraordinary journey through the minds and beliefs of those who lived on the northern fringe of the Sahara Desert. We discussed this story as long ago as March, 1970, in a restaurant in Covent Garden, and I still have the scribbled-on napkin to prove it.*

This story is dedicated to Brion's memory: a marvellous painter, a dazzling writer, and one of the great unappreciated talents of the 20th century.

Morocco is hospitable to a fault; but it is still a land that is full of secrets; and a land that revels in secrets. The Jajouka Scarab is one of its greatest secrets, and it would take a man with a great deal more money than me to find out what it is.

Fes is the sacred city of Islam in Morocco, and it is picturesquely positioned in the valley of the Sebu, surrounded by fruit orchards, olive plantations, and orange groves. The mosque of Mulai Idris, which was built over a thousand years ago by the founders of Fes, is so sacred that any Christian or Jew is forbidden from approaching it. The mosque of Karueen is the largest in Africa, and is regularly attended by more than a thousand students to learn classical Arabic and Islamic law and theology.

To visit Fes is a strange and uplifting experience that you won't forget. But beyond Fes, up in the mountains of the High Rif, another kind of experience is waiting – an experience that you can't *forget.*

THE JAJOUKA SCARAB

Twenty-seven years later, he was approached in the foyer of the Hôtel Splendid in Port-au-Prince by a small, birdlike black man in a dazzling white suit and gold-rimmed spectacles.

The man took off his hat to reveal a bald head like a highly burnished brazil-nut. His front teeth were all gold.

"Have I the honour of addressing Dr Donnelly?" The man's accent revealed him to be Algerian or Moroccan, rather than Haitian.

"I'm Grant Donnelly, yes."

"I have been looking forward to making your acquaintance for many years, sir. I am a great admirer of your work."

"Well, that's very good of you, thank you. Now, if you'll excuse me –"

Grant's wife Petra was waiting for him by the French windows that led out into the garden. She caught sight of him, and lifted her hand.

Grant made to leave but the man touched his sleeve. "Dr Donnelly – please, before you go. I have studied all of your papers and all of your books, and they are very detailed and comprehensive. But there is always one significant omission."

"Oh?"

"How could a great expert have written *Complete North African Insects* without a mention of the Jajouka scarab?"

The man released his grip on Grant's sleeve. He was smiling, but with no humour whatsoever. The sunlight reflected on his spectacles so that he momentarily appeared to be blind.

"I am a wealthy man, Dr Donnelly. I would give a great deal of money for information which would lead me to the discovery of a Jajouka scarab."

Grant gave him an almost imperceptible shake of his head. But the man's words had already filled his mind with flute music and the aromatic fragrance of *kif* and the silken sliding whisper that haunts anybody who has ever travelled to the edge of the Sahara.

"I would guarantee to make you rich, Dr Donnelly, if you would advise me of the possible whereabouts of a Jajouka scarab."

"There's no such thing," said Grant, with a slight breathless catch in his voice.

The man tilted his head to one side, and looked at him in scornful disbelief.

"No such thing, Dr Donnelly? Really!"

"Believe me," Grant insisted, "it's a myth. It's a story the Moroccan *bouhalis* thought up, to make a fool of Westerners. There's no such thing. If anybody's told you different, then they've been pulling your leg."

"There is no such thing, master," said Hakim, dismissively. "What you have been told is nothing but lies."

Grant shook another Casa Sport cigarette out of its crumpled paper packet. "Hakim, I talked to Professor Hemmer at the Institute of Natural History in Tangier. *He* knew all about it."

256

"Then he, too, has been told lies."

It was evening in the Old Town, in the early summer of 1967, and they were sitting in Fuentes café in the Socco, a little plaza crowded with cafés and Indian bazaars and jewellery stores which offered Swiss watches of suspicious provenance to Swedish tourists. They were drinking mint tea and eating thickly-sugared doughnuts, and Hakim was smoking *kif*. The strange, fragrant smoke drifted across the plaza and melted into the pale violet air. Inside the brightly lit café, old men in striped djellabas were listening to Radio Cairo on the shortwave.

Suzanna said, "Professor Hemmer was sure that it was a member of the scarab family, a very small chafer."

Hakim looked at her with dark, unreadable eyes. "Professor Hemmer is a German. He knows nothing of what is real and what is not real."

Grant put the cigarette between his lips, and lit it, and coughed. The tobacco tasted as if it had been soaked in honey and cinnamon and sun-melted asphalt. "It seems like we've come a long way for nothing, then. That's a pity. The university gave us a budget that was well out of proportion to the scale of our project, and we still have a whole lot left."

"All the money in America cannot alter reality," Hakim replied.

Grant sat back in his uncomfortable bentwood chair. He and Suzanna had been working in Morocco for seven and a half months now, and he had grown accustomed to the riddles and evasiveness which accompanied all business dealings in Morocco. But they had travelled a long way today, and he was tired, and Hakim's repeated denials were beginning to irritate him.

He and Suzanna had completed all of the work that they had set out to do, including a radical and spectacular study of the life cycle of the dung beetle, and a profile of weevil infestation which had already assisted the Moroccan authorities to reduce beetle damage to grain stores and warehouses.

But two weeks ago, at what was supposed to have been their farewell dinner party in the house of the Director General of Ethnic Studies in Kebir, they had set next to a chain-smoking old Frenchman called Duvic who had lived for forty-five years in the fondouk. As soon as he had discovered that they were coleopterists, studiers of beetles, he had laughed thickly and told them that as far as *he* was concerned, there was only one beetle worth studying, and that was the Jajouka scarab, *Scarabaeidae Jajoukae*, the so-called "penis-beetle".

"Why on earth do they call it that?" Suzanna had asked him, her green eyes bright as broken glass.

Duvic had coughed up sticky-sounding stuff into his handkerchief. His moustache was white, but one side of it was stained by nicotine to the colour of Dijon mustard. "You shouldn't have to ask. They used to use it in the Little Hills in a coupling ritual . . . instead of *kif*. When you smoke *kif*, you enter a different world, and walk with *bouhali*, the holy madmen who can do anything; walk through walls, discuss politics with the dead. But they say that when you use the penis-beetle, you discover yourself, your real self, with such a clearness that you can scarcely bear it. *Aimez-vous l'agonie?*

He hesitated, coughed again, and then he said, "Twelve, maybe thirteen years ago, I was offered a Jajouka scarab, in a brothel in Mascara. I said no. I have to confess that I was too frightened. Also, I was rich then, but they were asking more than I could afford, over fifteen thousand francs. Now I wish . . . well, it's no use wishing. I shall be dead soon, and who would have me, anyhow?"

"This scarab – it's a real beetle?" Grant had asked him, with quickly rising enthusiasm. He was already thinking of the papers, the book reviews, the lecture tours. Standing in front of three hundred academics and clearing his throat and saying, "None of you will ever have heard of *Scarabaeidae Jajoukae*, more commonly known in the Little Hills of Morocco as 'the Jajouka penis-beetle'." What an opening!

But the Frenchman had been drunk, too much Algerian brandy, and had suddenly become righteous. "I regret telling you," he repeated, over and over again.

Grant and Suzanna had been due to fly back to the States the following day, but early in the morning Grant had talked to Professor Hemmer on the crackly telephone line to Tangier, and Professor Hemmer had said, "Of course, the Jajouka scarab. A very rare chafer that feeds off the gum of the *kif* flower, the gum we call *hashish*. I have seen drawings of it, and read descriptions. It is mentioned, I think, in Quintini's *Insects of Africa*. But as far as I know it lives only in the *kif* meadows of Ketama, in the high Rif."

"Why do they call it the 'penis-beetle'?"

"Well, my friend, this is very simple. When the beetle is disturbed, it gives off a strong chemical irritant; and it was said that some of the hill-peoples used to insert it into male urethra before intercourse in order to intensify their sexual pleasure. I don't even know if you could still find one today. They have probably been rendered extinct by insecticides. I have heard of certain millionaires who would pay a king's ransom just for one beetle. But *natürlich* it's the question of finding one. And apart from that, its use is strictly forbidden on religious grounds, because Muslims believe in the absolute sanctity of the body, and on legal grounds by the government, who consider it very undesirable for the tourist trade. The last thing they want is to turn the high Rif into another Bangkok, swarming with Westerners in search of a new sexual excess. It is bad enough, *nicht wahr*, with all of my fellow countrymen giving shiny racing bicycles to the young boys on the beach."

Professor Hemmer had detonated with laughter, and Grant had cradled the old-fashioned telephone. Their pigskin bags were packed and waiting in the turquoise-tiled lobby of the Hotel Africanus. Nine cases of research material and three cases of specimens had already been forwarded to Paris. Suzanna had wanted to forget *Scarabaeidae Jajoukae* and return to Boston. "We can look for it next year." But Grant knew that if they didn't find it now, they would never find it. This was a place that, once you left it, you never came back. Not in the same way, anyhow. You might be haunted every night for the rest of your life by the sound of Radio Cairo on the shortwave, and the hollow, skin-prickling blowing of *raitas*, like oboes heard in a drugged and never-ending dream. But if you came back, the doors to the fondouk would be tightly shuttered, the Medina would be deserted, and all of the secrets of the Old Town would be lost to you. You would drink your mint tea as a tourist, not as a brother, one who knows the Secret Name.

Professor Hemmer gave them Hakim's address, because Hakim had once worked as an assistant for the eccentric English botanist Doctor Timothy Scudamore, who had spent five years on the high plateau of the Atlas Mountains, studying the flora, and then the folk music, and then the hidden treasure of all Morocco, the whereabouts of which is known only to Soussi magicians, who have a secret registry of all the gold that has ever been concealed

260

by anybody. If anybody knew where to find *Scarabaeidae Jajoukae*, Hakim did.

Although he *didn't*, or so he said, sitting with his mint tea and his thin *sebsi* pipe filled with *kif*, thin and angular in his white linen coat and his flappy linen pants and his red silk slippers. Under his red *tarboosh* his hair was shaved crucially short, and his face was narrow and crowded with angles, like a Cubist painting, so that he never looked the same twice. Only his eyes remained calm and motionless, as if he could get up and walk away, and leave them floating in the evening air, like a mirage, still watching them.

Grant, by total contrast, was two weeks past his thirty-first birthday, thickly put together, slightly overweight, with sun-bleached surfer's hair and a face like a genial quarterback: blue eyes, broken nose, and a toothy, immediate smile. He didn't look like one of America's leading experts on the impact of beetles on human society, not until he put on his round tortoiseshell spectacles, when he looked exactly like his late father, the author of *Donnelly's Definitive American Insects*.

He and Suzanna Morrison had worked together throughout their final Ph.D. year; sometimes intimate, sometimes nothing more than tolerant. Suzanna was tall, strong-faced, with high cheekbones and deep-set eyes. She had veils of shining brunette hair, breast-length, but ever since they had arrived in Morocco, she had covered her head with a scarf, and often she wound the scarf completely around her face, so that only her eyes showed. It gave her dignity, and although the brotherhood of men said nothing, they appreciated it, and they respected her for it. She wasn't one of these tourists, or one of these barefaced students, or one of their own women who scuttled out of the house for a pennyworth of this or a pennyworth of that, with only a rag to cover their faces.

She was even more of a free spirit than the brotherhood of men could have guessed. She had dropped out of SUNY for a year to hitchhike to La Jolla, California, where she had lived in a free-love community called The Shining Eye, a community in which the instant and open gratification of any sexual desire had been an integral part of a philosophy called The Opening. "Open your mind to all, open your body to all." She was more restrained now, but Grant still found her sexually intimidating. Her sexuality was so strong that it was almost audible, bare thighs sliding together, lips parting, eyelids fluttering; and the silken whisper of her hair like the sand snaking by moonlight over the Grand Erg of the Sahara.

The first time they had made love (in Paris, on the rue Chalgrin, in their bedroom at La Residence du Bois), Suzanna had told him quite matter-of-factly that that she had once had sex with five men at once. He had thought she was joking, because he couldn't think how it was possible. But when she had carefully and seriously explained it, he had remained silent for the rest of the day, both highly aroused and deeply disturbed.

This evening, Suzanna wore an indigo-coloured scarf and a loose djellaba-style dress of immaculate white cotton. All the same, Grant knew that she was naked underneath, and when she leaned forward on the table to talk to Hakim, he could see the heavy, complicated swinging of her breast.

These days, they weren't always friends and even when they were friends they weren't always lovers. They had argued, during the past seven and a half months, some-times violently. They had argued over the Jajouka scarab, and whether they ought to go back to Boston and forget

262

about it. But now that they were here, they had become closer again, sensitive to everything that each of them said, or was about to say, or *thought*, even. Grant enjoyed it when they were close like this. It gave him a feeling that he knew where he was in the world, both emotionally and geographically. Cared-for, and cared-about, 35.4 degrees north, 1.1 degree east.

Suzanna said to Hakim, "What if we agreed not to tell anybody what we had found? Would you show us the beetle then?"

Hakim glanced at Grant. "Does the woman speak for you, master?"

Grant impatiently blew out smoke. "Yeah. She speaks for me. Sometimes she even speaks for herself."

"There is no beetle," Hakim replied.

"You mean it's extinct?" Suzanna asked him.

Hakim's eyes flicked shiftily downward. "There is no beetle unless I decide."

"So there is a beetle but you won't show us where it is?"

"Unless I decide."

"So what's going to make you decide?"

Hakim smoked more *kif*. Coffee jugs clanked. Crickets chirruped. The shortwave rose and fell in the warm night air. It sounded like football results. Osiris United versus White Nile Wanderers? Hakim, at last, said, "Green card. Then I decide."

Suzanna stared at him, and then burst out laughing. "You want a green card? Are you yanking my chain?"

"Green card," said Hakim, crossly. "Doctor Scoodamor, he always promised that I could come to work for him in United States. Then he went searching for the Soussi magicians, and never returned. After all of my years of assistance and diligence, master, I was left with nothing. Very little money, for Doctor Scoodamor, he was full of promises of payment, and when he did pay, he paid with paper."

"Well, at least he paid," said Grant.

"What is the use of paper?" Hakim retorted. "We cannot put our money into banks because banks are sinful, but when we hide our paper money the mice eat it. All of the money that Doctor Scoodamor gave me I hid in my attic, but when I went to take it out, it was nothing but mouse-dust and coloured confetti."

Suzanna looked quickly at Grant and clasped his hand on top of the blue-painted metal table. "We could sponsor Hakim, couldn't we, Grant? Especially if we told Immigration that he was essential to our work on the scarab."

Grant smiled and nodded, and thought, *Jesus, Suzanna, you're the sharp one.*

"Then you will sponsor me?" asked Hakim.

"We don't know," said Grant. "If the beetle is lies, then no. But if the beetle is truth . . ."

Hakim tamped his slender pipe. The night was the size of all of Africa. "The beetle is truth," said Hakim.

The next morning they took the train from the white-painted stationyard at Fes. It was half after eleven, and the sun bleached the colour out of everything except the extravagant overgrowths of magenta bougainvillea, and the sky the colour of marking ink.

The train climbed steadily up through the hills. Ahead of them, the spring flowers had painted each successive mountain a different primary colour, yellow and red and blue. Behind them, the valleys were filled with white waterwort, a foaming surf of sickly smelling blossom. The fragrance of the flowers was so strong and so sweet that Grant thought that it would poison him, and that he would fall asleep, and dream of *bouhanis* who could talk politics with the dead.

He nodded off, but he was still conscious of the swaying and creaking of the train, and the drumming of the diesel engine.

When he opened his eyes again, Hakim was sitting opposite, peeling an orange with long, none-too-clean fingernails. He said, "I live in the Old Town but I am always here, in the Little Hills." Grant nodded in acknowledgement, but realized that Hakim had been talking to nobody in particular.

Hakim said, by way of explanation, "There are places in the world where secrets reveal themselves of their own accord. This is one of them."

"It's very beautiful," said Suzanna. The hills all around them were emerald green and glittering with little white flowers. On some of the hillsides they could see flocks of sheep. "It's like a dream."

Hakim offered her the orange, opened up like a flower, but she shook her head. He offered it to Grant, and Grant, out of politeness, accepted a piece.

"Tell me some more about the scarab," he said.

"It is truth, master. It exists."

"But will we find one?"

"Anything that exists can be found. Maybe we will have to go to a magician, but we will find one."

Jajouka was both postcard-picturesque and mysterious, an intricate little collection of dazzling whitewashed houses on an improbable hill, surrounded by olive trees and hedges of prickly pear. When the diesel train had rumbled away, they were left in heat-baked silence, and Hakim led them across the village green, where a tethered goat

265

grazed and tinkled its tiny bell. They passed through a low whitewashed archway and found themselves in a shadowy courtyard, where a young woman in a dark red dress was fanning the ashes of a smoky mud oven. A cockerel with brassy-bright feathers strutted around her.

"I am seeking your uncle Hassan," said Hakim. The sun slanted through the smoke.

The woman nodded toward the shadowy interior of the house, her earrings glinting. Hakim beckoned Grant and Suzanna to follow him, and they found themselves in a cool, bare room, where two elderly men in snow-white turbans and thick woollen djellabas were lolling on cushions, drinking tea and smoking *kif*.

There were ritual introductions. Hakim inquired about the health of uncle Hassan's brothers, his cousins, his goats, his fields and his wives. Hassan had a long curved nose and deeply hooded eyes, and all the time he spoke he rolled a little ball of gray wax between his fingers. The other man was much more buttery and plump. He was so high on *kif* that Grant couldn't understand a word he was saying.

"My master seeks a scarab," said Hakim, at last. "He is a man of high reputation and great learning, and wishes to complete his knowledge of all insects. He can pay you with great generosity."

Hassan thought for a moment, and then replied very quickly and softly, and at considerable length. With only kitchen-Arabic, Grant couldn't keep up, but he did manage to pick up the words, "Jeep", and "cousin".

"What did he say?" he asked Hakim, when Hassan appeared to have finished speaking.

"He said that he knows where the scarabs can be found. They are picked from the *kif* flowers not far from here by wandering hill-people, Nazarenes, who sell them to

266

the brothelkeepers in Tangier and Marrakech. He will introduce you to the hill-people and arrange for you to acquire two or perhaps three of the beetles. He does not wish for payment, since he lacks nothing. There is no electricity here and no running water because they would alarm Bou Jeloud the Father of Fear, who protects our sheep. He is satisfied with the tithe which he is given for his fields; and his *kif*; and his music.

"All the same he has a cousin Ahmed in Kebir who would dearly love to own a new Jeep. If this can be arranged, then he will take you to the Nazarenes who live by the beetle."

"What does a Jeep cost?" Suzanna whispered.

"Nothing, compared with one of these beetles."

"Then let's go for it. I can't stay here much longer. This *kif* smoke, I'm starting to hallucinate."

Hassan said something rapid and low. Grant didn't understand every word but he understood the implication. "Is this a man who has a woman to speak for him?"

In Arabic, Grant said, "In our country, the opinions of women are treated with the same respect as the opinions of men."

Hassan nodded, and smiled, and then replied in English. "Those who use the Jajouka scarab have respect neither for men nor for women; and no opinions."

"What does he mean?"

"He means that those who experience the scarab, master, have no more time for points of view. They are interested in one thing only: when will they experience the scarab again?"

It was past midnight when they came rustling through the syrupy-warm *kif* fields to the makeshift encampment of the Nazarenes. The sky was purple, the same colour as

267

old-fashioned typewriter ribbons; and the moon hung in it like a mirror. The Ahl-el-beit, the people of the tent, used to believe that the moon reflected the Sahara Desert, a map suspended in the sky.

A haze of *kif* smoke hung over the tents. They heard voices and breathy pipes. Grant took hold of Suzanna's hand and squeezed it to reassure her; or maybe to reassure himself. Hakim and Hassan were walking slightly ahead of them, all wound up in their turbans and djellabas. Every step they took crushed blossoms beneath their sandalled feet, and Grant could smell dew and the rotten-sweet fragrance of flowers.

It's like a dream.

They opened the largest of the tents. Inside, around a loudly hissing pressure-lamp, sat six or seven wild-looking travellers in ragged djellabas and shirts. A gray-haired man of fifty or so, with eyes like pebbles; three or four young men with dirty cheeks and sulky expressions; a Sudanese boy of sixteen or seventeen wearing nothing but a belted shirt, so that his long bare penis rested openly against his thigh. An older woman, with her face covered. Two young women, with uncovered faces, in thin muslin dresses.

Uncle Hassan sat next to the gray-haired man and began to speak in his ear, emphasizing his conversation now and again by tapping two fingers into the palm of his hand. The gray-haired man nodded, and nodded, and nodded again. Hakim whispered into Grant's ear, with breath that smelled strongly of oranges, "Hassan is asking for the repayment of a favour. Last year the Nazarenes were caught trespassing into the fields of the Adepts, and Hassan saved them from certain punishment."

After twenty minutes of murmuring and nodding, the gray-haired man beckoned to one of the young sulky men, who disappeared from the tent, and then, two minutes later, returned. He gave the gray-haired man two small boxes carved out of olive wood and inlaid with tarnished silver. Hassan took hold of Grant's sleeve, and said, "In these boxes, the Nazarene has two scarabs. They will bring him ten thousand dollars in Tangier, enough for his people to live for a year."

The gray-haired man unscrewed the top of one of the boxes and passed it to Grant to look at. The bottom of the box was entirely filled with hashish resin, which gave off a strong, distinctive odour. On top of the resin, scurrying quickly from one side of the box to the other, and back again, was a tiny black hump-backed beetle, very similar in appearance to a dung beetle, only very much smaller.

Grant and Suzanna watched it in fascination. "You know what this is like?" said Grant to Hassan. "This is like discovering the source of the Nile, only more so."

The gray-haired man leaned over to uncle Hassan, and murmured something in his ear. This time it was Hassan's turn to nod.

"He asks if you would like a demonstration of the way in which the beetle is used."

"I don't understand."

Hassan pointed to one of the girls, and then to one of the sulky young men. "They will show you, if you wish it."

"What do you think?" Grant asked Suzanna. "You want to see what they do with this thing, or what?"

Suzanna grasped his arm. "It's what we came for, isn't it?"

Grant thought for a moment, then turned and nodded. The pressure-lamp hissed and hissed, and moths pattered against it, and spun dusty to the blankets on the ground.

The gray-haired man spoke. One of the girls argued, but then he snapped sharply at her, and said, "*Tais-toi!*"

She stood up and lifted her djellaba over her head. It

269

dropped onto the cushions beside her. She was black-haired, with skin the colour of fresh dates. Her eyes were slanted and defiant. She was small, only two or three inches over five feet, and glossy with good feeding. Her breasts were huge: two enormous globes with areolas as wide as the circle that you would draw round a wineglass, veined with blue. Her navel was buried deep in her rounded stomach, but it was pierced with a golden ring. Her thighs were heavy, and between her thighs, her hairless vulva swelled like a plump and clefted fruit. Although these were Nazarenes, which was Hassan's derisory way of calling them Christians, they followed the Muslim way of shaving all their body hair, so that they were smooth and clean.

The girl knelt down on the blankets. She tossed back her hair with her hands and her breasts swayed. Her vulva opened like a sticky *kif* flower, and Grant could see her clitoris and her inner lips with the odd microscopic detail that he felt as if he were peering at the moon.

The gray-haired man spoke again, and waved his hand, and one of the young men stood up, and stripped off his robes. He was curly haired and very lean, much paler than the girl. He, too, was completely shaved of all his body hair, so that his penis looked even longer. It was slowly rising, its wedge-shaped circumcized head swelling up with every beat of his heart, his bare balls tightening. He knelt in front of the girl, and by then his penis was fully erect, a hardened sculpture of veins and silky shining skin. A single drop of clear fluid appeared in the opening of his penis like a magician producing a diamond from the palm of his hand, and quivered there.

The gray-haired man passed one of the olive wood boxes to the naked girl. Then he snapped his fingers, and one of his assistants gave him a thin lacquered pipe,

270

even thinner than a *sebi* pipe, and he passed that across to her, too.

The naked boy leaned his head back, closing his eyes. He grasped his own testicles in his hand, squeezing them so that they bulged. The girl placed the pipe between her lips, and gently started to suck. She probed the other end of it into the olive wood box, and kept on sucking until she had trapped the tiny beetle on the end of it.

"Watch now," Hakim told Grant and Suzanna. "This is how the Jajouka scarab is used to give you ecstasy."

The girl took the pipe out of her mouth and capped it with her thumb, so that the beetle was held against the other hand by pressure alone. Then she grasped the boy's erect penis with her left hand, stretching apart the urethral opening with her finger and thumb, and slid the pipe right down the length of his erection. The boy gritted his teeth, and clenched the blankets with his fists, but didn't cry out. The girl pushed the pipe right down until less than a quarter-inch of it was protruding from his penis. Then she released her thumb, so that the beetle was freed, right inside his urethral bulb, where his semen would collect in the last few seconds before he ejaculated.

She drew out the pipe, and a few drops of blood came with it. She leaned forward so that her erect nipples brushed the blankets, and licked off the blood with the tip of her tongue.

The gray-haired man went into a long, gesticulating explanation, which Hakim translated. "The scarab is inside the boy's body. It will remain there until he reaches the moment of climax. At that instant, his seed will propel it to the very tip of his penis, but it will react in a negative way to the female juices. It will cling to the opening of his penis, and instantly produce an irritating chemical, which

271

will give both boy and woman excruciating pleasure and excruciating pain."

Hakim said, "I have never tried it myself, master. Perhaps I am a coward. But I know many people who have, and they say that it is heaven and hell, combined."

The gray-haired man impatiently clapped his hands. The naked boy lay back on the blankets, holding his erection in his hand. The girl climbed over him, her thighs wide apart.

"Here, here," said the gray-haired man. He leaned forward and opened the girl's vulva with his fingers. Grant saw juicy pink flesh like a freshly cut pomegranate. The gray-haired man grasped the boy's penis and lasciviously rubbed it once or twice. Then he fitted it between the girl's inner lips. The girl sat on it, and the plum-shaped head disappeared deep inside her, until the smooth hairless pout of her vulva was pressed against the smooth hairless curves of the boy's penis-root.

Suzanna reached over and clutched Grant's hand. He could see by the look in her eyes that was she was frightened; but aroused, too. This was the sort of shameless sexual exhibition that would have made anybody want to rush out to the nearest private place they could find, and fuck themselves into a rage.

Usually, the Little Hills were filled with music. Flutes, drums, raitas. But all they could hear now was the wet kissing of a plump vulva against a bone-hard erection; and the conspiratorial hissing of a pressure-lamp. Everybody watched transfixed as the girl and the boy began to thrust more quickly; as the girl sat up straighter, and clasped both of her sweaty, pillowy breasts in her hands, and started to squeeze them, so that her dark nipples stuck out stiff between her fingers. Everybody watched as the boy's scrotum began to wrinkle and tighten, and the girl's juices slid down the dark divide between his testicles, and dripped across his puckered, hairless anus. Everybody watched with tautly held breath, mesmerized by the shluk, shluk, shluk of cock sliding deep into slippery cunt; thoughts that grew dirtier and dirtier; fantasies that grew wilder and wilder; and all the time the beetle was nestling, deep in his shaft, in the very place where semen and sperm would flood together, and tauten, and tighten, and then pump irresistibly into her body.

Grant didn't even realize that he was clutching Suzanna's fingers so fiercely; and neither did she. But then the boy tensed, and tensed even harder, and screamed. The girl screamed too. Only in anticipation, to begin with, because she must have known what was coming. But then the two of them were clenched together, rolling from one side of the blankets to the other, screaming and screaming and thrashing their legs, but never letting go of each other, thrusting closer together if anything, hips bucking, buttocks hard, fucking and screaming with their eyeballs white and their teeth clenched.

They were like *bouhanis*; they were like dogs baying at the moon. They were like ululating women and Aissaoua, the trance dancers, who would kiss snakes and throw live sheep into the air and devour them before they hit the ground. Grant thought for one long moment that they were going to die. "Jesus," Suzanna whispered. "Eat your heart out, Doctor Ruth."

It was over five minutes before the boy and the girl stopped quaking and climaxing and rolling around. At last they fell back on the blankets, eyes closed, gasping for air, their naked bodies shining with sweat. Sperm dripped from the girl's open vagina, but the men in the tent watched it with complete dispassion, as if she were nothing more than a she-goat who needed milking, and

273

had overflowed. The gray-haired Nazarene knelt beside the boy, lifted his wet, softening penis, and probed inside the opening with the narrow pipe. At last he smiled, and picked out the scarab, which he carefully returned to its olive wood box.

He said something to Hakim and Hakim translated. "These two will sleep for three or four hours. When they awake, they will want to do the same again, but much more urgently this time. The scarab is worse than *kif* when it comes to addiction. Once you have experienced it, you will always desire more. But perhaps that is the truth that you have come here to find.

He smiled, "You may take two of the scarabs. They are both male, so they will not breed, and besides, they cannot breed anywhere but here, in the *kif* fields."

He handed two olive wood boxes to uncle Hassan, who secreted them someplace inside his woollen djellaba.

"One warning," he said. "Never place two male scarabs in the same box; and never try to insert more than one scarab into your penis. Male scarabs are small, but they are more aggressive than scorpions. They will fight each other to the death."

Uncle Hassan placed his hand on the Nazarene's shoulder. "*Mektoub*," he said. "It is written."

They returned to Fes on the same train that wound its way down through hills. The morning was overcast, and the flowers smelled even more sickly decayed than they had before. Grant was restless and excited, and scribbled endless notes about *Scarabaeidae Jajoukae* on a legal pad balanced on his knee; but Suzanna seemed curiously listless and tired, and watched the hills rotating past the window as if she were dreaming about them. Hakim had smoked too much *kif* the previous night and slept with his chin against his shoulder. The first thing she said when they returned to their hotel room was, "I think we ought to try it."

"What?" asked Grant. He was opening a bottle of Oasis Gazeuse.

She came up to him and stood very close even though she didn't touch him.

"I think we ought to try it. The scarab, I mean. There's no point in giving lectures about it if we don't know what it can do."

"You're talking about you and me?"

She nodded. There was a look in her eyes which he had first seen when she had described to him the way in which she had made love to five men at once, but had rarely seen since. He was suddenly conscious of the way that her white djellaba was open at the front, revealing the curve of her breast, and he was sure that he could feel the radiated warmth of her body.

He swallowed salty-tasting mineral water out of the neck of the bottle. "You're not frightened?" he asked her.

She shook her head. "I've never been frightened of passion. Have you?"

"Sometimes. But this is chemical passion, rather than natural passion. It's my guess the scarab reacts to the protein content of male semen by giving off a substance rather like *Cantharides*, or Spanish Fly."

"We could take samples," Suzanna suggested, but her smile was very much less than scientific.

Grant walked across the tiled floor and stood by the billowing net curtains, looking down at the courtyard and the splashing blue-painted fountain. A man with one eye was standing in the corner of the courtyard, holding a large live toad in each hand.

275

"I don't know," said Grant. "All of our equipment's packed already."

She came up close again, and this time she stroked the sun-bleached wing of hair behind his ear. "You're frightened," she said.

He turned and stared directly into her eyes. Yes, he was frightened. But he couldn't decide which frightened him more: the tiny scarab in its olive wood box, or Suzanna.

They showered and soaped each other all over in the echoing bathroom with its antiquated plumbing. Then, with their loins white-lathered, they shaved off all of their pubic hair with Grant's Gillette razor. Grant stood drying himself while Suzanna rubbed herself with jasmine-scented oil which she had bought in the Socco. Her hair was wound up in a turban-towel. Her breasts were high and rounded and very firm, with nipples that stood up knurled and hard. She was very slim, with narrow hips and very long legs. Her vulva had neat, closed lips, as if it was a secret in itself.

Grant came out of the bathroom with his heart beating in a slow, pronounced rhythm, like the drums of the trance dancers who dance and spin and break earthenware pots on their heads until their faces stream with blood.

"Do you think we should have music?" Suzanna asked him.

He went across to the radio and tuned in to an Algerian music station. Suzanna climbed onto the red-and-green striped durry that covered the bed, and sat with her legs crossed, her wrists resting on her knees. Grant went to the bureau and picked up one of the olive wood boxes and the narrow laquered pipe. His hairless penis was half erect, and Suzanna smiled at him, that unscientific smile. "You look like Michelangelo's *David*."

He climbed onto the bed facing her. He handed her the pipe and then he carefully opened the box. The scarab was motionless in one corner.

"It's not dead, is it?" Suzanna frowned.

"High, more like. There's enough hashish resin in this box to keep you flying for a month."

Suzanna leaned forward and prodded the scarab with the tip of the pipe. Grant watched the way her breasts swung, the way her vulva opened as if the secret was soon to be revealed. He felt hot, almost feverish. The radio was playing some endless wailing music. The net curtains billowed, and their transparent shadow blew across Suzanna's face as if it were trying to show Grant that she was somebody else. Her nipple, the colour of a heat-exhausted rose petal, brushing her suntanned thigh. He could see her actual clitoris protruding from her lips like a shiny pink canary's beak.

She sucked gently on the pipe. The scarab clung onto the hashish resin at first, resisting her gentle, insistent suction. But then it clung to the end of the pipe, and she was able to lift it out of its box, trapped by the tiny vacuum which she had created. She raised her eyes. "You don't have to do this, you know."

"I know . . . but as you so rightly say, how can we pretend to know what we're talking about if we don't try it for ourselves?"

Suzanna took hold of his half erect penis in her left hand, and slowly rubbed it until it stiffened and swelled. They had never made love like this before, not in such a ritualistic way. On most occasions they had been drunk, happy, exhausted or just plain horny. This morning, everything seemed to be slowed down, as if they too were stuck in hashish resin.

Grant watched with detached fascination as Suzanna

squeezed his plump purple cock head so that his opening widened. Without raising her head, as careful as a seamstress or a surgeon, she slid the lacquered pipe into his urethra, all the way down the length of his erection. Instantly, it burned. He felt as if she were filling up his urethra with boiling fat. He flinched, but Suzanna clasped his shoulder to steady him, and pushed the pipe the last inch into his urethral bulb. Then she took her thumb off the end, and slid it out again. Blood welled from the end of his penis and ran down between his legs.

"Christ that hurts."

She kissed him, and tenderly rubbed him. "It hurts but it's inside you. Now we can see what it feels like."

She pushed him back onto the durry. He felt the coarse-woven fabric against his naked back. She climbed on top of him like a hairless animal. She kissed his face, nuzzled his lips, nipped at his ears. His penis blazed, because she had penetrated the delicate membranes of his urethra, but he felt something more. An itch, an irritation, deep between his legs, like a cinder that flies in your eye. His penis stopped bleeding, and started to drip with clear sexual lubricant, much more than he had ever experienced before, and quivering-bright. She massaged his testicles and pulled at his shaft and he began to feel that something terrible was just about to happen to him.

At last she sat astride him with her thighs further apart than he thought it was possible for any woman to kneel. He could see right up inside her; a glistening cave. She took hold of his erection with both hands and guided it up between her hairless lips. He closed his eyes. He heard a long ululation, music. He heard arguing and prayers. He felt as if his penis were being sucked by a fire-eater in the Socco Chico. Then she slowly sat down on him, and he slid right up inside her cool warm wetness, right up to the moment when bare skin kissed bare skin.

They made love slowly at first. His eyes remained closed. He could still feel that irritant deep between his legs. Then she rode him faster and faster, swaying her hips, her wide-flared bottom, her breasts swinging from side to side. Their juices made a lascivious smacking sound against their hairless skin. Suzanna clutched him, and Grant clutched her back. They were out in the desert where the sand endlessly slides in a whispering glissando. They were out in the desert, alone, on the Great Erg of the Northern Sahara, beneath a shadowless dune. The mid-morning sky rippled over their heads like a sheet of azure silk.

Grant could feel his muscles tensing; his climax rising. But this was more than an ordinary climax. The blood began to hammer in his head like the drums of the Black Brotherhood. He started to gasp. The irritation was almost more than he could bear. It felt as if somebody had inserted barbed wire into his urethra, and were slowly dragging it out.

Then – a startling explosion. He screamed; or he imagined that he screamed. His whole erection was ablaze with white-hot pain and unimaginable ecstasy. He felt as if he had plunged it into molten steel. He rammed his hips up, so that Suzanna's juices would put out the fire, but they didn't. She was screaming, too, and both of them were locked together in spasm after spasm.

It was more than he could stand. His whole life was flying out of his penis. He was hurtling through doors and walls, through walls and alleyways and sordid souks. He burst through courtyards and poured down zigzagging corridors. He detonated with a howl through the shrine of Sidi Bou Galeb, where the mad people are all chained up.

He rose up over the desert where the heat ripples, and the voices call "*Houwa! Houwa! Houwa!*"

At last he atomized like a French hydrogen bomb fifteen miles over Sidi Ben Hassid, blinding everybody who looked at him.

Suzanna touched his cheek. He opened his eyes and was amazed to find that it was twilight, the colour of washable ink. A warm breeze blew from the courtyard and he could smell the water from the fountain.

"What happened?" he asked her. "Am I dead?"

Her voice was low and trembly and lustful like the pan-pipes from the Little Hills.

"*Scarabaeidae Jajoukae,*" she breathed.

They ate a supper of highly spiced lamb kebabs in a little restaurant opposite the hotel. Moths whacked against the light bulbs. They could scarcely speak to each other. They both felt as if their souls had been drained. They didn't look at each other, either; but they kept intertwining their fingers and thinking of the beetle in its olive wood box. The gray-haired man had been right: *once you have experienced it, you will always desire more.*

They were still finishing their meal when an unexpected figure appeared out of the darkness.

"Hakim," said Grant. "What are you doing in Kebir?"

Hakim dragged up a chair and they ordered more tea. "I thought I could resist it," he said. Grant offered him a Casa Sport, which he deftly disembowelled and filled up with hairy green marijuana.

"You thought that you could resist what?" asked Suzanna, sensing that she had the upper edge.

"I used the scarab many years ago, master. I never forgot it."

"So . . . what are you suggesting?"

Hakim's eyes glittered. "You have already tried it for yourselves, is this not true? I knew it when the railroad called me to ask where you were. Nobody misses their train back to their homeland for *kif*; or for any other drug. But they would miss it for the Jajouka beetle. Is this not true, master? You would miss the end of the world for the Jajouka beetle."

Grant and Suzanna said nothing, but their fingers intertwined and intertwined. Hakim watched them and knew that he was right.

"You may not think that I am a worthy man," said Hakim. "But my father and mother were of good birth, and I have always observed the true ways."

He took out a match, a brown twist of paper with its head dipped in turquoise sulphur, and struck one up against the gritty little desert on the side of the box. He lit his joint. Pea-soup smell on a warm North African evening: *when, brother*?

"Well, you're right," Grant admitted. "We did try the scarab."

"And you wish for more?"

Both of them nodded.

"Then may I ask to join you?"

"A threesome?" asked Grant, aggressively.

But Suzanna squeezed his hand. "Why not? Our last night in Morocco. Tomorrow we can fly Air France and drink champagne and be professional and pure. The day after we can have lunch at The Commonwealth Brewery. But tonight . . . why not?"

"I have no diseases, master," said Hakim. "I have always been a man of the utmost scruples." Grant looked at him with his angular cubist face and his eyes that seemed to float in the evening air, and he was jealous and resentful. But there were Jajouka beetles up in their hotel room, feeding stickily on hashish resin. And he could still remember what it was like to atomize.

Hakim appeared in the bedroom door naked. The room was shadowy except for the light cast by a small pierced lamp, in which an oil wick dipped and deliriously floated. Hakim was very lean and muscular with nipples like almonds. He had no body hair whatsoever, he shaved all over for cleanliness. His penis was circumcized and very long, with a head shaped like the head of a cobra.

Grant and Suzanna were waiting for him on the rumpled bed, already naked. Between them, the two olive wood boxes lay side by side. In spite of himself, Grant felt his penis rising when Hakim appeared; and when Hakim politely climbed onto the durry beside them, and Suzanna took hold of Hakim's penis in her left hand, and rubbed it up and down, smiling, and looking excited, Grant's erection rose bigger than it ever had before.

"Here . . ." said Suzanna, and took hold of Grant's hand, and drew it down between Hakim's legs. Grant found himself squeezing and manipulating Hakim's smooth coffee-coloured penis, rolling his hairless balls between his fingers. He had never touched another man like this before, and he found it so arousing that he was breathless.

Suzanna opened the first olive wood box, and used the lacquered pipe to suck out the first beetle.

"For you, Hakim," she said, and gripped his erection tightly. Grant watched his thin stomach flinching as Suzanna pushed the pipe into his penis, and then released her thumb, so that the scarab would be dropped deep inside him. Hakim dripped blood and Suzanna leaned forward and licked it. Grant waited in jealousy and rising excitement.

282

Suzanna slid the second beetle into Grant's penis. This was the second time that his urethra had been penetrated today, and it was agony. His hands gripped the durry tightly and he could have shouted out, but he stopped himself. He didn't want to show weakness in front of Hakim.

Music from Radio Cairo warbled through the room. The lamp threw black shadowy lace onto the ceiling. Suzanna pushed Hakim flat onto his back, and then she lay on top of him, her back against his chest, turning her head around so that she could nuzzle him and kiss him.

She reached down between her legs, and took hold of his wedge-shaped penis, and positioned it between the cheeks of her bottom. Then – with the most extraordinary pushing and twisting and panting that Grant had ever seen – she forced herself downward, downward and downward, until Hakim's erection was completely submerged, right up to his mocha-coloured scrotum.

Suzanna's vagina dripped juice like a broken comb drips honey. She didn't have to beckon for Grant to know that this was the time for him to climb on top of her – on top of them both. He found a place to kneel between the tangle of four legs, and then he slid his itching erection into Suzanna's body. His balls bounced against Hakim's balls, and Suzanna couldn't resist groping between their thighs and mixing all their balls together, as if she were being fucked by a double-cocked four-testicled monster.

The two of them pushed harder and harder. They sweated, and gasped, and the radio music wailed and exhorted them. Hakim made Suzanna sore to begin with; but then she relaxed her bottom and he was able to push himself into her deeper and deeper. Grant felt slippery breasts and urging thighs and his balls knocking against Hakim's balls like *the English are coming! The English are coming!* He could feel Hakim's cock through the thin slippery membrane that separated her vagina and her rectum, and they were fighting each other, Nazarane cock against Muslim cock, with only the thinnest stretchy skin to separate them.

At some point, Suzanna climaxed, and trembled, and shook like the Agadir earthquake. The men's joint balls were anointed with juice. But they kept on thrusting; until Hakim ejaculated, and Grant ejaculated, and all three of them were locked together in utter chemical spasm, pumping and thrusting and (maybe) screaming or (maybe) silent. It was a world inside another world inside another world.

But the two scarabs were male. The one which clung to the end of Grant's penis; and the one which clung to the end of Hakim's penis. And there was less than a half-inch between them. And they detected each other's presence not by smell or by sound, but by the high vibration of their wing-casings, as they gave off their stimulating chemicals. And they were blindly ferocious adversaries.

Grant thrust and thrust, and his head went through heaven. Hakim thrust, too, dreaming of dances and pipes and suns that burst over the desert. They went through climax after climax. And all the time the scarabs were furiously burrowing through Suzanna's flesh, mad for each other, giving off more and more of their stimulating chemicals as they did so.

Suzanna reached another huge climax as the scarabs ripped through the walls of her vagina and grappled each other. Blood gushed out of her vagina, and flooded the durry, but neither she nor Grant nor Hakim were conscious of what was happening. The fiercer the scarabs fought, the stronger the chemicals they gave off, and the three of them rocked and shook and bounced on the bed, locked together in never-ending orgasm.

The scarabs pursued each other for hour after hour, burrowing their way through womb and kidney and bowel. They clawed through arteries; they shredded mucous membranes; they scratched through liver and lung tissue. Blood welled in cavity after cavity. Suzanna climaxed one more time, and then the pain suddenly flared up. Her stomach and her bowels felt as if they had burst into flame, as if she had swallowed a quart of gasoline and set it alight. Every nerve-ending shrivelled; every ganglion screamed.

Suzanna screamed, too, but even as she screamed she climaxed again. The scarabs were tiny, but their madness was the madness of the desert, the madness of total survival. The bed grew thicker and squelchier with blood, while Grant and Hakim thought they were hydrogen bombs.

Suzanna's arms flopped from side to side, and her legs gradually stiffened.

The owner of the Hotel Africanus opened the door and showed Captain Hamid what had happened. There was so much blood on the bed that it looked as if somebody had carried a whole bucketful from a nearby abattoir and sloshed it over the durry and the three people who lay on it as if they were dead. The girl was white faced and *really* dead. The two men were hideously bloodied, but slept with beatific smiles on their faces. The net curtains rose and fell in the morning breeze.

Captain Hamid touched the girl's ankle. Her skin was cold. The blood was already dry. He picked up one of the open olive wood boxes and smelt it, and then passed it across to his sergeant, who smelt it too.

"Hashish," he nodded.

Later, in the police station, under a tirelessly revolving fan, Captain Hamid carefully opened the olive wood box and set it down on the table.

"That's right – that was one of the boxes we kept the scarabs in," said Grant. "*Scarabaeidae Jajoukae*. Professor Hemmer will tell you, at the Tangier Institute."

Captain Hamid had a very meticulously clipped moustache. It reminded Grant of a little hedge he had seen in the gardens of the Koutoubia Mosque in Marrakesh. "I regret that there is no such professor; and no such institute."

"I don't understand. We went to the Little Hills, to Jajouka."

"Jajouka? I regret that there is no such place."

"But we went there. We found the scarabs for ourselves, and brought them back."

"I regret that there is no such thing."

"But I saw it with my own eyes. They killed Suzanna, for Christ's sake!"

Captain Hamid pushed a pack of Casa Sport toward him, and a box of brown-paper matches. "Your lady friend died from a perforated bowel, because of violent anal intercourse. A scarab, my friend? There is no such thing. Somebody has been telling you lies."

The man in the white suit replaced his hat. He had obviously seen something of the shadows that had passed across Grant's face, like cloud shadows passing across the Sahara.

"I apologize, Dr Donnelly, for my discourtesy."

"No, no," said Grant. "You don't have to apologize. Here –" he added, and took out his address card.

The man took the card and held it uncertainly between finger and thumb. "You wish me to call on you, when you are back in Boston?" he asked.

"I wish you to keep in touch. Just in case you find what you're looking for."

He gave the man one last, intent look. Then he walked across the shiny tiled lobby of the Hotel Splendid to join his wife. He was filled with such craving that he could scarcely speak.

Absence of Beast

Northwood, Middlesex

And so we return from the airport. But there is one more place where we have to stop: Falworth Park, in Northwood, Middlesex, another of those villages that were overwhelmed by tract housing, and the unstoppable spread of suburbia. Within living memory there were country lanes here, and farms, and rural pubs; and the traces of rustic life can still be found: stiles, and horse troughs, and abandoned barns.

As a child, I was very familiar with Northwood and Hatch End, because I visited my grandparents regularly, and they lived very close by, in Pinner. My grandfather, Thomas Thorne Baker, was the inventor of Day-Glo, and the sending of news photographs by wireless, and I spent hours in his laboratory, playing with his chemical scales and making a nuisance of myself. He never seemed to mind.

There is always a special bond between grandchildren and grandparents, and this is what Absence of Beast *sets out to explore . . . with hideous consequences.*

ABSENCE OF BEAST

Robert knelt on the window seat with his hands pressed against the windowpane, watching the leaves scurrying across the lawn below him. The clouds hurried across the sky at a delirious, unnatural speed, and the trees thrashed as if they were trying to uproot themselves in sheer panic.

The gale had been blowing up all afternoon, and now it was shrieking softly under the doors, buffeting the chimneystacks, and roaring hollow-mouthed in the fireplaces.

It was the trees that alarmed Robert the most. Not because of their helpless bowing and waving, but because of the strange shapes that kept appearing between their leafless branches. Every tree seemed to be crowded with witches and trolls and indescribable demons, their gaping mouths formed by the way in which two twigs crossed over each other, their eyes by a few shivering leaves which had managed to cling on, despite October's storms.

And at the far end of the long curving driveway stood the giant oak, in whose uppermost branches raged the monster that Robert feared above all. A complicated arrangement of twigs and offshoots formed a spiny-backed beast like a huge wild boar, with four curving tusks, and a tiny bright malevolent eye that – in actual fact – was a rain-filled puddle almost two hundred yards further away.

But when the wind blew stronger, the eye winked and the beast churned its hunched-up back, and Robert wanted nothing more in the world than to take his eyes away from it, and not to see it.

But it was there; and he couldn't take his eyes away – any more than he could fail to see the blind Venetian mask in the tapestry curtains, or the small grinning dog in the pattern of the cushions, or the scores of purple-cloaked strangers who appeared in the wallpaper, their backs mysteriously and obdurately turned to the world of reality. Robert lived among secret faces, and living patterns, and inexplicable maps.

He was still kneeling on the window seat when his grandfather came into the room, with a plate of toast and a glass of cold milk. His grandfather sat beside him and watched him for a long time without saying anything, and eventually reached out with a papery-skinned hand and touched his shoulder, as if he were trying to comfort him.

"Your mother rang," said his grandfather. "She said she'd try to come down tomorrow afternoon."

Robert looked at his grandfather sideways. Robert was a thin, pale boy, with an unfashionably short haircut, and protruding ears, and a small, finely featured face. His eyes shone pale as agates. He wore a gray school jumper and gray shorts and black lace-up shoes.

"I brought you some toast," said his grandfather. White haired, stooped; but still retaining a certain elegance. Anybody walking into the library at that moment would have realized at once that they were looking at grandfather and grandson. Perhaps it was the ears. Perhaps it was more than that. Sometimes empathy can skip a generation: so that young and old can form a very special closeness, a closeness that even mothers are unable to share.

Robert took a piece of toast and began to nibble at one corner.

"You didn't eat very much lunch, I thought you might be hungry," his grandfather added. "Oh, for goodness sake don't feel guilty about it. I don't like steak and kidney pie either, especially when it's all kidney and no steak, and the pastry's burned. But cook will insist on making it."

Robert frowned. He had never heard an adult talking about food like this before He had always imagined that adults liked everything, no matter how disgusting it was. After all, they kept telling *him* to eat fish and cauliflower and kidney beans and fatty lamb, even though his gorge rose at the very sight of them. His mother always made him clear the plate, even if he had to sit in front of it for hours and hours after everybody else had finished, with the dining room gradually growing darker and the clock ticking on the wall.

But here was his grandfather not only telling him that steak and kidney pie was horrible, but he didn't have to eat it. It was extraordinary. It gave him the first feeling for a long time that everything might turn out for the better.

Because, of course, Robert hadn't had much to be happy about – not since Christmas, and the Christmas Eve dinner party. His father had raged, his mother had wept, and all their guests had swayed and murmured in hideous embarrassment. Next morning, when Robert woke up, his mother had packed her suitcase and gone, and his grandfather had come to collect him from home. He had sat in his grandfather's leather-smelling Daimler watching the clear raindrops trickle indecisively down the windscreen, while his father and his grandfather had talked in the porch with an earnestness that needed no subtitles.

"You probably haven't realized it, but for quite a long

time your mother and father haven't been very happy together," his grandfather had told him, as they drove through Pinner and Northwood in the rain. "It just happens sometimes, that people simply stop loving each other. It's very sad, but there's nothing that anybody can do about it."

Robert had said nothing, but stared out at the rows of suburban houses with their wet orange-tiled roofs and their mean and scrubby gardens. He had felt an ache that he couldn't describe, but it was almost more than he could bear. When they stopped at The Bell on Pinner Green so that grandfather could have a small whisky and a sandwich, and Robert could have a Coca-Cola and a packet of crisps, there were tears running down his cheeks and he didn't even know.

He had now spent almost three weeks at Falworth Park. His great-grandfather had once owned all of it, the house and farm and thirty-six acres; but death duties had taken most of it, and now his grandfather was reduced to living in eight rooms on the eastern side of the house, while another two families occupied the west and south wings.

"You're not bored, are you?" his grandfather asked him, as they sat side by side on the window seat. "I think I could find you some jigsaws."

Robert shook his head.

"You've been here for hours."

Robert looked at him quickly. "I like looking at the trees."

"Yes," said his grandfather. "Sometimes you can see faces in them, can't you?"

Robert stared at his grandfather with his mouth open. He didn't know whether to be frightened or exhilarated. How could his grandfather have possibly known that he saw faces in the trees? He had never mentioned it to anybody, in case he was laughed at. Either his grandfather could read his mind, or else –

"See there?" his grandfather said, almost casually, pointing to the young oaks that lined the last curve in the driveway. "The snarl-cats live in those trees; up in the high branches. And the hobgoblins live underneath them; always hunched up, always sour and sly."

"But there's nothing there," said Robert. "Only branches."

His grandfather smiled, and patted his shoulder. "You can't fool me, young Robert. It's what you see *between* the branches that matters."

"But there's nothing there, not really. Only sky."

His grandfather turned back and stared at the trees. "The world has an outside as well as an inside, you know. How do I know you're sitting here next to me? Because I can see you, because you have a positive shape. But you also have a *negative* shape, which is the shape which is formed by where you're *not*, rather than where you are."

"I don't understand." Robert frowned.

"It's not difficult," his grandfather told him. "All you have to do is look for the things that aren't there, instead of the things that are. Look at that oak tree, the big one, right at the end of the driveway. I can see a beast in that oak tree, can't you? Or rather, the negative shape of a beast. An *absence* of beast. But in its own way, that beast is just as real as you are. It has a recognizable shape, it has teeth and claws. You can see it. And, if you can see it . . . how can it be any less real than you are?"

Robert didn't know what to say. His grandfather sounded so matter-of-fact. Was he teasing him, or did he really mean it? The wind blew and the rain pattered against the window, and in the young oaks close to the house the snarl-cats swayed in their precarious branches and the hunched hobgoblins shuffled and dodged.

"Let me tell you something," said his grandfather. "Back in the 1950s, when I was looking for minerals in Australia, I came across a very deep ravine in the Olgas in which I could see what looked like copper deposits. I wanted to explore the ravine, but my Aborigine guide refused to go with me. When I asked him why, he said a creature lived there – a terrible creature called Woolrabunning, which means 'you were here but now you have gone away again'.

"Well, of course I didn't believe him. Who would? So late one afternoon I went down into that ravine alone. It was very quiet, except for the wind. I lost my way, and it was almost dark when I found the markers that I had left for myself. I was right down at the bottom of the ravine, deep in shadow. I heard a noise like an animal growling. I looked up, and I *saw* that creature, as clearly as I can see you. It was like a huge wolf, except that its head was larger than a wolf, and its shoulders were heavier. It was formed not from flesh or fur but entirely from the sky in between the trees and the overhanging rocks."

Robert stared at his grandfather, pale faced. "What did you do?" he whispered.

"I did the only thing I could do. I ran. But do you know something? It chased me. I don't know how, to this day. But as I was scaling the ravine, I could hear its claws on the rocks close behind me, and I could hear it panting, and I swear that I could feel its hot breath on the back of my neck.

"I fell, and I gashed my leg. Well . . . I don't know whether the Woolrabunning gashed my leg, or whether I cut it on a rock or a thorn-bush. But look . . . you can judge for yourself."

He lifted his left trouser-leg and bared his white, skinny calf. Robert leaned forward, and saw a deep blueish scar that ran down from his knee, and disappeared into the top of his Argyle sock.

"Thirty stitches I had to have in that," said his grandfather. "I was lucky I didn't bleed to death. You can touch it if you want to. It doesn't hurt."

Robert didn't want to touch it, but he stared at it for a long time in awe and fascination. *Not a beast*, he thought to himself, *but an absence of beast. Look for the things that aren't there, rather than the things that are.*

"Do you know what my guide said?" asked his grandfather. "He said I should have given the Woolrabunning something to eat. Then the blighter would have left me alone."

The next day, after lunch, Robert went for a walk on his own. The gale had suddenly died down, and although the lawns and the rose-gardens were strewn with leaves and twigs, the trees were silent and frigidly still. Robert could hear nothing but his own footsteps, crunching on the shingle driveway, and the distant echoing rattle of a train.

He passed the two stone pillars that marked the beginning of the avenue. There was a rampant stone lion on each of them, with a shield that bore a coat of arms. One of the lions had lost its right ear and part of its cheek, and both were heavily cloaked in moss. Robert had always loved them when he was smaller. He had christened them Pride and Wounded. They had been walking between them – his mother, his father and him – when his mother had said to his father, "All you worry about is your wounded pride." Then he had learned at nursery school that a group of lions is called a pride, and somehow his mother's words and the lions had become inextricably intermingled in his mind.

He laid his hand on Wounded's broken ear, as if to comfort him. Then he turned to Pride, and stroked his cold stone nose. If only they could come alive, and walk through the park beside him, these two, their breath punctuating the air in little foggy clouds. Perhaps he could train them to run and fetch sticks.

He walked up the avenue alone. The snarl-cats perched in the upper branches of the trees, watching him spitefully with leaf-shaped eyes. The hobgoblins hid themselves in the crooks and crotches of the lower branches. Sometimes he glimpsed one of them, behind a tree-trunk, but as soon as he moved around to take a closer look, of course the hobgoblin had vanished; and the shape that had formed its face had become something else altogether, or just a pattern, or nothing at all.

He stopped for a while, alone in the park, a small boy in a traditional tweed coat with a velvet collar, surrounded by the beasts of his own imagination. He felt frightened: and as he walked on, he kept glancing quickly over his shoulder to make sure that the snarl-cats and the hobgoblins hadn't climbed down from the trees and started to sneak up behind him, tiptoeing on their claws so that they wouldn't make too much of a scratching noise on the shingle.

But he had to go to the big oak, to see the humpbacked creature that dominated all the rest – the Woolrabunning of Falworth Park. You were here, and now you have gone again. But all the time you're still here, because I can see the shape of you.

At last the big oak stood directly in front of him. The hog-like beast looked different from this angle, leaner, with a more attenuated skull. Meaner, if anything.

Its hunched-up shoulders were still recognizable, and if anything its jaws were crammed even more alarmingly with teeth. Robert stood staring at it for a long time, until the gentle whisper of freshly falling drizzle began to cross the park.

"Please don't chase after me," said Robert, to the beast that was nothing but sky-shapes in the branches of a tree. "Here . . . I've brought you something to eat."

Carefully, he took a white paper napkin out of his coat pocket, and laid it in the grass at the foot of the oak. He unfolded it, to show the beast his offering. A pork chipolata, smuggled from lunch. Pork chipolatas were his favourite, especially the way that grandfather insisted they had to be cooked, all burst and crunchy and overdone, and so Robert was making a considerable sacrifice.

"All hail," he said to the beast. He bowed his head. Then he turned around and began to walk back to the house, at a slow and measured pace.

This time, he didn't dare to turn around. Would the beast ignore his offering, and chase after him, the way that the Woolrabunning had chased after grandfather, and ripped his leg? Should he start running, so that he would at least have a chance of reaching the house and shutting the door before the beast could catch up with him? Or would that only arouse the beast's hunting instincts, and start him running, too?

He walked faster and faster between the trees where the snarl-cats lived, listening as hard as he could for the first heavy loping of claws. Soon he was walking so fast that to all intents and purposes he was running with his arms swinging and his legs straight. He hurried between Pride and Wounded, and it was then that he heard the shingle crunching behind him and the soft deep roaring of –

A gold-coloured Jaguar XJS, making its way slowly toward the house.

Because of the afternoon gloom, the Jaguar had its headlights on, so that at first it was impossible for Robert to see past the dazzle, and make out who was driving. Then the car swept past him, and he saw a hand waving, and a familiar smile, and he ran behind it until it had pulled up beside the front door.

"Mummy!" he cried, as she stepped out of the passenger seat. He flung his arms around her waist and held her tight. She felt so warm and familiar and lovely that he could scarcely believe that she had ever left him.

She ruffled his hair and kissed him. She was wearing a coat with a fur collar that he hadn't ever seen her wearing before, and she smelled of a different perfume. A rich lady's perfume. She had a new brooch, too, that sparkled and scratched his cheek when she bent forward to kiss him.

"That was a funny way to run," she told him. "Gerry said you looked like a clockwork soldier."

Gerry?

"This is Gerry," said his mother. "I brought him along so that you could meet him."

Robert looked up, frowning. He sensed his mother's tension. He sensed that something wasn't quite right. A tall man with dark combed-back hair came around the front of the car with his hand held out. He had a sooty-black three o'clock shadow and eyes that were bright blue like two pieces of Mediterranean sky cut out of a travel brochure.

"Hallo, Robert," he said, still holding his hand out. "My name's Gerry. I've heard a lot about you."

"Have you?" swallowed Robert. He glanced at his mother for some sort of guidance, some sort of explanation; but all his mother seemed to be capable of doing was smiling and nodding.

"I hear you're keen on making model aeroplanes," said Gerry.

Robert blushed. His aeroplane models were very private to him: partly because he didn't think that he was very good at making them (although his mother always thought he was, even when he stuck too much polystyrene cement on the wings, or broke the decals, or stuck down the cockpit canopy without bothering to paint the pilot). And partly because – well – they were *private*, that's all. He couldn't understand how Gerry could have known about them. Not unless his mother had told Gerry almost everything about him.

Why would she have done that? Who was this "Gerry"? Robert had never even seen him before, but "Gerry" seemed to think that he had a divine right to know all about Robert's model aeroplanes, and drive Robert's mother around in his rotten XJS, and behave as if he practically owned the place.

Robert's grandfather came out of the house. He was wearing his mustard Fair Isle jumper. He had an odd look on his face that Robert had never seen before Agitated, ill-at-ease, but defiant, too.

"Oh, *Daddy*, so marvellous to see you," said Robert's mother, and kissed him. "This is Gerry. Gerry – this is Daddy."

"Sorry we're early," smiled Gerry, shaking hands. "We made *much* better time on the M40 than I thought we would. Lots of traffic, you know, but fairly fast-moving."

Robert's grandfather stared at the XJS with suspicion

and animosity. "Well, I expect you can travel quite quickly in a thing like that."

"Well, it's funny, you know," said Gerry. "I never think of her as a 'thing'. I always think of her as a 'she'."

Robert's grandfather looked away from the XJS and (with considerable ostentatiousness) didn't turn his eyes toward it again. In a thin voice, almost as if he were speaking to himself, he said, "A thing is an 'it' and only a woman is a 'she'. I've always thought that men who lump women in with ships and cars and other assorted junk deserve nothing more than ships and cars and other assorted junk."

"Well," flustered Gerry. "*Chacun à son goût.*" At the same time, he gave Robert's mother one of those looks which meant, *You said he was going to be difficult. You weren't joking, were you?* Robert's mother, in return, shrugged and tried bravely to look as if this wasn't going to be the worst weekend in living memory. She had warned Gerry, after all. But Gerry had insisted on "meeting the sprog and granddad, too . . . it all comes with the territory."

Robert stood close to the Jaguar's boot as Gerry tugged out the suitcases.

"What do you think of these, then?" Gerry asked him. "Hand-distressed pigskin, with solid brass locks. Special offer from Diner's Club."

Robert sniffed. "They smell like sick."

Gerry put down the cases and closed the boot. He looked at Robert long and hard. Perhaps he thought he was being impressive, but Robert found his silence and his staring to be nothing but boring, and looked away, at Wounded and Pride, and thought about running beside them through the trees.

"I *had* hoped that we could be friends," said Gerry.

302

Friends? How could we be friends? I'm nine and you're about a hundred. Besides, I don't want any friends, not at the moment. I've got Wounded and Pride and Grandfather, and Mummy, too. Why should I want to be friends with you?

"What about it?" Gerry persisted. "Friends? Yes? Fanites?"

"You're too old," said Robert, plainly.

"What the hell do you mean, too old? I'm thirty-eight. I'm not even forty. Your mother's thirty-six, for God's sake."

Robert gave a loud, impatient sigh. "You're too *old* to be friends with me, that's what I meant."

Gerry hunkered down, so that his large sooty-shaven face was on the same level as Robert's. He leaned one elbow against the XJS with the arrogance of ownership, but also to stop himself from toppling over. "I don't mean that sort of friends. I mean friends like father and son."

Robert was fascinated by the wart that nestled in the crease in Gerry's nose. He wondered why Gerry hadn't thought of having it cut off. Couldn't he see it? He must have seen it, every morning when he looked in the mirror. It was so warty. If *I* had a wart like that, I'd cut it off myself. But supposing it bled forever, and never stopped? Supposing I cut it off, and nothing would stop the blood pumping out? What was better, dying at the age of nine, or having a wart as big as Gerry's wart for ever and ever?

"Do you think that's possible?" Gerry coaxed him.

"What?" asked Robert, in confusion.

"Do you think that could be possible? Do you think that you could try to do that for me? Or at least for your mother, if not for me?"

"But Mummy hasn't got a wart."

It seemed for a moment as if the whole universe had gone silent. Then Robert saw Gerry's hand coming towards him, and the next thing he knew he was lying on his side on the shingle, stunned, seeing stars, and Gerry was saying in an echoing voice, "I picked up the suitcase . . . I didn't realize he was there . . . he just came running towards me. He must have caught his face on the solid brass corner."

He refused to come down for supper and stayed in bed and read *The Jumblies* by Edward Lear. "*They went to sea in a sieve they did . . . in a sieve they went to sea.*" He liked the lines about ". . . *the Lakes, and the Terrible Zone, and the hills of the Chankly Bore.*" It all sounded so strange and sad and forbidding, and yet he longed to go there. He longed to go anywhere, rather than here, with his mother's laughter coming up the stairs, flat and high, not like his mother's laughter at all. What had Gerry done to her, to make her so perfumed and deaf and unfamiliar? She had even believed him about hitting his face on the suitcase. And what could Robert say, while his mother was cuddling him and stroking his hair? *Gerry hit me?*

Children could say lots of things but they couldn't say things like that. Saying *Gerry hit me* would have taken more composure and strength than Robert could ever have summoned up.

His grandfather came up with a tray of shepherd's pie and a glass of Coca-Cola with a straw.

"Are you all right?" he asked, sitting on the end of Robert's bed and watching him eat. Outside it was dark, but the bedroom curtains were drawn tight, and even though the wallpaper was filled with mysterious cloaked men who refused to turn around, no matter what, Robert felt reassured that they never would; or at least, not tonight. The night was still silent. The Coca-Cola made a prickling noise.

Robert said, "I hate Gerry."

His grandfather's tissue-wrinkled hand rested on his knee. "Yes," he said. "Of course you do."

"He's got a wart."

"So have I."

"Not a big one, right on the side of your nose."

"No – not a big one, right on the side of my nose."

Robert forked up shepherd's pie while his grandfather watched him with unaccustomed sadness. "I've got to tell you something, Robert."

"What is it?"

"Your mother . . . well, your mother's very friendly with Gerry. She likes him a lot. He makes her happy."

Robert slowly stopped chewing. He swallowed once, and then silently put down his fork. His grandfather said, uncomfortably, "Your mother wants to marry him. Robert. She wants to divorce your father and marry Gerry."

"How can she marry him?" asked Robert, aghast.

There was a suspicious sparkle in the corner of his grandfather's eye. He squeezed Robert's knee, and said, "I'm sorry. She loves him. She really loves him, and he makes her happy. You can't run other people's lives for them, you know. You can't tell people who to love and who not to love."

"*But he's got a wart!*"

Robert's grandfather lifted the tray of supper away, and laid it on the floor. Then he took hold of Robert in his arms and the two of them embraced, saying nothing, but sharing a common anguish.

After a long time, Robert's grandfather said, quite unexpectedly, "What did you want that sausage for?"

305

Robert felt himself blush. "What sausage?"

"The sausage you sneaked off your plate at lunchtime and wrapped in a napkin and put in your pocket."

At first Robert couldn't speak. His grandfather knew so much that it seemed to make him breathless. But eventually he managed to say, "I gave it to the beast. The beast in the big oak tree. I asked him not to chase me."

His grandfather stroked his forehead two or three times, so gently that Robert could scarcely feel it. Then he said, "You're a good boy, Robert. You deserve a good life. You should do whatever you think fit."

"I don't know what you mean."

His grandfather stroked his forehead again, almost dreamily. "What I mean is, you shouldn't let a good sausage go to waste."

Not long after midnight, the gales suddenly rose up again. The trees shook out their skirts, and began to dance Dervish-like and furious in the dark. Robert woke up, and lay stiffly, listening – trying to hear the rushing of feet along the shingle driveway, or the scratching of claws against the window. He had a terrible feeling that tonight was the night – that all the snarl-cats and hobgoblins would leap from the trees and come tearing through the house – whirled by the gale, whipped by the wind – all teeth and reddened eyes and bark-brown breath.

Tonight was the night!

He heard a window bang, and bang again. Then he heard his mother screaming. Oh, God! Gerry was murdering her! Tonight was the night, and Gerry was murdering her! He scrambled out of bed, and found his slippers, and pulled open the door, and then he was running slap-slap-slap along the corridor screaming *Mummy – Mummy – Mummy –*

And collided into his mother's bedroom door. And saw by the lamplight. Gerry's big white bottom, with black hair in the crack; and his red shining cock plunging in and out. And his mother's face. Transfigured. Staring at him. Sweaty and flushed and distressed. A sweaty saint. But despairing too.

Robert. Her voice sounded as if he were drowning in the bath.

He ran out again. *Robert,* his mother called, but he wouldn't stop running. Downstairs, across the hallway, and the front door bursting open, and the gale blowing wildly in. Then he was rushing across the shingle, past Wounded and Pride, and all the dancing snarl-cats and hobgoblins.

The night was so noisy that he couldn't think. Not that he wanted to think. All he could hear was blustering wind and whining trees and doors that banged like cannon-fire. He ran and he ran and his pyjama trousers flapped, and his blood bellowed in his ears. At last – out of the darkness at the end of the avenue – the big oak appeared, bowing and dipping a little in deference to the wind, but not much more than a full-scale wooden warship would have bowed and dipped, in the days when these woods were used for ocean-going timber.

He stood in front of it, gasping. He could see the beast, leaping and dipping in the branches. "*Woolrabunning!*" he screamed at it. "*Woolrabunning!*

Beneath his feet, the shingle seemed to surge. The wind shouted back at him with a hundred different voices. "*Woolrabunning!*" he screamed, yet again. Tears streaked his cheeks. "*Help me, Woolrabunning!*"

The big oak tossed and swayed as if something very heavy had suddenly dropped down from its branches. Robert strained his eyes in the wind and the darkness, but he couldn't see anything at all. He was about to scream out to the Woolrabunning one more time, when something *huge* came crashing toward him, something huge and invisible that spattered the shingle and claw-tore the turf.

He didn't have time to get out of the way. He didn't have time even to cry out. Something bristly and solid knocked him sideways, spun him onto his back, and then rushed past him with a swirl of freezing, fetid air. Something invisible. Something he couldn't see. A beast. Or an absence of beast.

He climbed to his feet, shocked and bruised. The wind lifted up his hair. He could hear the creature running toward the house. Hear it, but not see it. Only the shingle, tossed up by heavy, hurrying claws. Only the faintest warping of the night.

He couldn't move. He didn't dare to think what would happen now. He heard the front door of the house racketing open. He heard glass breaking, furniture falling. He heard banging and shouting and then a scream like no scream that he had ever heard before, or ever wanted to hear again.

Then there was silence. Then he started to run.

The bedroom was decorated with blood. It slid slowly down the walls in viscous curtains. And worse than the blood were the torn ribbons of flesh that hung everywhere like a saint's day carnival. And the ripest of smells, like slaughtered pigs. Robert stood in the doorway and he could scarcely understand what he was looking at.

Eventually his grandfather laid his hand on his shoulder. Neither of them spoke. They had no idea what would happen now.

They walked hand in hand along the windy driveway,

between Wounded and Pride, between the trees where the snarl-cats and the hobgoblins roosted.

As they passed Wounded and Pride, the two stone lions stiffly turned their heads. and shook off their mantles of moss, and dropped down from their plinths with soft intent, and followed them.

Then snarl-cats jumped down from the trees, and followed them, too; and humpbacked hobgoblins, and dwarves, and elves, and men in purple cloaks. They walked together, a huge and strangely assorted company, until they reached the big oak, where they stopped, and bowed their heads.

Up above them, in the branches, the Woolrabunning roared and roared; a huge cry of triumph and blood-lust that echoed all the way across Falworth Park, and beyond.

Robert held his grandfather's hand as tight as tight. "Absence of beast!" he whispered, thrilled. "Absence of beast!"

And his grandfather touched his face in the way that a man touches the face of somebody he truly loves. He kept the bloody carving knife concealed behind his back; quite unsure if he could use it, either on Robert or on himself. But he had always planned to cut his throat beneath the big oak in Falworth Park, one day; so perhaps this was as good a night as any.

Even when their positive shapes were gone, their negative shapes would still remain, him and Robert and the snarl-cats and the sly hobgoblins; and perhaps that was all that anybody could ever ask.